# Antler Dust

## An Allison Coil Mystery

# Mark Stevens

Third Line Press
Denver, Colorado

Antler Dust

by Mark Stevens

Published by
Third Line Press
Denver, Colorado

Library of Congress Control Number: 2011925590

ISBN:   978-0-9907224-0-3

Cover and Interior Design: Nick Zelinger, NZ Graphics

First Edition

Printed in the United States of America

*for Jody, my creative cowgirl*

# 1

Allison Coil stroked the soft neck of the massive bull elk. The skin was still warm to the touch. She felt the smooth fur on the animal's head, looked at the crimson dot on its skull that leaked blood, then pressed her index finger against the spot where death had found an opening.

Death in a flying cylinder, she thought.

"This is the point in the process where none of us really knows what to do next," said Vic, one of the three hunters who had led Allison to the site of the kill. They had returned to camp for their quartering tools when she showed up, making the rounds to check on all of her clients.

"He was still struggling when we got here," said another member of the trio. "We were forced to finish him off."

The three young men were appropriately respectful of the dead elk. Too many hunters treated animals as little more than bull's-eye targets.

"Is this your first kill?" she said.

"First kill, first shot, first day," said Vic, the man bearing the least amount of gear and hunting stuff—jeans, boots and a blaze-orange vest over a heavy winter jacket. "Beginner's luck all the way."

"How did it make you feel?" she said.

"Feel? I don't know. It all happened so quickly."

Allison stood up. The four of them were gathered in a grassy clearing a half-mile from their camp outside the main bowl of Ripplecreek Canyon.

"Good lung shot," she said. "Too bad he didn't die instantly."

Allison had guided these men into the wilderness three days earlier. She was a rarity in the Rocky Mountains, a female guide in macho land. Her job was to escort hunters on horseback into the high country, to help them set up tents and prepare for the hunt. This group was a welcome break from the greenhorns who tried to pretend that they had never worn a silk tie, drunk a three-martini lunch, or driven an SUV with a cell phone sprouting from one ear. This group had an earthy, genuine feel. She remembered taking note of Vic's good looks on the day she had loaded them in. She took another moment now to study him again: trim sandy-blond beard, a surfer-like shock of blond hair, square shoulders, strong hips and a solid demeanor.

"If I hadn't come back today to check on you boys, which one of you would have taken this puppy apart?" she said.

"I was going to wing it," said Vic.

"So . . . do you want a hands-on lesson, or do you want to watch me have fun by myself?" Allison said.

"A lesson, please," said Vic. "You might not be around to hold my hand the next time I bring down an elk."

"You've taken your kill for this season, mister," Allison said. "If you learn how to do this right, you can hold one of your buddies' hands." She looked over at the two other men, who took a small step away from each other, laughing.

Allison showed Vic where to make an incision in the white belly—a straight line from anus to heart—and how to avoid puncturing the intestines. She used a small handsaw to cut through the pelvis and splay the rib cage back. The hunters peered warily at the guts open to the wide sky. Like a doctor in an outdoor operating theater, Allison admired the animal's clean, shiny innards. White intestines, beet-red liver, pale-pink lungs—nature's color-coded diagram. She cut the corrugated esophagus, a windpipe like a vacuum cleaner tube, from the animal's throat. The discard pile grew as the animal was parted out. Vic took over as they emptied the viscera from the elk's cavity.

"We admire your guts," said one of the others. "So to speak."

"I don't know why they call it field dressing," said Allison. "Seems like the opposite to me. Think how much work it would take to put this elk back together, if it was possible to reassemble a dead animal. Say, for instance, if it was a kit you might buy in a hobby shop."

"An odd thought," said Vic. "But I think I know what you mean."

"A surgeon could stitch it all back together, but the pieces wouldn't be alive. You couldn't kick-start the heart or refuel the brain."

She was getting curious looks from her audience as she worked the saw around the ribs.

"If you see enough of these, it's a question you might start asking yourself," she said. She had been pondering survival and odds and body parts and death within hours of the jetliner crash. Prior to that day, death was just a word repeated on the nightly news.

Vic was the only one who was eager to reach in and scrape. Allison wondered why the others could come all this way, spend all this money on a guided hunt and avoid an opportunity to study the inside of an elk.

She helped fill water jugs in the nearby creek. They washed out the carcass and cut off the legs. She showed Vic how to scalp the antlers and leave enough of the nubs to show evidence that the kill was male, in case the boy-men were stopped on the way home by a forest ranger.

They quartered the animal and strapped the hindquarters to Bear, her Appaloosa. Back at camp, Vic helped hoist the pieces up with rope into a tree so the meat dangled from a branch well off the ground. Dangling meat attracted all kinds of wild creatures—raccoons, mountain lions and flies. Allison peppered the meat to discourage the flies.

As they worked side by side to complete this last step, Allison decided that Vic fit all of the criteria that she looked for in a man. He stirred her up, no question about it. She wondered exactly which organ fluttered inside her chest at such moments. It was a heart-lung combination that went light and limp and left her a bit breathless.

What did the space in her chest cavity do the rest of the time? What did she look like inside? How close had an ambulance crew come to learning that after the plane wreck? There were other bodies floating in the water for them to study that day, ejected and discarded. What the medics did see was her superficial exterior. She was short and slender, a hundred and ten pounds after a big meal. She had cropped, functional, straight brown hair that was easily covered, quickly cleaned and more manageable than it had been during her city days Back East, when a stylist took care of the externals. Her face was narrow and small, with warm brown eyes, a solid nose, high cheekbones and bright white teeth, the product of a milk-fed youth combined with strong Midwestern genes.

As Allison cleaned her knife with a jug of water and paper towels, Vic sidled over and started asking questions, making his move. She could read him like spoor. He asked how long she had been a guide, how long she had lived in Colorado, asked if all the "guy stuff" and macho posturing bothered her. These were questions that he did not really want answered, she knew. She had heard it all before, but what woman hadn't? Anthropologists had a phrase for it: mating ritual.

Vic told her about the three of them, even though she had not asked. They were co-workers from an advertising firm. Of all things, Allison thought. She had a career in advertising when she had lived Back East, prior to the accident. Vic quizzed her about how her life was currently set up, how long she had been out of the city. She replied with vague answers, not giving any indication that she was nailed down to a relationship, because she wasn't. Not officially.

Bear was hitched to a nearby tree. Allison tightened his cinch and breast collar. The long haul back from this spot in the wilderness meant it would be difficult to reach home before nightfall. She would probably end up riding in the dark, which made her wary, because the air smelled like it was gaining weight. Snow for sure. Blizzards and horse rides in the dark never concerned her when she lived where the mountains were brick, the open plains were asphalt and she traveled in birds made of fragile steel.

Back near their tent, the man-boys were evaluating how best to slice elk steaks for dinner. "The question is how a woman like you ended up here?" said Vic as she showed them how to extract the back strap, the best meat on the carcass.

"Why is that the question?"

"Okay, it's one question." He cut the slice free with a steady hand and she showed him how to bind the rest with twine.

Vic reminded Allison of an old college girlfriend whose blunt questions were delivered with earnest eyes that demanded sincere answers, whether the subject was the meaning of life or missing socks.

"The answer is that I needed a break from the world of big machines, big highways, big buildings and big news."

"In other words, all the intensity got you down," Vic stated.

"Yeah, I suppose. I used to be in your line of work, as a matter of fact."

"No kidding?"

"Griffin & Good," she said, knowing it would prompt a response.

"One of the biggest agencies there is."

"They thought I knew what made for great slogans. Toothpaste, amusement parks, grocery store chains, toilet paper. Tag lines were my thing, little words trying to mean a lot."

"You're a long way from that world. What happened? Did you run out of steam?"

He was sitting cross-legged on the ground, no longer working. His brown eyes bore through her, but his questions did not feel invasive.

"I needed to touch things again, real things," Allison said.

No, that wasn't it. Besides, it sounded corny. Everything is real. The answer had to do with stoplights. Or voice mail. Or email. Or twenty-dollar hotel breakfasts.

"It seemed like I was part of the clutter—TV, billboards, radio, whatever," she said.

She found herself sitting next to him on the cool ground. The raw tenderloin rested on a piece of tin foil at her feet. It was red and supple. It looked very much alive. As she gazed at the meat, Vic put an arm around her.

"Can you hang out tonight?"

Vic was smooth. The offer was simple. He was clearly playing off their spark.

"Nope, I'm due back," she said.

"Are you, may I ask, involved with someone right now?"

The thought of a quiet, groping roll in a tent, a loving siesta, a one-night stand on a mountaintop, had its appealing aspects. But Allison knew it wouldn't work.

"You can ask and the answer is—well, yes," she said. "And that goes with one of the other things I don't miss. Big confusion. Out here, it seems the only things that get messed up, are the things you want to go wrong. The rules are your own."

"I can respect that." His hand moved gently away.

"Thanks," she said. "Not that you don't seem to be a complete sweetheart. Truly."

She thought she heard him smile.

The moment passed.

She went back to being a professional guide. She packed up Bear and her powerful black mule, Eli. Vic and his buddies started building a fire and discussed meal preparations. Allison mounted her horse and turned to survey the camp one more time before heading Bear toward home. Vic held up his hand in a way that she interpreted as a combination wave and smile that said "maybe another time."

Allison pointed Bear straight up through the scrub oak and the main trail that would take her down through the Ripplecreek Canyon and bring her home.

\*\*\*\*

Dean Applegate lay prone in the snow. The distant ridge that he had been relying on for bearings had vanished in low clouds an hour ago, about the same time he had popped open a can of cold beef stew and called it breakfast. Through a pair of binoculars, Applegate panned the facing hillside as carefully as the master had taught him. The twin lenses delivered a jittery view of the landscape, a phenomenon he had never seen discussed in hunting magazines. But at least he was going through the motions, doing what he had read and what he had been shown by other sportsmen.

From down Ripplecreek Canyon, he could hear a distant clatter, the cacophony orchestrated by animal rights protesters to frighten off the elk and deer. The noise of those meddling buzzards blended in a staccato clamor, fading in and out. The clouds were sinking and the racket bounced at him from different directions.

*There.* Something moved.

The plodding shape was near the bottom of the slope where he was perched.

*It was moving toward him.*

The creature was at least a hundred yards away, so Applegate could not tell for sure whether it was elk or deer. It's moving too slowly. It might be wounded. It might be an outcast or an orphan, but that didn't matter.

*I am an assassin. No pity.*

He tried to remember all the things a good hunter would do at this moment, with prey in his sights. The list came slowly: check the wind, stay low, watch your step. But all of that was garbled with one notion: *Shoot.*

The animal turned to give him a good butt view. Slowly it turned back and continued to move steadily, relentlessly, as if *it* were the one doing the stalking. But Applegate didn't think he had been spotted. Camouflage was key. Applegate felt at one with the scenery. He was dressed to kill from cap to boot. His face was caked in olive and black greasepaint. The tree-and-leaf pattern on his parka, pants, gloves, rifle, socks, backpack, binoculars and sunglasses all matched. The pattern was known as ambush and that was his theme: surprise and destroy.

Applegate imagined how his friends' faces would look when he came back with the trophy. He knew they didn't think much of him as a hunter, but their opinion of him would be transformed on the spot. There was no doubt.

He aimed and waited. The animal poked its nose around a large tree.

*Deer.*

Applegate swatted away creeping doubts. Wild animals never looked very big at a distance, but the animal in his sights was too small to be an elk.

He squeezed the trigger and the world exploded.

The brown shape dropped.

Rifle still up around his shoulder, Applegate stumbled down the slope, through the scrub and thorny bushes, ready to fire again if the animal decided to get up and limp off.

He knew his kill would be no match in size for whatever George Grumley might bring down today. A whale underwater turns into a minnow once it's in the boat, he thought. But at least this small animal was something to show for his hunt.

It was dead, a clean shot. The brown heap did not budge. From where Applegate stood, the animal was bisected by the thin trunk of an aspen sapling flecked in quaking gold leaves.

Applegate kept the butt of the rifle tucked into his shoulder and cocked his eye square down the barrel as he stepped to the side of the aspen, a bit hesitant, fearful even, to invade the space where an animal had just died. Alas, it was more a yearling than a prize buck.

He did not recognize it. What the hell was it? The fur was smooth, much too smooth for a wild animal. For a moment, he flashed on the idea that it was a new species, a strange hybrid. This would be a second feather in his cap, a curiosity to show the men back at camp. He had not only proven his ability to kill, he might have discovered a new form of wildlife. He couldn't see the head. Maybe it was tucked underneath the body. Maybe the animal had broken its neck in the fall.

He stepped around to the side of the baby aspen and squatted slowly. His knees cracked unceremoniously. He hated the way his knees cracked when he squatted near the fire back at camp, like the pop of burning sap. He could always hear the muted chuckling of the other hunters.

A hand poked out from the fur where there should have been a hoof. There were fingernails, too, clean and white. Four fingers. There was no need to look for a thumb.

It all stared up at him, human as guilt.

\*\*\*\*

Rocky Carnivitas heard a muffled *pop* off in the distance. It gave him reason to smile. The echo of the rifle shot was like a satisfying growl that resonated deep in the woods. He waited for another, but it didn't come. The shot was either a one-bullet drop, with no need for a finishing shot, or a miss. From the sound, he calculated the shot was at least a mile away, down Ripplecreek. You could never be too sure, given the echoes and funny way mountains absorbed sounds, kicked them around. He hoped the bullet had found its mark, hoped a hunter would soon be dragging a carcass down to his truck so all the granola-crunching protesters would gape at the corpse, get angry and make more of a stupid fuss than they were already generating. Maybe the evidence that their protest had not worked would make them give up and go home. And get haircuts.

Rocky crouched next to a smooth boulder high up in Ripplecreek Canyon. He was a few hundred yards above timberline where the taller trees in the forest gave way to irregular clumps of scrubby bushes scattered among vast, open stretches of loose rock. At his feet, a big bull elk lay on the ground, alive but unconscious. The huge animal took furtive breaths as Rocky gingerly slipped the collar and GPS unit around its neck. He worked carefully to avoid bumping the valuable rack. These were trophy antlers destined to one day hang on the wall of a hunter's den. Some fat cat would pay ten Gs or more to stand in the woods and kill the elk later. The animal was probably wondering if it was dying. The collar, as thin as a shoelace but made of leather, snapped together.

Rocky patted the elk on its chest as if it were a puppy dog.

The air over the upper bowl of Ripplecreek tasted wet. He was lucky to be doing this work during the morning's relative calm. He had hiked far enough up the valley that the mayhem from the protesters was no longer a factor. None of them would venture this high, especially with the sky turning into a snow-sopped sponge. There was a storm coming. The damned hippies had better have skis.

Rocky stepped over to his backpack and dug out a small grease-stained notebook from a side pocket. He jotted down the GPS unit number and a note about the location and time of day, along with a few details about the animal.

The elk was theirs. Tagged. Marked for death, though the date was unknown.

"Nice work, as always," said a voice behind him. Rocky whirled around.

Grumley.

Rocky's boss was dressed for a week's worth of icy air, goose-down pants with beaver-skin mittens dangling from his belt. He was holding a rifle in his right fist. A rusty Eddie Bauer watch dangled from a leather lanyard around his neck. There was a story to that watch. Grumley treasured the timepiece and insisted he would be buried with it around his neck. The watch had been taken from the stomach of a bear he'd shot. The bear had invaded a Boy Scout camp up near Meeker. None of the scouts had been hurt, but the scoutmaster had been mauled to death. It had taken Grumley three days of tracking through rugged high-country terrain to catch up with the bruin. When he had hoisted the bear from the branch of a tree for bloodletting, the watch had fallen from a slit in its belly. Grumley tried to bring the watch back to the scoutmaster's next of kin, but they wanted Grumley to keep it as thanks for his efforts to protect others. The watch was still ticking.

"Did I take you by surprise?" said Grumley.

This was a loaded question. It was never a smart move to admit being taken by surprise in the high country, but there was no advantage in lying to Grumley.

"Fuck, my heart's pounding. Jesus, don't ever do that again." The notebook quivered in Rocky's hand.

Grumley had a peculiar look on his face.

"Is that the bull we were after?"

"Has to be," said Rocky.

"Good," said Grumley. "A bonus."

Grumley wiped his beard and lips with the back of his hairy hand. He had a habit of scratching or twiddling at the thick, three-inch tuft of gray-white beard on his chin.

Rocky didn't understand what Grumley meant by "bonus." Maybe he was supposed to know, but he didn't ask. Grumley was not the kind of man who liked being pestered with questions.

The elk began pawing at the dirt. It was starting to recover from the knockout drug injected by the dart.

Grumley watched the animal with professional interest. He owned the hunting guide operation and Rocky knew Grumley saw the elk as only one thing: money in the bank.

Rocky Carnivitas watched the elk with apprehension, hoping he had done everything correctly. Rocky didn't like people looking over his shoulder and passing judgment on the quality of his workmanship. But then, who did?

"How the hell did you sneak up on me?" Rocky said. "I thought you were with your buddies. And, say, did you hear the damn protesters?"

"I've been thinking about your . . . whaddya call it?" Grumley's handmade twirling motions as he tried to find the right word. The gun swayed in his grip.

"Proposal," said Rocky.

"Right." Rocky felt a rolling earthquake sensation in his gut. How the hell had he missed being followed? And why was his boss here anyway?

"Let's review that proposal, shall we?"

The last time they had talked, Rocky was able to screw up his courage to confront Grumley by knocking back a couple of double Wild Turkeys and then describing his proposal quickly. After Rocky had spelled things out, Grumley looked at him intently, thoughtfully—as if Rocky was simultaneously delivering a well-designed business plan and relieving Grumley of a chronic tension headache. The session had taken place in the barn a week earlier. Since then, Rocky had wondered when and how the subject would come up again. He had hardly suspected it would happen here and now, up in the high country, with a gun right *there*, flopping about in Grumley's hand.

"Okay, you want me to give you twenty grand," Grumley said, "or some such healthy amount like that. Right?"

"That's just a for instance amount," Rocky said, squatting down next to the elk to check the collar again, acting casual. As if this whole sordid situation was no big deal.

"What do you mean? You said an amount but you don't mean it?" said Grumley.

"The ballpark," said Rocky. "Not necessarily the final number."

"So the amount of money might go up from there?"

"Or down. Depends on the situation." "Okay, the ballpark," Grumley said. "The ballpark. And all of it buys me freedom from my wife and buys me solid gold guaranteed one hundred percent protection, because you are going to sit tight and not discuss my business operation with the authorities. Have I got it right? Is that the rough idea?"

When Rocky had first conceived of the plan it had made sense, the kind of sense incubated in a bottle of Wild Turkey. But now he was not so certain of its wisdom. Rocky stood up. The clouds had thickened in the past few minutes and the air carried a fresh whiff of pine. He ignored the erratic twitching of the elk's hind legs. It made a scrabbling sound on the rocks.

"That's more or less the idea," Rocky said. "But if you want to talk—"

"Good. Because I have a question, Rocky. Have you been screwing my wife?"

Rocky froze. "What the hell do you mean?" he said, worried that the pause had given him away.

"You little fuck," growled Grumley.

"She . . .

"She what?"

"She wants—"

"Oh, so you know what Trudy wants, huh?" Grumley scoffed. "Just beautiful." He held both arms out as if he could hug the hillside. The rifle dangled loosely in his hand.

Rocky spoke quickly. "Trudy only wants enough money to make another start."

"I can't believe I'm talking to a guy who's screwing my wife."

Rocky swallowed hard. He kept an eye on the gun. "It's seed money to get her going," he said.

"Seed for two fuckin' birds?"

"It would only put a dent in your stash," Rocky said with a note of certainty in his voice.

"How would you know? Have you been examining my books?" said Grumley.

"You screw my wife and you mess around with my business too, is that it? Did you hear what I said? My business. Think about it."

"It's just a drop in the—"

"Says who? Fuck you and your miserable plan." Grumley pointed the barrel of the gun at Rocky's face. "How does a nobody like you figure he's gonna snap his fingers and make himself a somebody?"

Snow began falling. It was sudden. No advance troops. The storm started in full battle mode.

"Well—"

Grumley took a step forward. Rocky backed up to where the elk lay scraping the rocks with its hooves. Grumley's fist came up gripping the gunstock like a brick. Rocky reeled backward and reached out to clutch at a rock, any rock, to brace his fall. His cheek was on fire.

Rocky crawled toward his backpack, coughing, spitting blood, disoriented. He shook his head and struggled to his knees, knelt over his pack and dug into it. There was one shot of xylazine left. He swung around and pressed the barrel of a dart gun against the elk's still-quivering neck, a nice soft spot. The overdose would be as effective as a bullet behind the ear. The elk would die fast.

"What the hell are you doing?" Grumley said.

"Trying to get your goddamn attention."

Rocky cocked the dart gun.

"Okay, okay," said Grumley.

Rocky felt a surge of relief. The situation was coming under his control. He still felt woozy from the sucker punch. The bruise on his cheek was going to be a humdinger.

Grumley walked away. He made it fifteen feet.

"Goddamn," he snarled. He turned around, his rifle up pointed at Rocky. "My business is my fucking business!"

But Rocky fired first. He pulled the trigger, sending the dart into the soft flesh of the elk's neck. There was nothing Grumley could do now to stop the elk from dying. Rocky looked up at the muzzle of the rifle pointed at his face and realized too late he had used the weapon on the wrong beast.

\*\*\*\*

The hour it took to get to the top of the mountain was given over to a thousand "what ifs" as Allison Coil contemplated the constant flurry of choices offered up by the world. The elk's choices had led him to a bullet. Her choice had left Vic's tent less crowded. With the sky dropping, her decisions now might turn out to be critical to her survival during the long journey down to the canyon. The gathering storm would no doubt curb the zeal of the protesters who had set up tents at the base of the mountain that morning.

Allison had not given much thought to them until now. She imagined that most of them were like the men she had left back at the hunter's camp, city dwellers out on a lark. But with the coming snowstorm, they might learn the hard way that Mother Nature was indifferent to the rights of everyone and everything on this planet. You might as well protest earthquakes, fires, floods and falling airplanes.

A rifle shot interrupted her thoughts.

She yanked the reins and instinctively rose in the stirrups to get a bearing on the sound. No point in walking into crossfire. She was at the top of Black Squirrel Pass, the summit of the ridge that formed the west wall of Ripplecreek. Sounds traveled strangely in the mountains.

She waited and listened. She reached for her binoculars that were tucked in a front saddlebag. Bear peered around inquisitively, lowered his neck. He chomped on a stray tuft of meadow rue. The pack mule, Eli, looked asleep.

The scrub ahead was vacant, but the chest-high brush farther on could hide a large herd of deer or an army of hunters.

The upper bowl of Ripplecreek was nearly a mile across. Through her binoculars, the falling snow at the top of the pass was compressed into a porous white whirl that turned distant clumps of trees into nothing more than dark blotches with un-defined edges, vague shadows.

Something moved. It was so small in her field of vision that it did not register at first. A tiny shape was moving near a cluster of rocks, off the trail, near Lizard's Tongue. It was a gray splotch with legs and muscles. Somebody struggling or pulling.

The shape disappeared, gobbled up by a small stand of trees.

Allison lowered the binoculars and squinted. With the naked eye, there was no detail except swirling snowflakes. She raised the lenses again.

There was nothing but fuzzy whiteness now. She replayed the mental movie: four or five seconds' worth of film, a man tugging an object, a shape, something of substance through the snow. Dragging a deer? A lone do-it-yourselfer using a sled to haul a carcass? Perhaps.

She put the binoculars back, cinched her hat down against the chilly wind and gave Bear a cluck. She dug into her jacket pocket for a Fig Newton. The trail would take her past Lizard's Tongue, where she could get a closer look at what she had seen through the binoculars. The man's body language told her one thing: he was in a bit of a scramble, hurrying as if the clock was ticking. She looked up at the oncoming storm. Perhaps it was.

# 2

At the mouth of the canyon, Dawn Ellenberg sat in base camp holding a walkie-talkie while two reporters with notepads stood nearby chatting with each other. Maria Nash was the poorly dressed, slightly nervous cub scribe from Glenwood Springs. Robert P. Calkins III was a more seasoned reporter, a brash young man from the *Vail Trail*. Neither had taken a note in over an hour.

Ellenberg had poured countless hours into her PR campaign, pumping the event as having Woodstockian dimensions. For all her troubles, Nash and Calkins were the only two "journalists" she had managed to muster to the scene. Not one television crew had shown up. No *USA Today*. No *People* magazine. No Denver newspaper reporters either, even though she had bought lunch for a Denver-based correspondent and had extracted from him a "we'll see, maybe" over curried chickpea tofu. No one had even bothered to make the drive over from Aspen.

Maria Nash and Robert P. Calkins III. That was all. There she was; there they were. The word would go out from her mouth to their pencil tips and through their meek little computers to their editors. Ultimately, it would be another afterthought in the big, flying sweep of worldwide news. Nash had asked her fair share of questions, but nothing out of the ordinary.

"What is the size of the army of protesters?" she had asked earlier.

"About five hundred," said Ellenberg.

"How many did you anticipate?"

"There was really no way to know, but we're thrilled with the turnout."

"Is it enough to get the job done?"

"You bet."

Calkins had held back, letting Nash do the nuts-and-bolts dirty work, then weighed in.

"Is the big meat-eating public out there really with you?" he asked. "Have you studied the meat-eating statistics lately? The numbers are up, I've gotta tell you."

Ellenberg responded at first with a thoughtful pause.

"Every great cause starts with someone saying 'enough, enough.' We need to educate the public," she said. "We need to enlighten the public and that's why we are here today."

Dawn Ellenberg was the founder and lead piper of FATE, which stood for Fighting Animal Torture Everywhere. She was the star of the show—which amounted only to a mini-show at this point.

A strong wood fire burning a few feet away helped beat back the growing grayness and the cold. She hoped the glow of firelight cast her apple cheeks and long, full hair in an earnest light. Even if there weren't photographers she still wanted to look the part of a revolutionary leader. She bent down, planted her boots flat on the ground and rubbed the heat from the fire into her legs.

Whenever team leaders radioed in, bizarre noises filled Ellenberg's walkie-talkie. The faithful had brought drums, snares and bongos. They had dragged up cymbals, whistles, wood blocks, bells, horns, boom boxes. They played everything from rap to Beethoven. There were yellers, barkers and howlers. They were scattered throughout the canyon, making their presence known. But when her radio was silent, the effect was not as impressive. She had wanted a pervasive sense of bedlam that would send every mammal scurrying out of harm's way.

Next year she would recruit animal lovers from the entire country, draw them all in for a seminal bash that would define the word "protest" for decades to come. It would be like Burning Man, only with purpose and results. The 1968 Democratic Convention, G8 Summit and European anti-nuclear marches were all known for their massive protests.

She would put this canyon—and FATE—on the map.

The storm was unwelcome. Had the TV cameras been there, it might have appeared to the viewing audience that the protesters were committed troopers—real warriors, not city wimps—willing to take on the hunters in even the toughest elements. But there were no cameras. And if it wasn't on TV, it was no revolution.

"Give me your wrap-up thoughts," said Nash. "Success or not?"

Nash had a husky voice. Her eyes jumped like she was in a rush. Her stringy black hair fell indifferently. If the public relations success of this day depended on reporters like Nash, Ellenberg didn't hold out much hope.

"This is a miserable day for Colorado hunters," said Ellenberg, with all the gravitas she could muster. Nobody respected whiners. "Anyone who has ever loaded a rifle in the name of wholesale slaughter has to be nervous. They're on the run now. They're scared. The wholesale slaughter has *got* to stop, *will* stop, *can* be stopped."

It was the speech she had rehearsed for a gaggle of reporters and cameras. But by the time she looked up, Nash had already stopped writing. Calkins hadn't budged. Maybe he had a secret digital recorder and was getting it all.

"This is hell day for hunters," she said, straight to Calkins. "Things do change. Americans used to smoke at work. Americans used to drink and drive. But society made changes and it will soon make another. This is hell day, the beginning of the end for hunters. Not only in this pristine Colorado canyon, but in every hollow, in every field and along every stream where the hunters' holocaust takes place. They have heard the noise today. Believe me, they have heard. From now on, it's their days that are numbered."

She gazed solemnly into the fire.

"How will you know for sure this worked?" said Nash.

"If I know in my heart that one animal has been spared from the wholesale slaughter, then it worked." She paused for effect. "One animal. That would suffice."

Nash clicked her pen.

"Praise the animals," said Ellenberg, her cheeks baked in the fire's heat. "We are at one with them today."

\*\*\*\*

Allison slowed Bear at the base of Lizard's Tongue, a distinctive spire of rock like a castle turret. The snow fell with intensity. Down to the right, where the slope dropped quickly, was the rocky scree where the man had disappeared.

If the deer was already dead, no hunter in his right mind would have contemplated negotiating such a steep pitch. On top of that, a deer would not drag well in one piece, unless it was a fawn. And no one could have cut it into pieces so soon after the shot. For whatever reason, the man might be in trouble, might need help. She could not glide past the spot without seeing if he would resurface.

She turned around in her saddle, thinking she might be able to spot Black Squirrel Pass and reverse the line of sight in her mind. She could barely see three hundred yards.

She gave Bear a pat on the neck and climbed down. She checked on the stoic Eli, who never seemed to mind much of anything. She squatted at the trail's edge and peered down across the tops of the rocks. Each rock was coated equally with a white stocking cap on its featureless face. She wrapped Bear's rein around a rock and headed up to Lizard's Tongue.

From near the top, Allison found a perch where she could steady herself and look farther down the slope. There were more rocks and snow. The view was of a broader landscape, but still empty. She panned the scene through the binoculars, panned back with even more care, overlapping every frame. Nothing.

Back with Bear, she brushed off the snow that had accumulated on his saddle and climbed on. The entire world was turning white, except . . .

An elk.

He was a fifty yards off the trail, maybe more. He was a beauty, judging by the sizable rack. She didn't know how she'd missed it. She had been looking for a man, she reasoned. Prime elk did not lie down and die in the open.

"Stay here, Bear," she said and re-tied his rope. "You too, Eli." Not that either animal had much choice. And Bear wouldn't wander far if he got loose. He just didn't.

She walked down the slope, stepping carefully. Rocks wobbled and the fresh snow wasn't good for traction. There was no need to check for signs of life. The antlers, about as large as she had ever seen up close, were like a miniature, smooth-boned forest. The fifth point was snapped, but the main beams were intact. The wound that had brought him down could be on the opposite side, underneath. She could see no trace of blood.

She brushed snow off his hide, checked for a wound and cleaned his face. His eyes were open, mouth slightly ajar. This animal had not been dead for long.

"Where the hell are your elk buddies?" she muttered. "Or your hunter?"

The elk was much too big to have been dragged by one man, couldn't have been dragged by two or three. The guy she had seen in her binoculars would know; there had to be a connection.

She sat back from the elk's head. Snow-coated Bear and Eli stood stock still on the trail, waiting. She imagined a scenario that might fit, but came up empty. She patted the elk's haunch. It was remotely possible the elk's killer would return with a team of helpers to quarter the animal. But it did not seem likely that anyone would be venturing back into the teeth of this storm. Here was a scene for the protesters to get sick over—the sheer destruction of an animal for no apparent purpose. The elk had not been tagged. He had been treated like garbage and he would rot. It was an utter waste and defied all the civilized rules that demarcated the line between hunt and slaughter.

Allison stood up and pondered the scene one more time, estimated her distance and bearings from Lizard's Tongue for future reference. She trudged back up the pitch, lungs burning a bit, and climbed back on Bear. The wind howled, as if to warn her she was running late. She tucked her blue bandana tightly up over her face and pulled down her hat. A few guides were starting to carry cell phones, but they only worked on certain high spots and that was one thing Allison liked about roaming the back country, not being constantly in touch, constantly available. If she had one now, however, she might be able to let someone know she would be running late.

Very late.

She gave Bear and Eli a cluck and they were off.

Her bones ached, but so did her head, as she tried to put it all together in a way that made sense. Right now, nothing did.

\*\*\*\*

Two miles back down Ripplecreek, Grumley forced his mind to cover the issues and think about what happened. He had stepped out of routine, but a return to routine would be so much better without that jerk Carnivitas. It felt like it would snow for a week. Mother Nature was taking care of business.

Carrying two rifles on foot had been distracting. His own rifle was now in his sling and Rocky's dart gun was in his hands.

The dead elk was a problem. Maybe he should have stayed to quarter the damn thing, but he didn't have the tools. Hauling Rocky off had been exhausting enough. Rocky's last act, as a dead weight, was one of his most cruel. Dead bodies handle about as well as a bag of wet sand.

Grumley kept moving. His burly, muscled body was fashioned by years of rigorous hiking. He moved like a fullback, always ready to head-butt a moving truck. He wore the outdoors—nicks, scars and dings—on every scrap of his face. He would have to work on a story to tell the other three hunters. He needed to come up with a version of events to tell Applegate: a reason why he had skipped off without joining him on his hunt. Or his crusade. For Dean Applegate, the most unlucky and least talented hunter George Grumley had ever known, each trip out of the tent was a frightening cocktail of raw emotion mixed with zero stalking skill.

Trudy kept flashing through his mind. He wondered what his wife knew about Rocky's attempted extortion. In reality, Grumley figured, the whole thing was self-defense. More than likely Trudy had no idea Rocky would make the threats. There wasn't a challenging bone in her body.

A slight pounding in his temples told him it was time for a drink. Water searches would be impossible after dark; staying on the trail would be challenge enough in this storm.

Grumley veered off the trail and picked his way through a tight stand of aspens to the streambed. He set his rifle and the dart gun against a tree, put his boot down through a few inches of fresh powder and pressed with all his weight on a layer of ice. It creaked for a few seconds and gave way. His boot landed in six inches of cold creek. Lying prone, Grumley dipped his lips in the water. He sucked slowly, steadily. It would be impossible to drink too much.

"George?"

Grumley flipped over like a cat on fire.

Applegate stood ten paces away, waving both hands to show they were empty.

"What the hell?"

"It's me.

"You little—"

"I spotted you back in here."

"Jesus H."

Grumley stood up. Applegate stepped closer, a fucking Gomer Crockett in head-to-toe catalog camouflage. He looked worried though. Applegate's tentative posture and bug eyes suggested things were bad.

"Have you been following me?" said Grumley.

Applegate shivered badly. His jaw was not solidly connected to his head. The thin cotton parka would be okay for the mountains in July, but not in October.

"I think I killed a guy," said Applegate.

"*Think?*"

"It might be one of the protesters. It wasn't another hunter, anyway, because he wasn't carrying a gun. We gotta tell somebody."

"Where did this happen?"

"Back up the valley. Not far."

"When?"

Applegate looked around to the right and also to the left as if studying the aspen would help him remember. His face was a picture of fear. He was not thinking.

"I don't know. Twenty minutes, maybe thirty. I've been wandering around. I made it halfway back to camp, then wasn't sure which way to go. I found the main trail here, sat awhile. Then I thought I'd try to find him again, the protester. I was thinking . . . he might not be dead."

"You said you killed him."

"I know, I know. But he might be in shock. I didn't really check.

I didn't feel for a pulse or anything. But he's probably dead. He was there, draped in this brown thing. Like a cape, only bigger."

"Cape?"

"Like a big piece of curtain or a blanket."

"Do you think you can find the way back to this guy?" said Grumley. "Sometimes it's not so easy. Everything starts to look the same."

"I think so." Applegate stood up.

"Be sure so."

"I am."

Grumley stepped over to his rifle and the dart gun propped against the tree. He stood between them and Applegate, who surely had been too confused to notice he'd been carrying two guns. That might be a problem. No matter what Applegate was taking in and remembering, Grumley didn't need the confusion, didn't need a question from Applegate about two guns. Grumley gave Rocky's dart gun a gentle tap with his foot and it fell silently into the snow, cutting its own grave.

＊＊＊＊

Applegate hunkered down for a moment as they were coming down the slope and held his palm above his eyes like a golfer shielding the sun to read the grain on a putt. But there was no sun, only steadily falling snow

"There," he said, pointing to a clump of buckthorn.

The body was wrapped around the base of the bush, the windbreak sparing it from being buried by too much snow.

"Aw, Christ," said Applegate, keeping his distance and starting to sob.

Grumley went to the body without hesitation and started brushing away snow and working to avoid disturbing the body.

"If I was the coroner I would say he's dead. What is this brown thing?"

The brown cloth covering the corpse was like a large cape, neither shaped nor stitched like regular clothing.

"Where did you shoot him?"

"I was standing farther up the slope," said Applegate. "Hundred yards or so."

"No, I mean where in the body?"

"Christ, I don't know. I thought it was a deer."

"I believe that's what you were supposed to think."

The brown cape completely surrounded the body. Grumley found an arm and could feel the legs, but he wasn't particularly keen on rolling the guy completely over to see much more.

"We've gotta carry him out," said Applegate. "And report it."

"You're crazy," said Grumley. "No cops, no nobody."

Applegate looked puzzled, said nothing.

"Of course not," said Grumley. "You'd be a fool. You're the guy they want."

"They?"

"The animal nuts. This dude was trying to get shot. Maybe not killed, but you did the trick. You're looking at jail time, buddy. Negligent homicide. Manslaughter, I don't know the right terms. It wouldn't matter how much remorse you'd spew out."

Applegate swallowed a mouthful of fear.

"This is the rifle you shot him with?" said Grumley. He studied Applegate's Sako and its beautiful wood-grained craftsmanship.

"Yeah."

"You gotta lose it."

"Lose?"

"Give it to me," said Grumley. "I'll take care of it. If anybody asks, you put it down and you don't remember where and you forgot about it. Lost it."

"Okay," said Applegate.

"If you walk out carrying this guy on your shoulders like a sack of potatoes, you're looking at a media frenzy and your butt on the barbecue."

Grumley could not believe Applegate hadn't simply disappeared on his own and pretended that nothing had ever happened.

"If you admit to having done this, you're going to drag yourself down and they'll probably get me, too. We do not want that. Are you with me?"

"Yeah."

Grumley took a step closer to Applegate.

"I got too much to lose if my name is so much as whispered in connection with this. You'd be the dumb out-of-towner with the inability to distinguish a deer from a human and since you were part of my hunting party, I'd be fodder for the local mincemeat factory. This guy's dead. Judging by the looks of things it's what he wanted, for whatever crazy reason. A guy who dresses like a deer during hunting season is begging to get shot. You fucked up once, Applegate. You won't do it twice. You gotta pretend it was a real bad dream."

"I suppose," said Applegate. "But what about him, leave him here?"

"Of course," said Grumley, taking two steps closer so he was smack in Applegate's face. "Now, listen to me. We're going to walk back to the main trail. We're going to hope the snow falls until Groundhog Day and covers every one of our goddamn tracks. We split up. You head down to safety. I'll go back up to camp. You don't have too far to go, maybe an hour or two at the most, depending on your pace. You never saw me."

"Okay," said Applegate.

"Can you make it okay? You're gonna have to use your wits to stick to the main trail. At least it's not snowing as hard down here as it is up on top."

"I will."

"You'll get cleaned up and wait at the barn, right?"

"Whatever."

"What happened to your rifle?" he said.

"Lost and forgot," said Applegate. "Right?"

"Right."

Sending Applegate down alone carried huge risks. At the very least, he could have a tough time staying on the trail, given all the snow and the darkness. He might have a change of heart and blubber it all out to the first person he saw. But sending him down toward civilization would spare the weary guy a steep hike back up to the hunters' camp.

"Can you start a fire in the snow if you get lost?" Grumley said.

"You showed me once."

"Can you do it now?"

"I think so," said Applegate.

Grumley dug in an inside pocket for two packs of fire starter gel. "One should do it, but you've got a spare in case you screw up," said Grumley. "Matches?"

"Got those," said Applegate.

"Do you have any food?" said Grumley.

"All gone."

Grumley eyed the body. Drinking water from the dead guy's canteen was worth the risk. So was eating his food, or at least a portion. They could both use a bit of fuel. He had seen how thirsty Applegate was, too. Grumley dropped to his knees next to the body and began searching.

"Aw, don't," said Applegate.

"Why not?

"Jesus," said Applegate. "Leave him alone. I'll make it."

"Got it," said Grumley, wrapping his fingers around a bottle that sat in an inside pocket. It was one of those squeezable plastic bottles used by bicycle riders. Further buried in the body wrap, he found a sandwich-sized Tupperware container.

"Bingo," Grumley said.

The water was cold but the dissipating heat from the body had kept it from icing up. Grumley figured there was a pint or so inside and passed it to Applegate.

"Don't get your lips on the plastic," he said.

The Tupperware held chunks of cheese and crackers. Everything was eaten in a minute. Grumley jammed the Tupperware back in with the body.

Dead guy, Grumley thought. This was the day for dead guys. It was a total coincidence. Two fucked-up deals, no question, but more than anything it was important not to let one get tangled up with the other. And it was damn important to get out of this valley before anybody else spotted him, especially those idiot protesters.

✳✳✳✳

Over and over in her mind, Allison kept seeing the hunched form of the man struggling desperately with the load. The vision was shadow-like, but clear enough.

An hour to go. Bear was eager and anxious; Eli toiled along like a worn-down soldier. Allison's eyes widened and she took a bit of relief from the decreasing intensity of the snowfall.

In a snowstorm, jet noise was even more pronounced, as if the roar was passed from one flake to the next. The blunt bawl from this jet had a deep, droning wah-wah quality to it. It was a distant reminder that jet traffic existed, a subliminal message from the world of technology. Next it was as if the jet was swooping along the tree-tops of Ripplecreek. The sound bounced down and around her and she glanced up, half expecting to catch a glimpse of a silver belly.

She wondered if the jet was bound east or west—New York or L.A., Denver or Salt Lake City. Perhaps it was a short-hopper on the way into Grand Junction, the passengers lined up in neat rows, elbow to elbow, heads bouncing in unison like puppets all controlled by the same puppeteer, all rocketing along through the skies. Alcohol for the travelers, jet fuel for the engines and heaps of good faith to keep the whole thing aloft.

At cruising speed, of course, the jet engines did not have the same straining quality they did at takeoff. Allison wondered if anybody realized how fast a plane was traveling on a runway before liftoff, or whatever they called it. Liftoff was for space shuttles and things like that. Planes *took* off. Whatever one called the means of getting airborne, it did not make a lick of difference when it came to human beings surrounded by hunks of metal rocketing through the thin air. Not all things that were supposed to go up managed to make it. Some flopped. Some nose-dived. Some came to a terrifying moment-of-truth—halfway earth-bound, gravity-happy, man-made structures that weighed thousands of tons, fancy-free mechanical things that used air, of all things, for power and opportunity. Allison had been on a jet that arrived at that moment and couldn't make the transition. Gravity won, or flight lost: one of the two.

Allison pictured a businessman sleeping in first class, an empty glass of sauvignon blanc on his dinner tray, a paperback thriller propped open on the synthetic blanket draped over his swollen gut. His mouth drooping slightly ajar, making the snoring even more irritating for his seatmate. Allison had been there, oblivious to the approaching danger.

Two years now in the mountains and she was beginning—barely beginning—to consider the fact that she had been lucky. Another few seconds further up and the drop would have been an exponentially greater slam to reality. Another few seconds further up and 31 dead would have been 119 dead.

Death, she had learned, is simply a corpse you carry around underneath your skin. Until one day it pops free.

****

The snow caught the FATE followers off guard but not off their game. A few returned early to warm their hands by the bonfire at base camp, but most trickled back in small, elated bunches and the spirits of the camp began to soar.

The ones returning were greeted with a wave of applause, some of it generated by bare palms and some of it generated by the soft, puffy, repetitive *whomp* of two mittens coming together. There were smiles all around. The two lame reporters were long gone, off to meet their deadlines or appointments in a bar.

"People!" shouted Ellenberg over the general din. Everyone stopped immediately. "We've got a pot of vegetarian chili and corn muffins almost ready. If anyone thinks they don't have enough warm blankets or clothes for the night, please let us know."

There was silence all around.

"Good. Again, congratulations. Let's sound off, to make sure."

"One," said Ellenberg.

"Two," said a male voice across the fire. The count climbed quickly to fourteen.

"Fifteen?" said Ellenberg. "Fifteen? Where is fifteen?"

"He was behind me in line yesterday," said a husky woman whose head poked out from a turquoise blanket. "Not a large guy at all, not much to him. He was struggling with the hike. Had trouble breathing. Didn't seem all that comfortable."

Ellenberg remembered him all too well. He looked like a kid, hadn't said much. He had stared at her from a seat near the front of the bus during the entire bus ride. He was the frail-looking one with the Red Sox cap. He could have been twenty-five; he could have been twelve. What she had seen of his scalp was hairless. His nose was a button and his cheeks were puffed hard, pink and frail. On the hike in, he had sputtered and coughed much more than the others and she had asked him directly if he was going to be able to make it. The answer was "yes" and the smile that went with it said *don't worry.*

"Does anyone know where he pitched his tent?"

"There was a tent forty or fifty yards down in a small aspen grove. That way." The voice belonged to an older man, thin with a long gray beard. He pointed off down the slope. "I was talking with a small guy who was putting it up yesterday."

"Does anybody here claim that tent?" she said.

Nobody spoke.

"Could you show me?" said Ellenberg. The chatter came to a halt as Ellenberg passed the man a flashlight. The group headed off.

They bumped around for three or four minutes in the dark, plunging through snow-covered bushes, until they stood next to a tent that sagged on the sides from a build-up of snow.

"Hello," said Ellenberg. Please be there, she thought. "Anyone home?"

No answer. Her companion began searching for the zipper to the front flap.

"We can't barge in," said Ellenberg. "That's private property. We don't have his permission."

"You're right," he said, a touch chagrined.

"Did you talk to him?"

"I asked him why he was putting up his tent so far away from the rest of the camp. He shrugged and said he was a light sleeper, needed complete quiet. Seemed like a nice enough guy."

The group headed back to the warmth of the bonfire, where the concern and fear draped over them like a bad cloud. Maybe this missing man had headed down the mountain on his own. It was only an hour or so back out to the main road. Maybe he would turn up at any minute with a good story to tell and none the worse for wear. Ellenberg said a quick prayer to the public relations gods.

# 3

It was fatigue all bound up with worry and weird thoughts. Allison had a hard time connecting the images from the day in her mind. She had put Bear away in the barn with a small sack of his own oats and had unloaded Eli. They both needed a good scrub but that would wait. It was midnight.

There was no one around to help or even talk to. Someone sleeping in the barn would have demonstrated concern for her whereabouts or well-being, but Allison had to remind herself not to look for such civilized touches. She was safe, dead, or struggling alone in the wilderness. Three choices. Take your pick. Had someone been sleeping in the barn, Allison would have felt like she belonged to a family. Loose-knit for sure, but still a family. But the barn's lack of humans said it all. So much for sentiment.

Allison walked the last stretch home. David might already be there. But occasionally he'd have a beer and unwind before driving up from Glenwood Springs. She wanted to curl up and wrap an arm over his broad back and conk out. But now she was torn between wanting to avoid the long talk, in order to maximize sleep time, and wanting to discuss the details of the day and attempt to put logic to the events.

She followed the road until the fence ended at the edge of Pete Weaver's Ripplecreek Ranch. She cut diagonally through an open field and couldn't quite get her legs out of first gear, a common sensation after a day on a horse. Her strides felt minuscule; the earth slowed.

She crossed Owl Creek on a footbridge, followed the creek down along the opposite bank, trudged through snow to the top of a small ridge and spotted the dim shape of her cabin. A weak porch light cast enough watts to offer a bearing, but it looked as if David Slater had not yet arrived. Otherwise, the whole place would have been ablaze.

She stopped on her porch, kicked the snow off her boots with a gentle tap against the threshold and opened the door to her small A-frame. The kitchen corner faced south, so in daytime the sunlight poured through two large windows. The bedroom was on the opposite side, tucked back in the corner. A heavy, wood-frame couch and a couple of old sitting chairs framed a living area around a wood stove. A long table made for an eating space next to the kitchen. The only closed space was a closet-sized bathroom stuck off the back. A spiral staircase led up to a set of twin beds in a loft where Allison liked to sleep because she could wake to a view of the peaks off to the east toward the Holy Cross Wilderness.

Allison lit a candle on the dining table, grabbed a beer from the refrigerator and headed straight to the bathroom to start the shower steaming. Remaining on her feet would delay sleep and it might keep her perked up enough to wait for Slater. Surnames ruled among conversation and wildlife officers so that's how she thought of him, too. Slater.

She was certain sleep wouldn't have its way with her until she told someone what she'd experienced and she was equally sure Slater would have some ideas about what she'd seen. Telling someone would make it seem more real. She lit newspaper and kindling in the wood stove and took a long draw of Coors. She undressed. The can of beer served as friend in the now-steaming stall and she let the shower blast her from behind, expecting Slater to call out any second.

She dried off. She stuck a few pieces of wood in the stove and stretched out on the couch. She finished the beer and thought about making some tea to keep her moving until Slater arrived. She stared at the flicker of light from the vent in the stove and decided that making tea might be a bit daunting for this particular moment.

★★★★

She felt a kiss on her forehead, light enough for a baby.

"It's six in the morning," he said. "Try not to cry."

"I'm late."

The schedule had her heading back up the mountain.

"I've got breakfast ready," said Slater. Allison recalled the gentle clinking sounds from the kitchen during the last half-hour, as she wormed her way to the surface of reality. And then, from even deeper down, she remembered the sensation of him dropping the quilt over her as she slept on the couch.

"What time did you make it in?"

"One-ish. You could use an answering machine."

"Yuck," said Allison.

"You were down for the count. Hard. Not that I even tried to wake you. The look on your face said *done*."

Allison crawled off the couch. She knew that moving wouldn't cause any physical pain. It would be torture but she wasn't hung over. That was one small blessing to count.

"Are you working today too?" she said.

"I wasn't supposed to," he said. "But we've got a problem."

"Problem?"

He was all duded-up in his green, slightly rumpled uniform. She liked him best in blue jeans and old sweatshirts, sitting in an aspen grove in a high meadow, splitting a six-pack and slicing summer sausage to go with crackers, mustard and cheese. This wasn't bad, the official dress of a US Forest Service resource conservation officer—once known as a forest ranger. But Slater looked uncomfortable in the uniform.

"Missing people-type problem. One of the protesters," he said. "Probably dead-type problem, given the storm. It's one of them all-hands-on-deck things. The sheriff has already called his troops together and made it clear he doesn't want anything that would keep the publicity rolling."

"Missing where?"

Allison pulled on a fresh set of Wranglers, an undershirt and a green and black checked flannel shirt that deserved to be washed but would have to do.

"Way up the canyon."

"Do they know who?"

"I don't think so."

The storm would have been rough enough if a hiker was prepared: brutal or fatal if he wasn't. Allison had not heard the protesters, but by the time she had come over the top of Black Squirrel Pass, the storm had probably chased them to a lower elevation.

"You must have had a rough day," said Slater. "Snow pretty hard?"

"Like the end of time."

"You get hung up?"

"Not by the storm."

"Huh?" he said, stopping as he put butter and orange marmalade on two pieces of burnt toast.

"I was late as it was, dawdling a bit as always," said Allison. "Then I heard a gunshot. A minute later I saw a guy dragging who knows what through the snow. Whatever he was dragging, it wasn't easy and required force. It was like I could see him straining at it. I worked my way down to the spot where I'd seen him and found a dead elk. Only the elk hadn't been shot. There were no wounds. And the elk was such a monster there was no way he'd been dragged, not by one guy and not by three or four."

Slater stared back with concern.

"He seemed angry," she said.

"How long between the shot and the time you found the elk?"

Allison took a breath and tried to stick to exactly what she'd seen. Her grandfather had once claimed he watched a UFO set down in a lake outside of Longmont, but he had refused to embellish it with made-up details. He told her that anybody who wanted to know what the first-hand experience was like could find the original police report and read it.

"An hour plus. You know the descent from Black Squirrel Pass."

"And you really couldn't see what the man was dragging?"

"No."

Slater pondered things for a second, his mustache-covered lip buried in the coffee, his deep brown eyes penetrating through the tabletop. He looked like a detective pondering clues.

The idea that she was cozying up to a cop-like guy was a constant source of amusement. This relationship wasn't necessarily forever, she thought, but even that idea didn't seem unbearable. He didn't seem to have the typical government mentality. Also, he was strong and straightforward. Allison had never before been with a man who could be classified in the "straightforward" category. Slater was a trim six-footer with an engaging face, dark eyes over a slender nose. His jaw was strong and his teeth, neat rows arranged by a perfectionist, sparkled on cue when needed. Allison liked the way he moved and talked, careful and in control, but he could flip over to the relaxation mode without much effort.

"Are you going to report this?" said Slater.

"Report what?" inquired Allison. "Dead elk in the woods? I can see the headlines."

"The dragging part," said Slater. "Maybe it fits in with our missing protester. Maybe not."

"I'll report it. You never know what it's worth," said Allison. "But I've gotta go. We've got two crews heading out today. It's practically every horse in the outfit."

"Me too. Hell," he said, looking at his watch. She leaned up for the kiss at first, and then stood all the way up. He gave her a warm, powerful hug. Slater was a long-term possibility.

Slater grabbed his coffee cup and headed out. She stood in the doorway as he climbed in behind the wheel of his government-green pickup and grabbed his radio, trying to raise somebody.

****

"Hear someone's missing?"

It was Popeye Boyles, retired Navy cook turned guide and all-around barn helper.

"No," Grumley replied. It couldn't be Rocky, Grumley thought. Hunting guides were always off in the wilderness. It could take a week before anybody even asked the first question.

"I caught some chatter on the radio this morning," said Boyles.

His hobby was playing amateur cop. He was wedded to a scanning gizmo that picked up every police frequency that bounced around in the narrow canyons and hollows of Ripplecreek. It never hurt to know who was poking around or headed their way. Most of Grumley's guide service was completely on the up and up. But a few clients and an ever-growing list of their friends and acquaintances could request and pay for a hunt that minimized their time in the field and maximized their chances of success—all the way to one hundred percent. Grumley considered his work nothing more than that of a good advance team. He found the prey and tracked the prey. Next, the clients were whisked into position to site down the barrel and pull the trigger. This made for an efficient use of time, for those who didn't mind parting with up to seventy-five thousand dollars for the convenience factor. The size of the fee depended on the number of hunters, the size of the prey they were after and the degree of difficulty they desired to make them feel, for a day, like Teddy Roosevelt of the Flat Tops.

"What did you hear?" said Grumley. Boyles teased. He always had to be asked.

"One of them eco-freaks.

"Them?"

"Protesters. Kids. I first heard that Dawn Ellenberg chick all concerned, talking with a sheriff's deputy last night, getting ready to contact Search and Rescue."

Boyles talked like he was explaining a batch of overdone scrambled eggs to the commander of an aircraft carrier.

"The guy's tent was empty last night and when they went to check it, they didn't even open the thing."

"How do you know?" said Grumley.

"Because one of the deputies asked them on the radio."

"But the missing guy had definitely gone up with the protest, hiked up the canyon?"

"That's what the cops asked," said Boyles. "And Ellenberg says yes, he was in the woods with the rest of them. But get this. The cops asked Ellenberg if they had actually looked inside the tent, you know, to make sure he hadn't passed out or was sleeping. But they hadn't looked. They didn't want to invade his privacy."

"His privacy?" said Grumley.

"Yeah. They're looking for a missing person in a blizzard and they won't even crash his tent to make sure the guy hasn't passed out or died of fuckin' embarrassment for being part of that stupid protest."

Boyles laughed and Grumley joined in.

The barn was busy with pre-hunt rituals. The next batch of hopeful hunters was packing up. Grumley had already checked in with a few of them. He had chatted with them, offering information about the best locations and the proper way to quarter a carcass. Everyone liked to chew on a bit of Grumley's world. It was part of the package, even on this side, the legal side. He had showered and chugged his way through half a pot of coffee and then fretted around and criticized a few guides, for the hell of it, as they loaded up the packhorses and mules.

"He's a goner unless he was a professional mountaineer," said Boyles, just making conversation. "But from what I gather, he was the kind of guy who would have had a tough time with a sleepover in his own backyard."

"Nasty up there," said Grumley.

News delivered, Boyles drifted off.

"One other thing," said Grumley. Boyles stopped like a dog on a choke chain. "Find someone to go tell my hunting buddies that they're on their own for a few days. However long they want to hang around is fine. Tell them I got pulled away, make some shit up. Marcovicci knows his way around; he can handle anything."

"Done," said Boyles.

"And tell 'em, too, that Applegate headed off. Might be back, might not. Tell 'em I'll be back to check in a few days. Make up a juicy story, okay? Tell 'em I got busy digging out a back-country camp. Whatever. Make it good."

****

Grumley plunged his old Ford pickup down the slope through the bog birch and parked it in the pristine powder covering the dirt driveway. No one had been in or out of Rocky Carnivitas' mobile home for a day or more. The handle turned. It was unlocked, a typical backwoods practice.

The interior of the old Streamliner was cramped, more like a steel cave than a home. It was only five short steps from front to back. In the middle, where the airplane-sized bathroom and storage closet faced each other on opposite sides of the floor plan, Grumley's shoulders scraped the walls. There was a bedroom in back.

Small wonder, Grumley thought, that Trudy's company and Trudy's closeness held a certain appeal.

The refrigerator yielded nothing but sour milk and a half loaf of stiff, moldy white bread, the cheap stuff.

Everything looked normal. The kitchen was straightforward enough, including the photographs taped to the cupboard doors: Rocky in various poses with hunted game, in various seasons and in various terrains. The game included a mountain lion, a bighorn sheep and a half-dozen elk and deer. There wasn't much Rocky hadn't killed. One of the elk sported a towering rack, near trophy size. Rocky had wedged himself in between the antlers and flashed a wicked grin. He looked simultaneously ecstatic and angry, as if his main spring was wound one crank too tight.

Grumley took forty-five dollars out of a tin box next to a tape deck on a ledge above the bed. He checked the tiny bathroom for secret compartments. Fuckin' Rocky, he thought. The business now produced more cash in a month than the sporting goods store generated in a year and it was not to be messed with by anyone. Rocky had been among the best. Until he got stupid.

Grumley went back to the elk antler photograph. Rocky wasn't quite as sheepish as his quiet manner had suggested upon first hire. Christ, that grin. Another poser. Grumley was sick and tired of the fakers and their bullshit. Rocky had been a coward and a fool for having been sucked into Trudy's world. He had wanted something for nothing. Worse, he'd been a major irritation. Staring at that semi-leer between the elk's huge headgear, Grumley wished he could kill him all over again.

\*\*\*\*

Suddenly, reporters. A whole flock. Maria Nash was back, but she was now flanked by a stringer from *The Denver Post* and two—count them, two—television cameras from two Denver stations that had managed to show up at precisely the same moment. One of these TV types was proving particularly obnoxious. Ellenberg wanted to clock him, but it probably wouldn't look good on TV.

"So you didn't find the note until this *morning*?"

"Correct."

"And he had left it on his sleeping bag?"

"Correct."

Ellenberg tried to remember her training in media management. Never reveal anger. Be calm, especially with cameras recording every blink. She counted six television cameras, five photographers and ten reporters. They fanned out in a semi-circle in the trampled field.

Ellenberg was tired and emotionally drained. The walk down from camp to the county road through the snow had been grueling. A thin snow was still falling, but splotches of blue could be seen through the clouds to the east.

"But you knew this individual was missing more than twelve hours before you looked in his tent, correct?"

"Yes," said Ellenberg. "There didn't seem to be much we could do."

Ellenberg noted that the reporter's oversized parka included a fur fringe. She wanted to point out how animals were being used to make him appear warm.

"What do you think the note means?"

This question was from good old Maria Nash. Ellenberg wondered if she would hear the phrase "meat-eating statistics" if Robert P. Calkins III was not there.

"I'm not sure."

Never get trapped in a cycle of speculation. Answer facts and always bring questions back to *your* themes and issues.

"Did you have any standards, were you doing any checking for physical fitness for your . . . your whatever you call it?"

The badger again—Robert P. Calkins III.

"Protest," said Ellenberg.

"So the answer is no?

"That is correct.

"And so you basically would have let anybody join your event?"

"It was a peaceful protest against a particularly invidious form of violence," said Ellenberg, with an ever-so-slight smile. "Not an event. We welcomed all those who wished to help show the world about the level of barbarism being committed every day right here in Colorado."

"Would you have called it off had you known that the snowstorm would be this severe?"

"I think," said Ellenberg. She checked herself. "Yes," she said, working to be emphatic. The reporters stood around waiting to see if the badger had another chomp left. Calkins looked at the others, who stared back. The badger tucked away a pen he had never used. The press conference was over.

Ellenberg took a deep, invisible breath and drifted off toward the FATE trailer that had been used as headquarters throughout the protest. A giant banner had been draped along the trailer's side: *FAIR IS FAIR. LET'S ARM THE ANIMALS.* She reached the door of her trailer, turned around with a feeling she was being followed.

She fought the impulse to gasp.

The man stopped inches away. For a second she remembered one friend's suggestion that she consider having a bodyguard. The man was solidly built and over six feet tall, dressed head to boot in hunter's camouflage. His face was smeared with green-black paint and the look on his face was serious, cast in a snarl.

"Dawn Ellenberg?"

Maybe he was a reporter for *Field And Stream* ("*Fire And Aim*," as they called it).

"I wanted to tell you . . ."

"What . . . ?"

"Your protest. I mean, I'm a hunter. But I'm finished. What happened here has . . ."

He stopped to fight back tears.

"What is it?" she said. "Are you okay?"

"I stopped and thought . . . what's the point?"

"It's okay," said Ellenberg.

"No, it's not. I'm giving up hunting. I want to help."

"Help?"

"Volunteer. Help. Whatever."

"There's certainly plenty to do."

"It took guts to do what you did."

"Several hundred others, too," she said.

"I admire you all."

"And you're from—"

"Denver, just outside."

"I think reporters might be interested in your change of heart. Very interested."

If he remained decked out in camouflage garb, she realized, the story of his conversion could be extremely effective.

"I'm not doing this for anything like that," said the hunter.

"Your story might pay certain dividends for us. I'd be grateful. I'll introduce you to the whole PR team."

"I was going to head back to Denver, but I could stay."

"Splendid," said Ellenberg.

"Thank you," said the man. "I'm starting to feel so much better already."

"If there are no reporters who are interested now, it might be tomorrow. I'm sure we can find you a spot to make camp. A tent, sleeping bag. We've got to get you out of those clothes for now. You're likely to spook a whole bunch of folks around here."

"It's all I had."

"That's okay. Thanks," said Ellenberg, holding out her hand for a shake. "And your name is?"

"Applegate. Dean Applegate."

\*\*\*\*

The more they asked questions, the more Allison realized how little she had seen and heard. A shot. A man. A shadow. A shape. A moment of activity. A dead elk lying in the rocks.

The ring of officialdom had stopped their search planning long enough to listen to her tale. Sheriff Sandstrom had wanted to designate a low-level deputy to have her sketch her route and key landmarks on a topo map. But then she said it: "It might have been a human body."

Slater had helped her nail down a minute with Jerry Sandstrom, *Sheriff* Jerry Sandstrom, with the spiky ear hair and backwoods gruffness. He had been sheriff since Nixon was president and was recently given another four-year deal from the voters. Jerry On-The-Spot Sandstrom. He always liked to be there in murder cases before the last wisp of steam rose from the corpse, according to Slater. Sandstrom stood next to Slater's boss, District Ranger Gary Bridgers, who was intent but clueless. He took notes and tried to look as if he might have a good idea any second now. A seasoned old cowboy stood near Bridgers. She recognized him from the trails. He was an overly nosy sort and one of Grumley's crew.

They all stood under the canopy that jutted off the barn that was the heart of Pete Weaver's Ripplecreek Ranch. Weaver was long gone. He had headed off with the two groups of hunters, but not before Allison had pulled him aside and told him she'd probably be busy with the authorities and why.

"What makes you say *human body?*" said Sandstrom. "How far away were you?"

"As the crow flies, hard to say," said Allison. "It was the way the load was being dragged, the way the man was pulling it."

"And you had a good look at it even through a friggin' storm?"

"With binos. Good ones."

They took her to the hood of a pickup truck with its nose protected by the canopy. A topo map was taped to the green metal. The map already sported a series of red dots and trails marked in felt-tip pen. One said "D.E.'s camp." Dawn Ellenberg's.

"Where were you?" said Sandstrom.

Sandstrom's head shook and bobbed even when he wasn't talking. The rooster-like flap under his jaw amplified the condition. He towered over Allison, so she got an unwelcome look at the quivering pouch.

"Here," said Allison, quickly finding the tight concentric circles that indicated Lizard's Tongue. She showed him Black Squirrel Pass and where she had camped the night before. The officials huddled around Sandstrom and tried to figure out if it was possible for their missing protester to have traveled that far.

"What time was this?" said Sandstrom.

"Late morning. Maybe noon."

Allison found Slater's face in the huddle of men and he offered encouragement with a faint smile.

"Anything else unusual or out of the ordinary occur?" This was Bridgers, wedging himself into matters. "Anything you saw or heard, anything you found?"

"No," said Allison bluntly. "Except an elk. Dead one. Good-size bull, too."

"A carcass?" said Sandstrom.

"Yeah, carcass. But a fresh kill."

"You're sure?"

"He was still warm."

"And where was this?" Sandstrom showed a flash of impatience.

"Right at the spot where I saw the guy, near the base of Lizard's Tongue."

"Good Christ," said Sandstrom. "A dead bull in the wilderness. I'm sure all of the cows are upset, but we've gotta start with our missing boy and keep this investigation focused on the Homo sapiens. Okay with everybody? Thank you, sweetheart."

Allison squeezed her way out of the circle of Sandstrom's huddle.

"We'll need a good bloodhound to find the trail of the missing protester," Sandstrom said to Slater.

"Maybe that one in Grand Junction isn't busy. The one that followed the bomber home," suggested Slater.

"Call and find out," said Sandstrom, snapping as if his authority extended to all branches of government.

"Done," said Slater, who was known fairly well in Glenwood Springs and around. He had mediated a dispute between mountain bikers and hikers on a popular National Forest trail and had settled a long-standing feud between backcountry outfitters competing for access to one of the best elk herds—a spat that had to do with camp locations in the wilderness area. But Slater's role kept the "accidental" shootings to one. Still, Allison thought Slater might roll his eyes at her any second, as if to say, *get a load of this old cop.* But Slater played right along. His attitude made Allison smile.

The last full-fledged boyfriend she'd had after the airplane accident was hung up on every mystical song Van Morrison had ever sung. He was a mental drifter, a searcher, who calculated the price of belonging to every structure or organization as a personal sacrifice. Not Slater. He saw his place, or knew how to pretend he did. As a result, the picture of comfort and suggestion of stability that he presented was strangely inviting.

# 4

"Something tells me we're getting close."

This was Applegate, who had pulled up behind Ellenberg as they trudged through the snow.

"What makes you think so?"

"A hunch, I don't know. If he wasn't well to begin with, it's hard to imagine he got much farther, even with better conditions."

"True," said Ellenberg.

A fresh set of clothes turned up. They fit a bit loosely, but they worked. Jeans and a fleece sweatshirt. He had shaved and cleaned up. He looked more at ease, less severe, out of the camouflage.

Ellenberg and most of the others had spent the evening in the camp's oversized canvas tent, singing along with a trio of acoustic guitars to everything from John Denver to Neil Young to Kurt Cobain, *Nirvana Unplugged*. The mood of the singers had been subdued and earnest. It was not a party, it was a bonding. Everyone was thinking about the lost protester, whose identity was now in steady circulation. His name was Ray Stern. Everyone was thinking about Ray.

"Sleep okay?" said Ellenberg.

"After that great serenade," said Applegate, "of course. Thanks for the loaned tent."

"Not a problem. Thanks for your help, by the way," Ellenberg said.

"My pleasure."

"I hear the interviews went okay."

"The reporters all ask the same five or six questions," said

Applegate with a smile. "I thought one of 'em from *The New York Times* was gonna write my life story though."

"Didn't I see you being tortured by that slick-haired guy from Channel 9?"

"A strange breed, that one. He figured I was set up by you guys to look like a hunter."

She had urged the reporters to all visit the sing-a-long, to show the group's strong common beliefs and sense of community.

"Did you convince him?"

"I remembered I had a picture of myself with a big old elk that I killed several years back. Nearly trophy class. The picture was sufficiently faded. Now even *Time* has it, *Time* magazine."

"Fantastic," said Ellenberg. "Are you dealing with this okay?"

"I've never felt better," said Applegate. "I feel, I don't know, cleansed. Purified."

Applegate took a deep breath. Whether it was from plowing through the snow or from thinking things over, Ellenberg couldn't tell.

"My decision seems so small if it means prompting someone else to think about animals in a different way."

The day had dawned clear and strong. It revealed a valley frozen in white, from cornices on the wind-whipped ridges to the west, to the rounder hills off to the east. The scene was defined by what was not white: the south-facing trunks of trees, the occasional boulder large enough to avoid a complete cover of snow and wisps of grass or bush that poked through the surface. A giant, invisible razor had given the scene its final grooming touches, turning the snow blanket smooth and clean-shaven.

The bloodhound led them up through a stretch of valley where the walls closed in and the woods grew dense. The entire troop—twenty cops, friends and fellow protesters—came to a complete stop as the dog poked around. A TV helicopter buzzed overhead for an aerial shot.

Applegate realized he was breathing harder than normal. Through binoculars Ellenberg could see the bloodhound working a series of concentric circles from the point where he had first pulled up. The handler and Slater stood rock still. It was remarkable that the dog could smell anything in the cold.

The bloodhound suddenly plunged off into a thick stand of trees, stopped suddenly and started pawing at the surface. His handler smiled.

"I hope Ray Stern felt release," said Ellenberg. "A moment or two."

Applegate buried his face in one mitten-covered hand and put the other on her shoulder.

\*\*\*\*

Grumley was anxious to get a grip on his entire operation. He wanted time alone in his office, a small square of space in the center of the barn, between the shop and the saddle room. The office was big enough for a couple of old desks, a sagging red couch, a telephone, a space heater and a stocked rifle rack that circled the room on three sides. The rack was now home for Applegate's Sako, a beautiful weapon much too nice for the likes of such a pathetic "hunter."

He didn't really need Popeye Boyles nipping at his heels, but the guy might sulk if you didn't scratch him behind the ears.

"You look refreshed." It was Boyles, toting a shovel coated with muck.

"Nothing like home cooking," said Grumley.

"And being the old sailor I am, I know you don't mean food."

Grumley grimaced.

"What's up with the search?"

"They're up there now, bashing around," said Boyles.

"They?"

"A bloodhound from Grand Junction, a bunch of cops and rangers, a pack of them protesters and the dead guy's brother."

"Dead guy?"

Boyles stopped for a second and cocked his head to the radio strapped to his waist. Grumley could hear a soft voice but could not make out the words.

"Just someone sending out for donuts," said Boyles. He stood there as if he hadn't been asked a question.

"Dead guy?" Grumley repeated.

"Pretty sure dead. A bloodhound can track the trail of a filet mignon hanging out the window of a car door three days later, as long as you have a piece of the original steak. He'll find it."

"Where's the sheriff on all this?"

"Sandstrom on a hike? In the snow? Uphill? Please."

"Well?"

"He's monitoring things from base camp over at Weaver's place. What's gonna be interesting is if they wind up where that one guide said she saw somethin'."

"One more time, Popeye."

"One of the guides over at Weaver's place said she saw some strange goings-on up near Lizard's Tongue."

For a split second the announcement didn't seem connected to Grumley's world. How could anybody have seen anything?

"Strange what?"

"She's tellin' the cops about hearing a shot and seeing somebody. Most of it was garbled, you know, fuzzy. But she got herself a few minutes with Sandstrom."

Grumley tried to think of the questions that a normally curious guy would ask. The key was to settle on a point between overly interested and not nosy enough.

"Name?"

"Allison something."

Grumley remembered her, a city girl with a lot of want-to, trust-me in her eyes. She'd come around, at one point, looking for a job. "Allison Coil?" He remembered her. She was stunning in her own small-boned way. Cute and very green.

"That's it."

"Why does she think it's anything?"

"Have to ask her. Oh, something about a dead elk, too."

Grumley suddenly realized how everything could unravel. *Heard* a shot. Saw something. She might make enough fuss that they'd go look. There was no chance of finding the body until spring even if someone gave enough of a shit to keep complaining that Rocky Carnivitas was missing from the face of the earth. Even then all the cops would have would be a dead guy and a bullet, right? Hunting accident. Applegate was the complicating factor.

Boyles shuffled off, turning up the volume on his police radio.

For two hours Grumley made routine calls while the working part of his brain sorted through various scenarios of cop investigations. Two clients were due next week, one for a bull elk, the other for a trophy-class mountain goat. Both were repeat clients, a Hollywood B-movie producer and a San Francisco banker. The banker didn't want things to be "too easy" this time. There should be two crews getting both animals ready. They would have to tranquilize the bull and tie it down one or two days before the scheduled hunt date. Rocky's bull would have worked fine, but that was water under the bridge. The mountain goat could be moved after he was sedated.

Next, he made a call down to the store. Sales were good, not spectacular. They had run out of camouflage vests because of a screw-up with the distributor, but there was no shortage of ladies' swimwear.

The schedule showed two two-man crews out servicing camps. One camp was due to break the day after tomorrow. Both were five-man groups, one supplied with a cook and one without.

According to the chalkboard, two other guides were following back a messenger from a third camp who had come for help quartering and packing out a kill. Boyles was scheduled for barn clean up. A guy named Gilliam was on "Trudy Duty," the thankless job of watching Grumley's wife to prevent any unattended seizures.

Grumley drove back down the valley. Six miles downhill, he turned back to the north and headed up the eight bumpy unplowed miles to a cabin where he kept horses and had built quarters for the crews that helped run and organize the custom hunts. The hunts were known among the crews as "George G's Custom Carnage." The cabin sat in a dark, craggy canyon that saw sun only a few hours each day in the summer. From early September to late April it was constantly in the shadows. The corral was less than ideal, on a steep slope and wooded, but what did horses know about level? Grumley had built a small shelter for the horses to use in storms and a small barn for saddles and repair.

Four horses worked on a small pile of hay scattered in the snow. Given how fresh the pile, someone had been there within the hour. No one was lolling around in a bunk, drinking coffee, or waiting for orders. There were a dozen men who worked on Grumley's crew and they were all solid, like marble. And that made sense. They were well compensated. They earned enough in four months to last them a year, if they didn't convert it all into Wild Turkey.

It was a profitable empire. No mistakes were going to destroy it. Grumley found a bit in the shed and led Trooper from the corral. He found a blanket and saddle and fitted them on. He tied a coil of rope to the saddle, raided the refrigerator for a wedge of cheese and four slices of ham. From the headquarters of George G's Custom Carnage, as he liked to think of it, Lizard's Tongue was only half the distance of the main trail up Ripplecreek. However, it was twice the grade in spots. He had to go back up to fix the problems caused by the meddlesome Allison Coil. Even if it wasn't until next spring, he didn't want anyone flipping over the elk to discover it was bulletless.

\*\*\*\*

They didn't yank Ray Stern from his white grave; they first dug out around him in a square double the size that would have been necessary to simply extract the body. The scene looked to Applegate like a slightly faster version of an archaeological dig in snow.

The body looked like a toy. The brown blanket had fused itself to the corpse. They unrolled enough to wave Ellenberg over for a peek. She approached the body cautiously, buried her face in her hands. She returned to where Applegate and the others stood. The television guys didn't miss a moment.

"It's a fake animal skin," said Ellenberg. "A huge wrap. He made himself a target."

"He didn't want to waste his death," said Applegate.

"It won't be wasted," said Ellenberg. "Believe me, it won't be wasted."

They carried the frozen lump of Ray Stern to the nearest clearing, up and over a small ridge no more than a hundred yards away. One of them carried Ray Stern's frozen torso around the shoulders. Two others carried the legs. The brown blanket flopped along like a shroud.

Within a few minutes a mountain rescue helicopter hovered overhead and lowered a sled. The group watched as Stern's body was winched slowly up, cameras rolling.

Applegate couldn't watch. He knelt in the snow and bowed his head, knowing his life would never be the same.

\*\*\*\*

The landscape was frighteningly white.

"Oh shit," she muttered.

Allison looked at Slater. He understood. As they climbed the hillside on horseback, the snow depth increased with every hour. Bear was starting to wade slowly. Walking was hard work. The snow-covered landscape altered her bearings and the intense sun was disorienting. The remaining half-mile of slope up to Lizard's Tongue was a vast, bumpy, lumpy snow farm. It was eight city-sized blocks of chunky terrain and she was looking for a dead elk lying on its side, the equivalent of a couple of flopped-over Harleys.

The helicopter drone, echoing up the canyon, had disturbed the peaceful walk for the last fifteen minutes. She turned to watch as it levitated from a position close to the treetops. The helicopter banked hard and flew off, leaving behind a wonderful silence.

And a weird sense of displacement.

This didn't even look like the same slope, but here was Lizard's Tongue and there was Black Squirrel Pass. They were on the right trail.

Bear worked along on his own internal radar headings. The snowfall had not thrown off his sense of direction. There was a slight indentation in the terrain that tracked the trail. Slater, who knew the intricacies of the Flat Tops like most people know their way to work, never questioned Bear's judgment. It was helpful having Slater along. The cops were so consumed with the missing protester that the concerns she had registered were treated like an ordinary citizen complaint about a barking dog or partying neighbors. Slater had been told by his people to interview hunters in three specific backcountry camps. He was on his way to fulfill that assignment. They would split up at Lizard's Tongue, if and when she could find the elk.

Finally she told Bear to stop. By her sense of mental triangulation, this spot was right.

"The cops have a bloodhound," said Slater. "Maybe he's done now and we could borrow him."

"I wonder if he'd need the scent of any old elk to do his tricks or if it would have to be this particular bull?" said Allison.

"Probably have to be this one," said Slater, "now that you mention it."

The sun mixed with the cold air and snow to make the temperature manageable. If there was a ski lodge right in this spot, and if circumstances were different, they would both be sipping a Heineken, coats off, listening to overly loud rock and roll on the tinny outdoor speakers and letting their faces soak up the rays. Instead, they had to hunt for an animal that was already dead.

In her mind, Allison outlined a section of snow. It was half a football field long but not as wide. It was where they needed to start looking. She walked the perimeter of the area, pounding through hip-deep snow, constantly checking Lizard's Tongue against her memory of it in the blizzard. This had to be about right. She was hoping for an antler poking through the surface of the snow, or maybe a major indentation where the snow had not accumulated quite so quickly because of the elk's dissipating heat. The wind had erased the possibility of the latter, the depth of the snow the former.

Slater had two telescoping probes, the kind used to locate avalanche victims. They were aluminum with a pointed, pencil-like tip and T-shaped grip on top. They came folded up but snapped together easily. Stepping slowly side by side, three feet apart, they started plowing their field. The elk had not been directly at trail side, so they started closer to the middle, probing down with their rods every step, hoping she would sense a touch of something different than frozen tundra and something not quite as far down. All the while, Allison knew she should have marked the elk's location, should have plunked down a flag of some sort that would have helped them now. The probing was tedious, the trudging difficult. At this pace, two hours might be enough.

"Your government dollars at work," said Slater. "Whatever it takes."

"At least I can't moan about the lack of responsiveness from the US Forest Service," said Allison.

"In more ways than one, if you get my drift," said Slater. "And drift may not be the best choice of words, given all this snow."

They huffed and grunted as they worked—stepping out of their last spot, sinking into the next, probing down with the sticks, waiting to see how the feel of the bottom registered on their gloved hands. Allison was dubious this would work, but it beat shoveling or waiting for spring. Slater recounted how he once found a dead hunter this way. The hunter's tracks led into an area creamed by an avalanche that had plummeted off a windblown cornice a hundred yards up. It was Slater's probe that found the body and others had come around to see how the probe felt. It had been too late to hope for a rescue, so the moment was used for training. Slater told Allison she would know if she hit elk. It was *different.*

Step, sink, probe, wait, feel. They hit the hour mark and then 90 minutes. They had snacks and a drink, hot Lemon Zinger from a thermos. Just a quick bite before they were back at it. Allison wondered how long it was worth exploring. What if they poked this whole section and came up empty? In which direction should they look? Would there be time, or even the inclination? They were more than half finished with this plot when Slater stopped his methodical rhythm.

"We got a bite," he said.

But this find wasn't a matter of feel or touch. Allison worked Slater's probe to see if she could feel the body below, but couldn't register anything. This find was a matter of height. The probe wouldn't sink as low as it did immediately nearby. End of story.

Digging down and around the elk was hard work, but the effort was eased by the fact that she knew she hadn't been whacked out and had remembered enough to find her way back to this spot. The frozen elk emerged like a breach birth. It came butt first like a hairy, unwieldy rock. Slater worked from the antlers down and she worked from the rear up, scooping snow off the carcass by hand.

"Nice one," said Slater, standing back to admire the specimen. "Healthy size rack, too. But what makes you so sure he's not completely shredded underneath?"

"Two things. This guy didn't fall, he decided to get down. He's not crumpled up. Second, no exit wound. Sure it's possible. But not even a nick on this side? Nothing. It didn't look like this guy had been in pain."

"Interesting," said Slater. "I don't think it would have ever occurred to me, but you might be right."

They dug underneath the elk's legs, fitted ropes up and around the front and tied them as close to the body as they could, walked their horses around, tied one rope to each saddle and stepped the horses away. The rope pulled taut and the elk's feet slowly rose up. The feet pointed oddly to the sky and the elk flopped over. They scraped through caked-on snow, studied the elk's head and double-checked the rump and belly for holes, blood, or trauma of any kind. There was nothing.

"He was a beauty," said Slater.

Allison was on all fours, peering into the elk's face. The shadow from Slater's head moved and she caught a flash, a glint of steel. She refocused her eyes on the bright snow to catch sight of it again, reached down and wiggled free a rectangular metal box not much bigger than her hand.

"GPS," said Slater.

"Yep," said Allison.

"Your basic gear for any wildlife biologist."

"For tracking," said Allison.

"And study," said Slater.

"So this is strange or not strange?"

"Medium strange. We get our share of people who want to study the elk migration or diseases or impact on the habitat. It's possible something was authorized that I didn't know about."

"But to have him go down now, at the beginning of the hunting season?"

"Odd, no question," said Slater.

"And why didn't the elk survive?"

"Do we know all the ways they can die?" said Slater.

The GPS collar, which Slater now flipped around in his hands, put a human in the area where Allison said there had been a human. She thought this, but didn't say it. Wasn't that obvious? She stood and stared down the hill, looking for anything out of place, out of line, out of the ordinary. The snowfield returned a blank stare.

"Whatcha gonna do?" said Slater.

"Me?" said Allison. "How about the authorities?"

"We'll see if we can trace which scientists might be using the Auditrak 535," he said, reading off the monitor. "But it's the equivalent of asking which hikers wear boots."

Allison looked away, thinking she'd wasted Slater's time and trouble. Or maybe someone would come climbing back up out of the snow right now and explain it all, the same way dead-looking bodies had scrambled up out of Long Island Sound. Only here, the pristine and unforgiving cover of white snow swallowed all the possible answers.

\*\*\*\*

Grumley squeezed a hunk of horse manure in his bare fist and felt the heat in the lump's core. Two horses. And they hadn't been gone long. He could catch them if he wanted.

The field of snow was churned up and the elk had been flipped over. Fuck. It wasn't hard to imagine his house and barn now filled with cops looking for him. And Trudy might be there answering questions or filling in the blanks for the detective.

How could things have gotten so screwed up?

The bullet in Rocky. Was it *in* Rocky? What would they make of it? What had anyone seen? How much?

Applegate. Christ, Applegate had better stay cool or the whole thing could be unzipped in a flash. Maybe he'd spill his stinking guts and decide to take all the honorable, puked-up blame himself for killing the protester. And then bumble his way around and mention having run into Grumley. More than anything, Applegate's muzzle had better stay put.

*****

Trudy Grumley didn't start crying until the body was being hoisted up to the helicopter. He looked so small and frail, dangling below this mechanical monster by a thread. The sheriff's people and one of Dawn Ellenberg's people held up the oversized brown cloth the protester had been wearing. The television news stations showed a clip of Ellenberg reading the note the guy had left in his tent. The report showed pictures of the dog bounding through the snow to find the body and pictures of Ray Stern as a kid. Trudy let the tears flow and the tissues pile up around her on the blue comforter. And then there was an interview with the sheriff during which he basically said they would stop at nothing to find the stupid hunter who couldn't tell the difference between an honest-to-goodness whitetail and a two-legged human in a cloth suit.

It was a CNN reporter, an older one who looked like an entire vat of coffee wouldn't put a jolt in his heartbeat, who first used the term "creative suicide." The other stations picked it up. It was a neat, simple description that made her ache. She felt the strength of the dead protester's decision, the conviction that went with it. There was nothing more admirable.

They showed an extended interview with Dean Applegate, who had also been in the search party for the dead protester. He was dressed in his camouflage outfit sitting in a barn on a chair plunked down in the middle of the dirt and muck. The guy looked familiar. He talked about how the protest movement had affected him, how it had made him stop and ponder the real need for hunters, the real necessity of "ripping an animal apart" with a high-powered bullet. "The sport is an anachronism," said Applegate. "Everything else has changed in this world except the way we treat animals. And that's changed for the worse. Now we can scope 'em from a mile away, fire bullets that are really small missiles. I simply came to realize that it isn't fair."

Something about him was old-friend-familiar, or met-once-familiar. High school?

And still no Rocky. The wait was agonizing.

Trudy sat on the corner of her king-size bed, her right hand absently snipping the air with her pruning shears and the left flipping the satellite dish from one end of the sky to the other, looking for bits of news about the dead protester. It was starting to get repetitive.

Smoke, the gray cat, gave himself a bath on her lap while two black kittens played with a ball of string on the bed behind her. She glanced down the long driveway, watching for cars. The only delay that made any sense was that Rocky got mucked up with the animal people, an event so well orchestrated that it had drawn coverage by CNN, all the network news operations and, of course, every television station out of Denver.

Trudy was impressed with Ellenberg's pure sense of spunk. Ellenberg was one of those women willing to lead a rebellion on an entire cultural issue—fighting for all those living things, disrupting all of those hunters, screwing up all those cops.

Trudy scratched Smoke's chin and gently put him down on the bed. The delay was worrisome, the uncertainty worse.

Trudy's world was her house, a massive stone structure at the end of a long, snaking driveway off in the woods, a couple of miles west from the Colorado River and just outside the southeastern flank of the Flat Tops Wilderness. George had picked the spot for its seclusion. Eighteen trees had been plucked to make room for the site and they still had half the timber in firewood stacks off the garage. Six years in the house and nine trees' worth of wood had gone up the chimney.

A moss rock fireplace dominated the living room, a giant wood-burning stove nestled inside. A stone ledge fronted the fireplace as long as the living room was wide. Three matching leather couches formed a U-shape around a coffee table, which was a varnished slice of tree from the tallest Douglas fir they had destroyed to make room in the woods for themselves.

The living room was for show. They rarely had guests or parties. Trudy spent half the time in her greenhouse, which was accessed through the kitchen. She had gradually covered the greenhouse and kitchen in plants, her mute pals. The collection now expanded to the living room and hung from the ceiling. It took up every corner of unused space.

It was an easy life that had put roundness, a layer of padding and real hips onto her bony build. Her frame, gaunt in high school, was now more recognizably that of a woman. The humidity from the plants, especially in the greenhouse, kept her skin soft. Her hair hung down to the middle of her back. Her face was long, with clear brown eyes and it looked okay, nothing spectacular, with straight teeth and a smallish nose.

The problem, of course, was mobility. Seven years now of seizures. She had simply come to accept the house as a comfortable, familiar cell. She could drive, but it was risky. The doctors had trained her to watch and sense the faint aura in her vision, like a smear of Vaseline, as a warning sign. She could stop the car and wait for the seizure to pass. The doctors had said her spells didn't seem to be violent, but that might not always be the case. They only wanted her to drive on the back roads where she could go slowly. But the only way to Glenwood Springs and Eagle, the two closest towns, meant fourteen miles of interstate in one direction, twenty-two in the other. Take your pick. She didn't want to be going sixty-five and watching for auras. Nor did she want to be picking her way around the winding roads that hugged the banks of the Colorado River and worrying about where she would pull over to let the episode run its course. She didn't want strangers tending to her or calling ambulances.

And when they did start, there went the sales clerk job at the clothing store in Glenwood Springs and gradually her sense of independence. When George was gone for one of his long stretches, either on a hunt or flying his plane up to a remote neck of the woods, a member of his crew was given the task of visiting once in the morning and once in the afternoon to check on her, to make sure she hadn't keeled over in a fit and to do any odd chores she wanted done. They called it "Trudy Duty." It hadn't taken her long to get over the strange feeling of having what amounted to a personal valet. Few of them refused a warm plate of her best food—Chinese chicken, Thai beef salad, or pork chops in apricot-ginger marinade. It was one way of saying thanks to those who helped her out. She could get chauffeured into town when she wanted to go to the bookstore or eat lunch. Groceries were delivered once a week. She had a satellite dish for entertainment. Trudy was made to feel her illness was being compensated for and accommodated. But it was not treated.

George had stalled when it came to her desire to travel to Denver where specialists were perfecting fixes for her type of seizures. They could peel off a chunk of your skull, attach a bunch of probes, reattach the skull, wait for the next seizure, determine precisely which part of the brain was going haywire when the seizure took place and then, if the part of the brain involved didn't seem crucial to memory or speech or motor control, snip it out.

"Wait until they perfect the procedure," George had said. "We don't have insurance or the thirty thousand dollars to put up front. And what's wrong with the way things are?"

That's where Rocky Carnivitas had offered a refreshingly different point of view. There was a sweet and amiable side to Rocky, despite a slightly tousled and unschooled manner. He had drawn "Trudy Duty" three days in a row earlier in the summer and had held her and comforted her through a fierce seizure that came on while they sat in the car in the dirt parking lot after the annual rodeo in Eagle. The rest of the night Rocky had stayed close, like a first-time dad. Rocky was the only one of the hands who had shown any interest in her situation. The others all wanted to know as little as possible.

"If George doesn't say it, he manages to imply that he doesn't have the money," Trudy said.

"Christ, he's worth ten times that," said Rocky. He had driven her up to an overlook in Glenwood Canyon a few months earlier for a picnic. Grumley had flown to Texas to meet new clients. Rocky and Trudy sat on a blanket up on a cliff more than a thousand feet above the river. A bottle of wine and curried chicken sandwiches were slowly devoured. A fleet of rafters bobbed in the sparkling river below.

"George says some months we barely make the mortgage. I mean, it's a great house, but from time to time he'll grumble about business and suggest getting a smaller place."

"He's got the money for your operation," Rocky had said. "Trust me on that."

They slept together that afternoon. A few tentative gropes on the picnic blanket served as prelude. They finished back at her house in the cool sheets of the spare bedroom—neutral territory. She discovered a yearning to be close to him. He was patient and listened to what she knew about plants and herbs. George's whereabouts weren't too much of an issue. He was rarely home midday and, besides, Rocky's presence did not need to be concealed.

Now Rocky was way overdue. When it came down to it, she realized Rocky had filled an aching gap and she did not want the gap to reappear. Perhaps someone else cared that Rocky was missing, but she didn't know who that would be. However, amid the crash and crush of the media coverage about the "creative suicide," a missing guide wasn't worth a blip.

# 5

"I suppose Ripplecreek has made a name for itself," said Slater. "The worst kind. I just saw two local reporters interviewing another reporter from a national television network about why this story has attracted so much attention. They're getting desperate for new people to interview, I suppose."

Slater refilled two crusty plastic coffee cups perched on the flopped-down glove compartment door of his Forest Service truck. The coffee dribbled from a beat-up steel thermos. He and Allison sat in the truck, engine idling, outside Pete Weaver's Ripplecreek Ranch, which had been commandeered by Sandstrom as a temporary base camp and police headquarters, a place to hold news conferences and issue a few orders.

Two days had passed since she and Slater had split up their investigation, a half-mile down the canyon from Lizard's Tongue. Slater had found hunters near a few of the camps, but none had any useful information. Or maybe they didn't want to involve themselves.

"It's perfect for Sandstrom. He laps up the national press while the case drags on," said Slater. "The guy is sixty-three. He's not going anywhere, but pretends every case is his next ticket to international fame."

"Maybe he's hoping for one of those movie deals about his side of the story," said Allison. "Be a good retirement bonus. These days, it doesn't take much. But it would look better if it was him holding up the deer suit," said Allison. That's what the media started calling it: "deer suit." As if it came with a coat and tie.

Allison cracked her window for a breath of fresh air and ran the palm side of her knuckles over the straight, bristly hairs on the back of Slater's neck.

"Did you ever have long hair?"

"In high school. Over the ears. I was extremely rebellious. We had military dads, with all their rules and bullshit. My dad had a real, live barber's chair, for crying out loud. Now I get antsy if it's not trimmed once a week and my job comes with its own set of rules for grooming. Something I promised myself I'd avoid. What gives?"

"Indoctrination. That's the city life, too. It wears you down. Conform or else," said Allison.

"Really? I thought the city was where all the weird folks could hide, do their own thing. I thought non-conformity was the point and why people liked living in the city, to watch it all go down."

"Conformity at the corporate level, I suppose," said Allison. "Wear certain suits, read certain books, hang out in just the right places, say just the right things."

"Well, you fit in here too," said Slater. "Half the folks in the mountains out here are runners anyway."

"I didn't run from anything."

"No?"

"I needed trees and sky. And I knew I'd never fly in an airplane again."

"So you needed a new home. I'm no philosopher, but isn't that all of us? Either happy with our homes or looking for something better?"

Slater was a relative of a friend of Pete Weaver. Slater had asked Weaver if there was an extra guide he could hire to help him take a Boy Scout troop from Glenwood Springs into the Flat Tops for a late summer daytrip. Allison drew the lucky straw. She led Slater and his scouts up to an aspen grove below a nearby ridge for a cookout.

She admired how Slater managed to bounce easily among what the kids coughed up, from problem to complaint to fussiness. He often turned a sour moment into a funny one. Slater was the stern but slightly goofy shepherd of the olive-green flock. He showed them environmental damage from mountain bikes, talked about a proposed gravel pit application outside the wilderness area and showed them all how to make the best s'mores going by barely melting the chocolate before loading it into the graham cracker and marshmallow sandwich for the final heating. He danced artfully among small teams of scouts in the afternoon as they did various merit badge projects and he showed no sign of fatigue at dusk as they returned. In order to determine if Slater might be eligible for pursuit, she had separated a few key pieces of information about Troop Leader Slater's marital status from one of the Eagle Scouts. Slater, easily the best looking man she'd ever approached on her own, was genuinely flattered when she mentioned that she was going to be visiting friends in Glenwood Springs the following week. It wasn't true, but it sounded good. She had asked if they could meet for a drink. The drink led to a dinner date and the third date was a daylong horseback ride that ended in her bedroom and lasted until breakfast.

"And you?" said Allison.

"And me what?"

"Conformist?"

"That's what being a cop, of any variety, is all about," said Slater. "Rules, order, everybody in line, make sure chaos is controlled and renegades are reined in. Speaking of which, I've got to interview every hunter out of Weaver's camps."

"Six or seven are coming out today and seven more tomorrow," said Allison. "Today's won't be out until early afternoon at best."

"Doesn't matter. They want all the bases covered. In case they saw or heard something, you know. The government thinks of everything. And thinks it's everything too. You can't have too many bases covered, even if the bases are way the hell out in left field or foul territory."

"Oh, a baseball metaphor."

"It's true," said Slater. "If there's anything that makes me madder than wasted taxpayer dollars, it's *stupid* use of taxpayer dollars." He was not amused.

"Which is there more of?"

"I don't know. Some days it's just 'do everything' because in government everything can be done eventually."

"Any mention of elk biologists working up in Ripplecreek?"

"There's a permitting process and, as always, no coordination among the five ranger districts," said Slater. "They could have come out of any one of them."

"You going to tell Sandstrom?"

"About?"

"About the dead elk?"

"Why would I?"

"Don't you think it's a bit strange?"

"Maybe."

"And confirms that I wasn't seeing things?"

"What would I tell him?"

"I don't know. Maybe it's all connected. If you're part of the briefings, mention it, that's all. Remind Sandstrom and the others about what I saw. Maybe somebody else knows something now. Put two and two together."

"Okay," said Slater.

"With enthusiasm?"

Slater bounced his head around, thinking.

"I can't believe you don't believe me," said Allison.

"Well, I do. But I also think there's a reasonable explanation. You know, in all the other stuff with the protester. The elk is strange, no question."

"I've got this thing about seeing pieces of the world being picked up and put back together. Call it a quirk."

Allison lightly kissed the first two fingers on her left hand, pressed them to Slater's cheek. She opened her door.

"I'd call it a challenge," said Slater.

"Works for me," she said.

****

"Wasn't there an Apple something or other who was one of your hunting friends? He was on the news."

"Dean Applegate?" said Grumley.

"That's the one," said Trudy. She plopped her watering can down on the cement floor of the greenhouse and started refilling it with a hose.

"Why do you ask?"

"He was up there where they found that protester, the dead one." said Trudy.

"He left with the others," said Grumley, thinking that Trudy must be mistaken.

"Tall, lanky guy? Kind of a military haircut. Always looks a bit shell-shocked when he talks? Said his hunting days are over. He's giving interviews."

"Interviews?" said Grumley. "What do you mean?"

"He and Ellenberg are buddies, by the looks of things."

*What the fuck?*

Trudy flitted from one plant to the next, poking the soil, shoving in inch-long vitamin sticks, pulling off yellow leaves and generally looking content. He wanted to tell her to stand still, like for a whole minute.

"They even had a live hook-up with the Today Show this morning," she said. "I almost woke you up. It's not often one of your friends gets on national TV, right there in your own house, beamed in."

The telephone rang. George leaned back in his chair to reach the wall-mounted phone. He mumbled briefly, covered his mouth and the mouthpiece with a hand.

"It's your company-sponsored chauffeur, who didn't realize I'd be back. Need anything I can't handle?"

Trudy wanted to ask which of the helpers it was, or make up an errand.

"Are you going to be around?"

"Just the morning."

"Tell him to call back at noon and we'll probably do groceries, okay?"

"Call back at noon," George said into the phone.

"Which hired gun today?" said Trudy.

"Does it matter?"

"A couple of them," said Trudy, "are plain better than others."

The doorbell sounded and Grumley cursed. "Never any peace," he said.

Grumley retreated from the kitchen. He was secretly glad to remove himself from Trudy's fussy world. A brown calico was making friends with his boots and he jerked the cat up by the scruff and let him dangle freely as he opened the door.

Sheriff Sandstrom stood there, needling a toothpick around in his gums.

"Home playing with your favorite pussy?" Sandstrom smiled, just barely.

"Yeah, some fun," said Grumley, flicking the cat aside. It landed with a thud and an accusatory *meow*.

"Ooh, that one wants to bite back," said Sandstrom. "Not my type."

"Not generally rated in the top ten," said Grumley. "Come on in."

"To what do we owe the pleasure of your driving all the way out to east bum fuck today?" said Grumley, leading him to the pot of coffee.

"I wish it was gardening tips I needed. Then I'd know the trip wasn't wasted," said Sandstrom. He stood looking down into the greenhouse, his back to the kitchen. "My word," he said. "Enough jungle for Tarzan and all the apes."

"Trudy," said Grumley with a sigh. "She knows her fertilizer."

"Is she around?"

"She doesn't get far," said Grumley.

Sandstrom plopped down at the kitchen table and wrapped his thick-knuckled paw around a big blue cup.

"You've probably got the biggest pot farm in the West right here and I'm having a cup of coffee like I don't care."

"If that's true, then I gotta talk about getting my share of the action," said Grumley, head racing to think what real questions would be coming.

"Talking about my babies?" said Trudy, striding confidently into the kitchen. Her rubber boots had been replaced by white tennis shoes. The white T-shirt had been covered by a blue-checked shirt, open to the navel. Grumley wanted to say "Shoo," but had to admit his wife had a certain damn look. He tried to squelch the pride.

"Just commenting on the quantity," said Sandstrom, extending a hand to shake without getting up. "They are in beautiful shape."

"Thanks," said Trudy.

Grumley thought he'd be sitting right across from Sandstrom in the café-style booth. Trudy now occupied the seat. He didn't want to sit next to either of them but felt awkward standing.

Grumley pulled over a stool and plunked it down next to the table.

"My wife," Sandstrom continued, "couldn't grow mold on old food. That's quite a talent you've got."

"Thanks again," said Trudy.

"But I'm not here for how to get my thumb green," said Sandstrom.

"The murder," said Trudy, quickly somber.

"We don't know m*urder*," said Sandstrom.

"Accident?" said Trudy sharply.

"Stranger things," said Sandstrom. "Unless one of the animal protesters had the guts to pull the trigger on his buddy, the one wrapped in the deer suit. That would be murder."

Sandstrom took a sip of coffee. Maybe he needed the time to let the concept settle over the room.

"See what I mean? It's not hard to imagine. A zealot will do about anything. But that's not why I'm here, to spout loose theories on what makes city people go wiggy in the head. George, your name's on a list and we gotta check off a few questions. Where were you the day this fella decided to make himself a true fool? Not that I'm taking sides."

"Hunting," said Grumley. "By myself."

"Where abouts?"

"Down east from our camp, away from the protest, for obvious reasons."

"Not with your buddies?"

"No. They wanted to lay low completely, ride out the protest and then get back to serious hunting."

"So you were by yourself?"

"Like I said. Too much business to tend to," said Grumley. "This year I was only going to join my buddies for opening weekend. Besides, short trip this year. These days, everybody's so damn busy."

Grumley tried to keep plausibility within bounds and be wary of trip wires. But he couldn't wait too long to answer. He'd already established a rhythm. He tried to remember what he was saying.

"Didn't see a small brown humanoid traipsing around?"

"Uh, no."

"But you got no way of proving where you were?"

"Uh, no."

"See any others up and around there? Anything strange? Hear anything?"

"Nothing that comes to mind," said Grumley.

"Well, this visit has been good for high-quality caffeine and bad for solid information," said Sandstrom.

"I'm sorry we can't help," said Trudy.

Sandstrom stood up. Grumley followed him to the door and outside.

"If things settle down and you need a few thrills . . . ?" said Grumley, trailing off.

"Thanks," said Sandstrom. "The elusive big kahuna will have to wait another year, fatten up for Sheriff Ahab. You always have a way of finding the big ones."

"Not likely if it snows like this all winter," said Grumley. "No forage."

Sandstrom plopped himself behind the wheel and snapped the ignition. "I know he's out there," he said. The car purred with a low, pleasing warmth. "And I know who to call. What's your slogan? Best Dag-Gum Guides In The Valley?"

"Very amusing," said Grumley with a smile, hesitating, not knowing whether to push his luck. Had he already slipped? Had Sandstrom already picked out an error in what he'd said? Was a key tidbit out of whack? Had anybody noticed that Rocky Carnivitas hadn't been around?

"Maybe one of your people actually saw something, but may not know it was important. Do me a favor and ask around." Sandstrom slapped the steering wheel. "Almost forgot. I'll need a list of where to reach all your hunting buddies and your guides, too. Could you give me that? Addresses and phones too? Have it called in or dropped off down in Glenwood Springs, say, by afternoon?"

"Sure," said Grumley. "So, say, uh . . . this must really be quite the scene. All the media, all the questions."

"There's more cameras here than at Kodak HQ," said Sandstrom. "But I'm telling 'em who has got the information and when they're going to receive their daily dose."

"Anything else going on?" said Grumley. He hoped Sandstrom viewed him as casually curious, nothing more.

"Jesus, ain't this enough?"

"Course it is. I'm just making conver—"

"You seem worried."

"Not me," said Grumley. "Just wondering. One of my guys said he heard someone who said she saw something way the hell up there. Didn't know if it was related, or might have been."

"Oh, the little guide that could. A little screwy in her mind, I think, with her directions. Women. Maps. You know. She heard a shot, she thinks. Hey, you go to see a waterfall, there's going to be a splashing noise. It's hunting season. Well, you get my point. She didn't have much worth taking to the bank."

"Who was it? Anybody I'd know?" Grumley tried for a casual tone.

"Now that seems like confidential police information."

Grumley stared.

"Allison but I can't remember the last name. Kind of a small gal."

Popeye had been right.

"Yeah," said Grumley. "Seen her around. Where was she?"

"When?"

"When she saw what she saw."

"Coming off Black Squirrel Pass."

"Sounds like you know your mountain terrain."

"Not really," said Sandstrom, who started backing out. "Only telling you what I heard."

Grumley imagined he was listening to one of Trudy's revelations about a new plant she had brought home. A look of complete indifference. "Thanks for the visit," he said.

"Onward and sideways," said Sandstrom. "Sideways and onward."

\*\*\*\*

It was a glorified motel with a few hotel-like amenities such as room service. Nice enough. The lodge sat off the interstate in downtown Glenwood Springs. From his motel room, where FATE had set up a "PR camp" to exploit the media frenzy over Ray Stern's dramatic exit from Planet Earth and milk the story of one odd hunter's miraculous conversion, Dean Applegate could see the ever-wafting steam billow up from the city's public hot springs a block away. Day or night, it didn't matter. The steam was endless. He badly wanted a dip to soak off the last days of worry and fatigue. It bugged him that the camera crews, reporters and even Ellenberg sported a slightly sulfuric perfume that had become telltale proof of a thorough soak.

Applegate had gotten used to the cameras and the lights and waiting for crews to set up. He even knew how to loop the microphone cord behind his shirt buttons so it didn't show. The repetitious questions were getting old, so he had started to embellish his tales a bit, as a means of entertainment. Maybe in his old hunting days he hadn't felled the most stunning elk, but he could say he had helped his buddies stalk them. Maybe he hadn't filled his freezer with venison every season, but he could talk about the thrill of the hunt and what he used to believe was an energizing, manly sport. His description of his conversion never wavered, how the realization of Ray Stern's protest stopped him in his tracks. But his hunting yarns were sometimes spun with a tougher or more interesting weave.

The camera crews were legion. All the news stories. The morning shows. The magazine shows. The networks and the independents: how could anybody really tell the difference? Same questions, same faces, same line of thinking. Between interviews, he listened to various agents from New York and Los Angeles wanting the right to pitch a movie deal based on his story. One working title was *I Will Kill No More*. They whispered great sums that made sleep a dicey prospect. He thought about a debt-free existence and Caribbean vacations.

Even Ellenberg's close scrutiny showed respect. She was not nearly as cool or militant off stage, it turned out. He had even seen her drink a few glasses of Chardonnay and get rather giggly. Applegate had fantasies about the ex-hunter making an item with the Queen of Animals. Ellenberg was cool. Her laugh was throaty and full. She tucked her long chestnut hair up and over her ear like a high school kid who realized, for the first time, that boys watched every move girls made. She had skinny hips and a hippie-dippy look. He wanted to buy her champagne and tickle her toes, just to hear her laugh. He'd never felt this natural joy from being around any other woman.

More than anything, Applegate felt a new, warm cocoon of family. There was a near-religious bond inside the group, a touch of zeal mixed with a few common beliefs about how the world should work. He would not let them down. Suddenly Grumley and the others were the ones out of touch. Hunting was uncivilized, unnecessary and cruel. What was the point? How could mankind consider itself decent and refined when it spent so much energy and showed so much interest in slaughtering lesser beasts? The hunting culture could claim they were following centuries' worth of instinct. Individual hunters could say they did it for the meat. And the state-sponsored so-called experts could say hunting was vital to managing wildlife populations. But it all came down to a rifle and an innocent animal being shot and killed to tease and excite a man's base instincts.

Applegate watched the surging steam and yearned for a dip. He was exhausted. He poured off three fingers of bourbon in a plastic cup from the bathroom and fetched ice from the machine near the lobby. He sat on his bed, sipping away as he watched the late news on CNN and thought about his stupid, but brilliant, mistake.

His last.

\*\*\*\*

"What's in the woods?"

"A chance to get naked," said Allison.

"I don't like getting naked when it's below a temperature that can freeze certain tips of one's anatomy."

"I love it when you're reasonable," said Allison, climbing out of Slater's truck and making a point of showing him she had grabbed the keys. "Freeze here or come with me."

Allison led the way, using a flashlight to follow the tracks of others through the crusty snow. The night was noiseless, as if the temperature had convinced the wind to lay low. She led the way, trudging a couple of hundred yards down through a densely wooded slope to a small clearing that opened to a canopy of stars. Allison slipped a five-dollar bill through a slot in a metal box that had been nailed to a tree. The money paid for upkeep and the ever-present pile of wood, dried and split. A fire burned casually, kicking a glow across the hot springs. A giggle bounced across the water, high and clear. Two heads bobbed in the center of the pool.

"Come on," said Allison, peeling off her parka and hanging it on a branch. She took the wine bottle from Slater and nestled it in rocks next to the pool, untied her shoes and pulled down her jeans. "In two minutes you'll be so warm and relaxed you'll never want to leave."

"Strangers," said Slater.

"Come on, Mr. Boy Scout. You've seen one weenie, you've seen them all. Besides, those two could care less about you."

"Oh, thanks," said Slater.

"And if you'd noticed," she whispered, "it's two women and they're not hugging because it's been a while since they've seen each other."

Slater took a tentative look over Allison's shoulder.

"Don't stare," she said.

"You are quite observant," said Slater.

"Like I've been trying to tell you. Now, let's go."

Allison was down to her underwear. She peeled them off and stuffed her clothes in a plastic bag. "If you leave them out to the elements, the steam from the pool gets them soaked and then they freeze. Put yours on top of mine before you get in. That is, if you decide to join me."

Allison waded in, ignoring the hot shock to her toes. The bottom was rocky. Finally, at hip level, she pushed off the bottom and floated away. Slater was down to his American flag boxer shorts and then slipped those off. She admired the view of his taut, slightly hairy stomach and the fire's golden glow on his skin.

She found the bottle in the rocks and they drifted to a corner of the pool. Slater came up close next to her, gave her a gentle kiss on the cheek and turned so they both faced out, looking across the water.

"So in their minds there is only one case?" said Allison. Slater had been permitted inside a day-ending inter-governmental briefing, closed to the press.

"Sandstrom's got a laser beam on Ray Stern. He's got a large army of crackerjack specialists buzzing in a swarm, but they've got zip-oh. They need a break, someone with a morsel of useful information."

Slater cautioned her that all the closed-door information was confidential and then went into detail. The autopsy, he explained, left few clues. The bullet had come to rest against the victim's spine, the seventh vertebrae. The dense material of the deer suit had slowed the missile down, but it couldn't have been a rifle that was overwhelmingly powerful. There were traces of THC in Stern's system, enough that he had probably smoked dope in the twenty-four hours prior to his death. Two other marijuana cigarettes had been found in his tent. The doctor who performed the autopsy reported that leukemia patients often were prescribed marijuana for its therapeutic and pain-relief benefits. Sandstrom told the press that Stern's brother confirmed he was one of eighteen patients in the state who had been permitted medicinal use of dope. In fact, Stern had joined a class-action lawsuit against the FDA, which was trying to declassify marijuana as a beneficial drug.

"So Stern got high," said Allison. "Doesn't change what he did."

"Enough people will think it means he wasn't in control of his actions," said Slater. "Taints it a bit, diminishes the impact of a totally sober decision. But I haven't told you the best part."

Slater sat up off the water and on a rock. His concern for strangers' eyes was no longer an issue.

"Okay, the best part," said Allison.

"Stern's lunch," said Slater. "He had a Tupperware container with him—but it was empty. Remnants indicate it was cheese and crackers, probably cheddar and a kind of salty thing, most likely Ritz."

"So he ate it."

"No. That's the point. He didn't. He had an empty stomach."

"How do they know it wasn't an old, empty Tupperware?"

"The cheese crumbs."

"Cheese crumbs?"

"You know, cheese bits. They were fresh."

"So whoever shot him also ate his lunch?"

"It was no bear or raccoon that resealed a snug-fit plastic lip."

"Yuck," said Allison. "Ooo, so you're looking for a stupid, really bad hunter who might steal your lunch too. Any fingerprints on the plastic?"

"No. He probably kept his gloves on. Stern's water bottle was emptied, too. The guy needed food and water."

Slater sipped some wine, passed the bottle.

"So, is Sandstrom going to see this through?" said Allison. "I mean, does he know enough, care enough, to get it done?"

"He'll need luck," said Slater.

"Until you get lucky, you gotta plug away. So, where is the sheriff's department going to be plugging?"

"I don't think they publicly reveal all aspects of an investigation," said Slater. "Especially to key witnesses."

"Even to you—or to the feds?"

"Like two snarling cats. Teamwork is unheard of. My boss, Bridgers, isn't even told when and where the task force meets. It's pathetic."

"So you don't even know the strategy?" said Allison.

"Do what I'm told, which isn't much now that every hunter in the state has been quizzed."

"What if I heard the shot that killed Ray Stern? Reports say Stern wasn't too big. Maybe he got shot and then the killer needed to move him. Dragged him for a ways, got tired, plunked him in the middle of nowhere, but off the trail."

"Long ways from where you were. And how's that fit with your elk?"

"I want to know why nobody thinks these things are related, that's all."

"Long way to carry anybody from up near Lizard's Tongue all the way down to where Stern's body was found. Think how weird you'd feel moving a corpse around."

In the drink of Long Island Sound, she had bobbed around with a few others who hadn't been so lucky. Slater was right.

"One question, okay?" said Allison.

"Shoot."

"Do you believe me?"

"What's to believe?"

"I was wondering if you think I'm making things up."

"Of course not," said Slater.

The women were climbing out. Steam flew from their skin. The vapors were quickly zapped by the cold night. Slater slipped back into the water and Allison watched him as he watched them.

She eased her hand down Slater's chest, over his stomach. She let her hand linger where the hair on his belly, a few inches south of his navel, was wet and curly. She felt further down and found him limp.

"Those two naked girls didn't do it for you?"

He answered by reaching over with a free hand to cup her breast. He kissed her on the mouth.

"Relax," she said. "We're all alone now. Just us and the steam and the night."

"I'm getting relaxed," he said.

"Not all of you, apparently," she said.

She passed the bottle back to him and he took a drink. Slater inhaled with a soft moan as she stroked him. He nuzzled and kissed her under the ear. He was harder now. Her fist splashed gently in the water where his hips broke the surface. The sound was like a frustrated fish working its way upstream. Slater raised his hips above the water and the splashing subsided, but not his desire. Allison pressed against him and he turned and gave her a full, warm kiss as she stroked. His hand was reaching for her and she felt that wonderful ache as he touched her. She rested her head on his chest and took in the view down his chest and the water, ripples gilded by the fire. The tight loop of pleasure and yearning was worth savoring and she slowed down, worked her hips around and enjoying his touch. Was the journey better than the destination? In this case, she would cast an emphatic vote for yes. He counted down "three . . . two . . . one . . ." in a half-moan, half-whisper and his body quaked and he turned to her, holding her tight and then not. He sunk into the water and let out a long sigh. He shuddered and rolled over, his back to her. Allison picked up the wine and sipped, letting the wine tingle on her tongue.

"You're next," he said.

"Promises," she said.

"I'm not a man of my word?"

"It's worth making sure," she said. "Never hurts."

Slater rolled on top of her, kissed her gently on her forehead, eyes, cheeks, stomach, hip bones and down.

As she closed her eyes and felt the ache surge, her mind drifted maddeningly and immediately back to Ray Stern. It was hard to connect the death of Ray Stern with what she'd seen and heard. Hard, yes, but not impossible. Was the man dragging Ray Stern? She could not stop thinking about the man and his awkward, nearly angry, work—tugging something like he was taking out the trash and none too happy about the chore. As Slater found a rhythm with his tongue, Allison leaned further back and concentrated on banishing all thoughts of worry and problems and questions and theories. What mattered was right now. What mattered was each millisecond after the next and staying out on that road, enjoying the journey.

# 6

"Who else is left?"

"It's a freelancer. Some guy says he needs to stay in his room at the Hotel Colorado. He's working on a book or something, parts are gonna run in *Rolling Stone*. His theme is the dilapidated state of the American protest movement. Says he wants to use our organization as a success story and he wants to talk with you."

Applegate sighed. He felt spent. However, a candle-size glow of self-esteem continued to burn steadily deep in his guts and it wouldn't hurt to feed the flame.

"No problem," he said.

Applegate was relaxing with a Bloody Mary in one hand and the television remote control in the other. *Wheel of Fortune* numbed him like an ice bath.

"We'll go over later and jump in the hot springs," Ellenberg said. She walked over to his bed and sat down next to him. "The manager called. Turns out he's one of us. Said he saw you on CNN this afternoon and wanted to offer us a few minutes of peace and quiet."

They had commandeered a section of the hot springs' pool deck that afternoon for a live-via-satellite debate with the editor of a prominent elk journal, *Bugle*. Applegate had taken the editor on with all the emotion and passion he could muster. The words came quickly and easily. He was polite. He listened and didn't step on the other guy. He waited his turn and objected—strongly. He challenged every claim and talked in warm and clear tones about the senseless destruction of natural beauty. With fervor he made up a story about having seen a hunter drop an extra elk for the pure joy of it while packing out the carcass of another. The second elk was left to rot, its antlers cut off and hidden in a spot where the hunter would return later and retrieve them.

He focused on the issues and he remained composed. That was one of the tips from Ellenberg: to appear reserved and relaxed. Ellenberg said it was important to "out-friendly" the hunters.

"You were great today, Dean," said Ellenberg, casually putting a hand on his leg.

"When does the freelancer need me?"

"Twenty minutes or so. Stop by my room when you're done. We'll see about dinner and the soak."

The prospect of the date alone sent Applegate out the door of the Roaring Fork Inn with an extra lift in his step. The hotel was a few blocks away. In the fading light of day, a steady flow of cars plodded along, most heading east on the interstate from Aspen and Carbondale. A day of strong sunshine had turned the streets and sidewalks into sandy, sloppy muck. He passed a gas station where cars waited for the pump. He passed BJ's Velvet Freez, a one-hour photo shop and a spiffy new café that advertised espresso drinks. Across the river, an Amtrak train was coming to a stop at the station.

He had a flash that the pickup truck at the end of the block looked a lot like Grumley's. He was about to cut across the street and duck out of sight when the voice came up behind him, distinctive and clear. The voice said the door was open and to go ahead and climb inside.

"Hey, whatcha doing? How's it going?" said Applegate. Something told him this encounter was not a coincidence, but he thought he'd start by pretending otherwise.

Grumley started driving, pulling a U-turn. He honked his way across the lane of oncoming traffic, made a nuisance of himself to edge ahead.

"George, I—"

"Shut up."

"I've gotta get back to the hotel for an interview."

"With *Rolling Stone* . . ."

"Yeah—how did you . . .?"

The truck screamed west on the interstate for less than a mile, pulled off at the only other Glenwood Springs exit. Grumley turned behind a convenience store into a muddy lot that was empty and dark. Applegate flipped the door open and stumbled from the truck, wondering which way to run.

Grumley climbed down and came around the front of the truck. His fist landed on Applegate's jaw. Applegate spun helplessly to the ground, coming to rest with his shoulder in a pool of brown water and sharp pebbles embedded in his cheek.

"Your interviewing days are over," said Grumley. "I saved your miserable butt up there in a blizzard and the way you say thanks is to go saddle up with the animal huggers."

"You don't know how I felt shooting that guy," said Applegate. "Shit."

"Nobody knows. Nobody will ever know," said Applegate. Was Grumley going to hit him again?

"Christ," said Grumley. "Cops all over the place. You don't really know who saw what or what they can figure out."

"They'll get nothing outta me.

"The idea was to lay low and you plaster your face on every TV screen from here to Timbuktu."

Applegate touched a spot on his left jaw where the pain was sharp, hoping the physical punishment was over.

"We got a guide who said she saw you."

"Huh?" mumbled Applegate. The statement did not connect. The idea of a witness had never entered his mind. "No way."

"Bullshit. You think you could see everything?"

"What'd he see?" said Applegate.

"She," said Grumley.

"*She?*"

"The guide. A *she*," said Grumley.

"What the hell is she saying?"

"Beats the shit out of me. She's talking to the cops. The sheriff was out at my house asking all sorts of nosy-ass questions. He's got something, count on it. But you've made it a lot harder for yourself to slip around unnoticed and find what the fuck it is. What a joke," Grumley said with a scowl. "Mister tough guy hunter one week, mister softie the next."

"The cops haven't even come to me. They can't. I didn't do nothing," said Applegate. "Nothing."

"And what if they ask to see your gun?"

"They won't."

"They might. And your alibi?"

"There are lots of hunters out by themselves."

"And what if she got a good look at you and your equipment?" said Grumley. "Something. Anything. You got your hands full and you're out there with your face all over the TV."

"What can we do?"

"Are you serious?"

"What?"

"We. You can't do anything except disappear."

"How?"

"Tell them you need a break. Get back in the truck."

Applegate studied the open door, pondered his options. He didn't move.

"Back in the truck," said Grumley, grabbing him by the arm, practically winging him inside. "You're leaving town."

"What about my stuff, my friends?"

"*Fuck* your friends," Grumley shouted, bouncing the truck

crazily through the potholes in the parking lot, flooring it as they hit the ramp to the interstate. Grumley didn't say anything. Applegate didn't know how or when to start. It was a short run to the Glenwood exit. There was little time to think, to come up with a plan.

Grumley guided the truck up the overpass above the interstate and turned to the left, cutting in front of a lumbering dump truck and speeding up a busy side street toward the train station. A silver Amtrak train sat idle.

He reached into his coat and pulled out a ticket.

"Go," he said.

"My things, my stuff."

"Have your animal friends pack it up for you and send it down."

"You want me to lay low, okay. But I ain't going to Denver now."

He was thinking of his promised soak with Ellenberg.

"You're getting on the train. You're staying on the train," said Grumley. "You're getting off in Denver. You're going home. You're going back to tinkering with computers or whatever the hell it is you do. You're gonna dig yourself a hole in the back-yard and stick your head down there for about a year and mind your own business. If you don't get on the train now, maybe your rifle will get dropped off at the sheriff's by one of my guides who happened to fuckin' find it two hundred yards from where poor Mr. Stern was dropped. That would make things a lot simpler. I'm already in it by helping you cover all this up. We can get this over with real quick. I'll risk taking my bumps. I know where to find the sheriff. That would be good pee-*are* for you and your nutcase friends. Go."

Applegate studied the ticket propped in front of his face, took it. He got out and headed onto the platform, pissed off and un-steady. What the hell was happening? How could Grumley do anything? He showed his ticket to a man in a train uniform, one of the last people hanging around outside, who said his car would be three cars up but he better climb on here. The train started moving. Applegate hopped on and headed up the interior stairs to the second level. He walked through three cars of private sleepers and sank down in a row of empty seats.

"Hey," said a young cowboy who looked like a rodeo escapee with his tough-boy jaw and his red bandanna. "Don't I know you?"

Applegate sprang out of his seat and told the kid to save it, he'd be right back. The next car up had a snack bar where Applegate ordered a Budweiser and the bartender poured it in a plastic cup. Applegate found a seat that swiveled so he could face away from all the others and look out into the dark. The interior lights on the train created a reflection on the window. Headlights streaked along the highway on the opposite side of the canyon.

The train snaked through the canyon, in no apparent hurry. Applegate chugged the beer, found the stairs from the snack bar down to passenger seats below, where travelers were settling in. He opened the sliding door between cars and stood on the swiveling steel platform. The floor bounced and wiggled. The canyon widened. A conductor passed through and asked to see his ticket.

"I'm up in general admission," said Applegate. "Just taking a tour."

"Keep touring. You can't stay out here."

The conductor moved on.

The train slowed. Applegate prayed it down to a complete stop. It would be a long drop, but he hitched his legs over the barrier between the cars and lowered himself until he was hanging by his fingers. He let go. The rocks and wood ties were rough and he tumbled to absorb the impact.

He crouched low along the side of the train, stayed in its hissing shadow. His right ankle throbbed, his left shoulder was probably bruised. He dangled his arm, shook off the pain. The night was cold. Three more sections of train and it came to an end. He was headed back toward Glenwood Springs, where he belonged. All he had to do was follow the tracks.

****

The voice on the other end of the phone was tentative, small.

"Allison Coil?"

"Yes."

"I know this may sound crazy, but there's only a few people I know to call."

Allison stood in the middle of Pete Weaver's barn, using the phone in the saddle shop. She had been out in the corral brushing down a mule when the phone rang. She didn't think she'd reach it in time but she had run.

"My name is Trudy Grumley."

Allison took in the name.

"George's wife?" Grumley ran an outfitting service that competed with Weaver's—and Grumley always booked big, noisy camps full of rowdy clients with high-maintenance needs. Grumley's operation was gritty, old school and swaggered. It was geared for hard-charging high rollers. By comparison, Weaver ran the friendly neighborhood corner outfitting service. Anyone was welcome and even complete greenhorns were treated with patience and care. Allison knew she was a better fit with Weaver's team.

"Forgive me for interrupting. This won't take a minute. I've already talked to most of the guides who work for my husband. And they haven't been able to help. So I thought I'd check with a few others."

The woman was so hesitant that Allison instantly wanted to reassure her. And could this really be George's wife? The voice was docile and small.

"I know this sounds—"

"Please," said Allison. "How can I help?"

"I was wondering if you might have seen a friend of mine?"

The word *friend* was surrounded on both sides by a moment of silence.

"Who?"

The pause was agonizing. Allison thought she heard the woman swallow and for a second she worried that they'd been disconnected.

"It's so hard to know who knows who," said Trudy.

The world around Allison screeched to a halt. The voice, in its utter meekness, commanded her total attention.

"Do you want to know if I've seen somebody?"

Another pause.

"I know it shouldn't be that big a deal. It seemed all right to ask the others who work with my husband. Now, I feel like . . ." She stopped.

"Where are you calling from?" said Allison.

"My home."

If she remembered correctly, Grumley had tucked his home up at the end of a long driveway near the mouth of the canyon. Weaver had pointed out the driveway but she had never been up there. She was having a hard time imagining this voice as belonging to anyone in Grumley's orbit; it didn't match his gruff, rough-edged world.

"Who's missing?"

"*Missing* isn't for sure."

"Overdue."

"I don't know if you know him. Rocky."

"Rocky Carnivitas?"

"Yes."

"Sure. Everyone knows him."

Trudy waited for the answer.

"No, I haven't seen him," said Allison.

Allison had nearly finished her work for the day. There was a saddle repair that could wait; minor surgery. And Slater was off on one of his backcountry treks. It could be a day or three, depending on what he encountered or how long he felt like being gone. She was never sure how he decided to stay out or return home.

"Oh well," said Trudy. "Thanks, I'm sorry—"

"I did see something, but . . ."

"I know about that."

"How do you know?"

"The blotter. You must have filled out a police report."

She had done that, as much an exercise in accuracy as anything else. Sandstrom had insisted on a written record.

"The newspaper picked it up, ran a few paragraphs. It was probably straight out of your report, I don't know. They stuck it in their weekly police blotter." The voice had gained a bit of courage. "That's one reason I called you. Rocky isn't usually so late. I was wondering if the police figured out what it was that you saw."

"No, they haven't. How long has he been overdue?"

"A few days. He wasn't due back at any set time."

Now it was Allison's turn to pause.

"Is your husband worried?"

Rocky, after all, was George's worker. He was a legendary guide, skilled hunter and notorious loner.

Allison remembered Rocky on the trail the first time. She was heading up on a training mission with her boss, Pete Weaver, and a crew from Minnesota that oozed "golly gee" all about them. They were true young bucks on their first hunt. Weaver had them wide-eyed and mesmerized with his expertise. Rocky was heading down on his own with supplies and a three- or four-horse string.

Weaver stopped to chat with Rocky. Weaver introduced Allison, who had been bringing up the rear, from thirty or forty yards away. But then Weaver signaled her to climb down and come up to see how not to pack a saddlebag. Rocky sat smiling as Weaver, known throughout the valley as an overly fastidious know-it-all, unpacked one of the bags on Rocky's string and showed her how the weight was all wrong: bad knots on the manty rope, no quick-release knots on the basket hitches that connected the string, slipping D-rings. The loads weren't balanced. A case of Mountain Dew here, boxes with canned food there, a bow case thrown here, a duffel bag tossed there. The trail was littered with stuff. Weaver was busy showing her what he meant about the science of a well-packed horse. Rocky was watching, amused.

Allison thought, then and there, that Weaver's outfit had been a bad choice all around. Rocky worked for Grumley's Double X Ranch and she should have held out for a slot, even though they said they were all full. Weaver had taken her "on spec." Too many city folks, he'd said, had come up on a whim and couldn't stick it out through all the barn duties, wrangler business and odd guide jobs. But Weaver's treatment of Rocky at the time—it wasn't until later that she got a peek behind Weaver's cool exterior—had sent her sympathies to this hapless kid and his badly packed train.

Rocky eventually got restarted and the next time she met him was in a bar over in Eagle. Off his horse, Rocky was smaller than she'd remembered. He had deep-set brown eyes surrounded by a weathered face that had the ability to flash an off-center but slight grin. There was a bare glimpse of mangled teeth. They finally got around to a dance by the jukebox and Allison tried to come up with one solid reason why she should not encourage him.

When she moved to the mountains, she had made a promise to not be so picky. But she found it puzzling how the personal electricity between them turned cool, like a switch, after hours of talk and several rounds of bourbon and beer. She felt sobered up and disinterested. She always felt as if she was peering around the next corner, doing everything possible to look into the next room in her life. All she could picture was his likely hairy back and no emotional connection. It was easier to change your handwriting than your attitudes.

Rocky pressed against her as they stood by the hood of her secondhand Blazer. She let him grope for a minute and gave him a good kiss or three and wriggled out, said something about another date down the road. She left him in the dirt parking lot with a bulge in his pants and nothing but hope on the brain.

"If he's worried, I wouldn't know," said Trudy. "I've probably taken up enough of your—"

"Could I stop by?"

"I suppose."

"Is anybody looking for him?" said Allison.

"Not that I can tell, no."

"Where does he live?"

"Well," said Trudy. "That is one thing I need help with. And, if you won't mention it, I happen to have a key. Can you stop by and pick it up?"

\*\*\*\*

Trudy hung up, shaking.

She hadn't been able to say good-bye and realized she had expected Allison Coil to know where she lived. They hadn't discussed directions. Perhaps everyone in the whole valley knew. Maybe this was all stupid, unnecessary. Maybe she had gone too far, stirring up questions. Maybe Rocky would slide through the door at any second. But Trudy knew better.

Trudy busied herself by straightening the house. She plucked a few not-quite-yellow leaves, fed the cats and topped off their water trough. She paced in the darkened living room. She badly wanted to hop in her car and go find Rocky. But being out and about alone was a scary prospect. What if she had a seizure? How could she explain it if she wound up stuck where she wasn't supposed to be? She remembered the key to Rocky's trailer. He had given it to her "in case" she ever needed a quick hiding place that was not too far away. She dug it out of her dresser drawer and clutched it in her hand.

The trees down the road caught a glow and a pair of headlights worked their way up the drive. Trudy stepped back to the kitchen so there would be appropriate waiting time after the doorbell sounded. She stood with her arms folded, making a mental note to keep the visit brief. It was possible George could return, which would really screw things up.

****

"Trudy?" The door opened a crack. "Allison Coil."

"Come on in," Trudy said. "Thanks for doing this."

"Really, not a problem."

Trudy Grumley had extraordinarily long hair, thick and flowing. She was trim and pleasant looking, earthy. Allison noted her tentative movements, her hesitant way of moving. She and Trudy were identical in height, neither of them very tall, but Trudy carried more femininity. Her features were soft. For someone who lived in the mountains, she looked like she could use a bit more sun.

"I probably sounded like a weirdo on the phone."

"Hardly, please."

Trudy led her into an oversized living room as a swarm of cats came to check out the visitor. Trudy and the cats led the way to the kitchen, as if they knew the routine. A table and waited for them. The back of the kitchen opened to a lush greenhouse.

"I'm more comfortable here," said Trudy. "Tea?"

"Sure."

"I think I can spare only a few minutes. I really—forgive me—don't want George to see I've got a visitor. He's a little funny like that."

"He and I have met. I applied for work at his ranch, but ended up with Weaver."

Allison had wondered if they might have a glass of wine, or something stronger. A drink was routine after a day around the barn. Nothing about Trudy suggested this would be a time to linger over a cocktail. She was on edge.

Trudy poured hot water into two cups to steep the tea. Allison smelled orange and herbs.

"So you read the police blotter? A regular thing?"

"Sometimes. It's a glimpse at the state of mischief."

Breathing the humid air of the greenhouse reminded Allison of the spas in the $175-per-night hotels from her old traveling days. Trudy's graciousness in person stood in stark contrast to the disjointed telephone conversation. Trudy looked so tame. She was a portrait of the word "meek," with long, slow blinks of her eyes and a too-easy smile. She was a true flower child, frozen in time.

"Nobody has checked Rocky's place?" said Allison.

"Not that I know of," said Trudy. "I myself don't get out often."

Allison listened with increasing respect as Trudy described her personal health and general situation. Trudy looked into the steaming tea more than anywhere else, but she spoke with clarity and purpose.

"And George hasn't gone to look?" said Allison.

"We're husband and wife, I suppose," said Trudy, "but not that close. Anymore. Rocky was one of several who came around to help me out with groceries, errands, whatever. Fix this, carry that. But George doesn't know that we're good friends and I don't want him to. George has his secrets, believe me. This one's mine."

Given everything else, Trudy was certainly justified.

"Where does he live?"

"In a trailer about halfway back up the canyon. You'd never see it from the road unless you were looking, but it's right there before the road forks. I'm going on memory, having seen it only from the road. I've never been there."

"I'll ask around," said Allison. "Least I can do."

"It shouldn't be too hard to find, I wouldn't think."

"You haven't even asked your husband about Rocky?"

Trudy took a breath and sighed slowly.

"I can understand why it would seem a bit awkward—to help," she said.

"No, look, I'll stop asking questions. I do want to help. Rocky—we were friends for a while, although I haven't seen him around much. We went out a couple of times. I liked him; he's a helluva hunter. You know, he could be absolutely anywhere."

"Sure."

"But you have reason to believe—"

"He hasn't stayed gone for so long. And, well . . ."

Another one of those telephone pauses.

"George's airplane."

"What about it?" said Allison. Word in the valley had it that George would fly certain clients up over the Flat Tops to Meeker, give 'em an aerial buzz of the herds, whet their appetite.

"I have a friend at the Eagle-Vail airport. He calls whenever George comes back. It's a favor. It puts me on alert that he's in the area. It seems to change my whole view of the world, even my rate of seizures, so it's helpful to know. Anyway, I called over there today because sometimes Rocky would go with him, on a long hunt. But George's plane hasn't budged in weeks."

"Could George have used another plane?"

"Why would they use a different plane? And anyway Rocky

would have told me he was going off for days and days. He would have, believe me."

On cue, a guttural rumble from a car—or something—cut through their quiet space. Allison guessed pickup truck, maybe an older model.

"I believe you," said Allison. "Do you have the key to Rocky's place?" said Allison.

The engine sound cut abruptly.

As Trudy stood up, the side door to the garage opened and slammed with authority. Trudy didn't flinch. She handed Allison the key.

"George," she said under her breath. "No mention of this."

"Of course," said Allison.

Trudy looked down. She was steeling herself.

George came through the door, a dumbstruck look on his red face. Trudy turned and offered a smile.

"Hello," she said, as if the world had suddenly started to spin on an endlessly cheery axis. "We have company."

\*\*\*\*

Allison drove toward home up the dark canyon, knowing she should wait for morning. What did one more night matter? She wasn't about to return to Trudy's as long as George hovered around. George had been spooked, no question. Allison had said hello and then good-bye—"Just leaving."

She drove slowly down the stretch of dirt road where Trudy had indicated Rocky lived and she found an opening in the thicket. Her well-used Blazer, painted a custom gray and black by the Gypsum kid who sold it to her, was nicked and rough-hewn. The plunge through the thicket, with both sides of the body scraping branches, was the equivalent of a soft-touch car wash.

Her headlights found a silvery trailer, dead and dark. It could wait until morning, until she had daylight for bearings and nerve. It would wait until morning.

Allison slept fitfully in her A-frame, painfully aware of Trudy's predicament. There was no sign of Slater. She might have to go into Rocky's place alone, without a semi-official wing of authority to protect her.

Open the door, see Rocky wasn't there, tell Trudy.

Open the door, find him drunk, tell Trudy.

Open the door, find him dead, tell Trudy.

Open the door, find something, tell Trudy.

Why did this seem so daunting? It wasn't as if she was breaking in. It was a passed-along key, surely a sign of trust.

In the morning, feeling a bit woozy, she awoke thinking she'd steal a half hour from her personal routines and a half hour from her boss before showing up for work. She was, by far, the most punctual guide in the bunch. Old city habits. She drove down to Rocky's trailer in a bit of a mental fog, letting her promise to Trudy pull her along. At the entrance, she noticed that one other set of car or truck tracks headed into the clearing, but the tracks looked old and stiff.

She parked next to the trailer where the previous vehicle had stopped. The feeling of quiet and cold was pervasive. A layer of snow clung to the trailer's roof. Certainly, with someone here and the heat running, it would have melted.

She knocked on the trailer door. And waited. Hoping nobody was watching, she inserted the key, gave the door a push. She called out: "Rocky?" The key wasn't necessary. The door opened before the lock turned.

The trailer was empty.

There were no notes, messages or signs of struggle.

She examined a few pictures up on the cupboards: Rocky with his kills, all decent-sized animals. She stepped to Rocky's kitchen table, picked up a three-year-old motorcycle magazine and flipped through it, wondering about the world of a lonesome, thirty-five-ish guide in the mountains and about his personal hopes and dreams. Was he working for anything, toward anything?

The catalog underneath the magazine was cheap and crudely made. At first it didn't even register—the cover photo of a man kneeling in a field, holding up a palm-size gizmo only slightly larger than a cell phone. It wasn't really even a catalog, but more of a brochure. She leafed through it.

*Unprecedented accuracy* said the caption beneath. A photo of two men hunched over a mountain lion, attaching a radio collar. *AUDITRACK. Features: auxiliary sensor data, long-term data storage in animal unit, operates under canopy.* Allison flipped the page over and a clear picture stared at her. It was the identical GPS gear she had found next to the bulletless elk. *Download by radio. Built in transmitter. Spreadsheet to determine battery life. Adjustable neck. Durable.* On and on.

The brochure was addressed to Rocky Carnivitas at a P.O. Box in Glenwood Springs. Allison stuffed it into her back pocket.

She explored the trailer more purposefully, meticulously and found a matching GPS collar in a closet off the bedroom.

This one sat next to an unplugged battery charger.

Rocky the wildlife biologist? Allison had a simple answer for her own rhetorical question: *I don't think so.*

****

Allison called Trudy from Weaver's barn and had a quick conversation to let her know that Rocky's trailer was empty and that she'd keep looking. Trudy thanked her profusely and didn't even ask if Allison could return the key.

Throughout a day of packing up a new hunting party and delivering another group's kill to a nearby taxidermist, Allison ran through the odds of Rocky not being involved with the dead elk. The answer was obvious.

After leaving the taxidermist, she drove up to Grumley's barn and sat in her Blazer next to the corral for a minute, to let the moment settle. She had to have her questions ready—and what if there was a convenient explanation about Rocky? This was the same spot where she had parked on her very first visit to the canyon, responding to a small ad in the Glenwood Springs paper: *Guides needed. Horse exp. required. Will train other skills.* Grumley had done the interviewing and clearly didn't trust her city looks and soft exterior. Her background. She had sat in the car too long beforehand, brewing up a mild panic attack and questioning if she could complete the long strange trip from ad exec to mountain woman, via plane crash. She hadn't interviewed well, in part because she had left a mental door ajar where self doubt could creep in. She couldn't let that happen again.

Remembering the packed gun rack in the office, Allison got out and knocked on the doorjamb inside the barn, asked for George Grumley.

"Not around," said an older, whiskered man in brown chaps. It looked like he was getting ready to ride. Maybe it was a permanent condition. She recognized him from the talk with Sheriff Sandstrom under the eaves of Weaver's barn.

"I'm actually looking for Rocky," said Allison.

"Why didn't you say so?"

Allison didn't reply.

"Haven't seen him, now that you mention it. But it's not too unusual." He pronounced it *unuzle* and relished mangling the word.

"Is he up with the camps?"

"No doubt."

"Have you seen him since the big dump?"

"Can't rightly say. But—no, *probly* not. My name's Boyles. Yours?"

"Allison Coil." She noticed a walkie-talkie on his belt. "I work down at Weaver's."

"I'll ask the boss when he comes back. *Ack-shoo-lee*, we have a chalk board right over here."

Boyles led the way to a board mounted between two stalls. "Says Rocky . . . well, it says nothing about Rocky. Looks like someone erased his last destination. Now sometimes that boy will get deep in his cups and need a few days to come out of it. His trailer is—"

"There was no answer at his trailer. No sign of him. Would anybody else know?"

"What?"

"If he's been around."

"Not likely. I'm here more than anybody else: chief, cook and bottle washer. Believe me, he'll turn up."

"Thanks," said Allison. "It's really no big deal. It's just that I know someone who wants to talk to him."

"Whatever," said Boyles. "No doubt the storm slowed him up a bit. But in any tough situation I'd put my money on the old Rockster. No question."

Allison thanked him and left, wondering about the gnawing in her guts, possibly the same sense of dread that was gnawing at Trudy.

✳✳✳✳

Grumley showed Boyles where to park the truck, tucked down and out of sight from the road that split the valley. Boyles punched off the headlights. Across the road, an A-frame sat nestled against a stand of trees straight across a broad, moonlit field. One window revealed a soft glow from inside the house.

"Allison's place," said Boyles. "City girls."

"What do you mean?"

"The old leave-one-light-on bit. You know, when nobody's home. A city thing."

"You can tell she's not home?"

"I'd bet dollars to donuts. Do we want her home?"

"Not exactly," said Grumley.

"What are we doin'?"

"Pokin' around. And, if nothing else, delivering a message."

"No time for US mail?"

"Not exactly. She needs something to think about."

"One inquiring little bitch," said Boyles. "Probly thought I was going to get all alarmed, like she was the only one to notice Rocky ain't been around."

The sight of Trudy talking with the Allison Coil pest had been enough. But hearing Boyles tell about her asking questions, probably on Trudy's behalf, well, that called for a shot across the city girl's cute little bow.

They crossed the snowbound field quickly, skirting the edge by the creek bed, so they could come up behind the house through the trees.

Boyles knocked innocently. He would make up a story on the spot if she or anyone else answered. A second knock. Grumley hung back in the darkness.

Still nothing.

Boyles tried the handle as Grumley came up onto the porch.

"Locked," said Boyles.

"Give it a shoulder."

The door rattled but didn't open.

"How un-neighborly," said Grumley. "Give it the old linebacker tackle."

"I played wing."

"Whatever."

Boyles took a step back and lowered his shoulder.

"Are you sure you want this much damage?" said Boyles.

"You got any better ideas?" said Grumley.

"We could try the kitchen window. Sometimes people get careless."

The kitchen window slid up an inch or two. Boyles shimmied it the rest of the way. He put his heel in a cup formed by Grumley's gloved hands, eased up and disappeared through the opening.

Grumley heard a thump and right behind it a crashing sound. He waited at the front door, which opened a minute later.

"Goddamn flowerpot right underneath the window."

"Like we care," said Grumley. Potting soil covered the counter around the sink. "Don't worry about it."

Grumley positioned Boyles at the door to stand guard. "This won't take long."

First he emptied the closet, throwing everything out in a heap. He emptied the dresser, all five drawers, flinging underwear and sweaters on the floor. Toss the bed, leave all the cupboards open. He was not quite sure what he was looking for—something he had overlooked from the spot where Rocky went down in the snow, something he couldn't get a grip on. Clothes and belongings were scattered everywhere, leaving nothing in its original place. Upstairs, there wasn't much to do but turn over the twin beds and mess things up.

"Lights on the road," said Boyles. "Slowing."

Grumley was balling sheets and blanket into a knotted wad.

"Turning on the driveway," said Boyles.

"Shit."

"The mess in the sink," said Boyles. "I don't think it'll stand out."

"Fuck it," said Grumley, skipping down the stairs. "Fuck it."

The headlights were snaking their way in across the field, bumping up and down.

"Come on," said Grumley. They jumped off the porch and ducked off to the side as the headlights swept the front of the cabin.

"Christ," muttered Grumley, after they jogged across a few yards of open clearing between the A-frame and the stand of trees to the back.

Boyles crouched down as another light clicked on inside.

"Message delivered?" said Boyles.

"Shit," said Grumley. "I was just getting started."

# ワ

The sheriff's office, one block off the main drag in Glenwood Springs, was cool and clinical. The receptionist, Officer McNabb according to her nametag, pointed Allison toward a deputy who waited a minute to stop reading a newspaper and finally grabbed a clipboard. His nametag said Deputy Gerard. He was plump, bored and had seen it all. Allison ran through the details of the burglary at her cabin, what she'd found, the hours she had been gone.

"Anything missing?" said the deputy.

"Nothing so far. Even a stash of cash, a couple hundred dollars, was overlooked."

"Sometimes you don't realize what's missing for a while."

"I know." Allison had been hit in Denver once and had not realized for weeks that a camera was gone, along with the obvious TV and DVD player.

She wanted to remain calm about the explanation. But the sensation of dread she had felt when she realized a stranger or strangers had been stomping around in her private place came back to her. It wasn't a big deal compared to a swim in icy Long Island Sound with airplane parts and dead bodies as your companions. But it had rattled her.

"A geranium by the kitchen window was smashed. The door wasn't broken, so that's how they must have gotten in."

"They?"

Deputy Gerard shifted back in his chair and studied her.

"I think 'they.' There were two sets of footprints in the snow this morning that led away from the house."

"But they didn't take anything?"

"I don't have much."

"No idea what they were after?"

"No. None."

A radio crackled. Gerard cocked his head to listen.

"Big cheese is pulling in."

Gerard stood up and took on a more professional air.

"Anything new on Ray Stern?" said Allison.

"Zip. Of course, that's not official. Of course, I didn't say anything."

The front door opened and Sandstrom clomped in, trailing two deputies. One was guffawing, maybe at a bad joke. He spotted the presence of a woman and squared up. Together the three officers created a huddle of leather jackets, olive green uniforms, guns and thick black belts. Their angry boots had lost of bit of shine to the mucky streets.

"It's the guide," said Sandstrom. "Allison something."

"Coil," she said.

"What's new?"

"I was burgled. Your staff has a report."

"Ransacked," said Gerard. "Nothing stolen."

"Unusual," said Sandstrom.

"There is something else. Someone missing," said Allison.

"Who?"

"A guide named Rocky Carnivitas. Works for George Grumley. He hasn't been seen since before the snowstorm. You need to know."

"And why do we need to know?"

"It's part of this situation."

"And you're sure he's missing?"

"Nobody has seen him."

"Which means he could be out on a trip and out of communication range, correct?"

"Possible. Unlikely."

One of the deputies shifted a toothpick back and forth in his mouth and offered a squinting grimace.

Allison was tempted to tell Sandstrom about the GPS collar and the brochure in Rocky's trailer, to add spice to her information. But how would she explain it, or what it really meant?

"You weren't that far off from where the bloodhound found Ray Stern," said Sandstrom.

"A half mile up the hill. That's a long way."

"Not that far if you really think about it," said Sandstrom.

"A whole different terrain; if you'd go up there, you'd see."

"I believe you saw the guy who was trying to hide Stern's body. And it's possible with the storm that you weren't exactly where you thought you were. Correct?"

"Wrong." Sandstrom's stubbornness was maddening. "I could show you the precise spot Bear was—"

"Bear?"

"My horse. I could show you the spot Bear was standing. It was a ways up from where they found Stern."

"A ways?" said Sandstrom. "No chance of a mix-up? Have you thought of that?"

The chant started low, but clear.

"What the—?" said Sandstrom.

The chanters were stepping off a school bus.

"Two, four, six, eight—don't forget to investigate. Three, five, seven, nine—maybe murder isn't a crime."

"What the—?" Sandstrom said again.

There were about twenty of them in a neat formation on the sidewalk. They all sported bright yellow sweatshirts with big blue letters across the front: *FATE.*

Sandstrom stepped outside and Allison was right behind him. Based on Ellenberg's elated response, Sandstrom's move couldn't have been more perfect for her needs. Ellenberg wielded a mini megaphone and shouted the loudest. After one refrain of their chorus, the group pointed its placards squarely at the gaggle of cops thirty yards across the parking lot.

*Ray's Killer: There's a Home on the Range*
*Cops Are a Hunter's Best Friend*
*Cops and Hunters, Birds of a Feather.*

Four television cameras panned over to focus on Sandstrom and his deputies, who watched the proceedings with idle curiosity, nothing more.

"Good Christ," said Sandstrom through a half smirk, stepping back inside after seeing all the cameras. "Someone hand me my rabbit gun. This is like the arcade games in the carnival and I'm slightly out of practice."

"Looks like we're down to the hard-core protesters," said the toothpick chomper.

Allison stood behind the knot of cops, hoping she was out of view of the cameras.

"That woman Ellenberg has one shrill set of pipes," said Sandstrom. "I'd rather listen to twenty girls with fresh manicures scrape their nails on a blackboard."

"Isn't that Dean Applegate behind Ellenberg?" said Gerard.

"Who?" said Allison.

"The hunter with a sudden case of conscience," said Gerard. "Claims Ellenberg and company made him think twice about killing animals."

Allison studied the lanky string bean behind Ellenberg. He hardly looked like prime hunter material. There was something tentative about the way he walked. His chanting lacked conviction.

"The reformed hunter," said Sandstrom. "I believe you're right. By the way, did anyone talk to him?"

The deputies looked at each other and back at Sandstrom.

"You guys play mumbly peg or whatever it is you do to decide who gets the privilege," said Sandstrom. "But do it. Don't make a big scene here. Wait 'til he's back at whatever place they're staying or whatever hole he crawled out from."

"Gee, chief, don't you think this would be one you'd enjoy? Making him sweat?" said Gerard.

Sandstrom considered the suggestion.

"I believe you're right. Now that you mention it, I believe you're right." A gleeful, boyish look spread across his face. "Now, we could stand here all day like we've never seen a stupid parade before, or we could go inside and get back to work. Right now, we're sort of helping Dr. Doolittle's wife prove her point. Men?"

Sandstrom backpedaled into the station and headed to a rear office. His posse followed smartly.

Allison stood for a few minutes watching the protesters from a closer vantage point. One camera crew was breaking down. The other was doing an interview with Ellenberg. Applegate had the megaphone now. The chants were starting to lose their zing. The moment was over; the protesters had sent their message.

Allison pulled up closer to listen to the interview with Ellenberg.

". . . It's just clear this is not a priority for the sheriff. Painfully clear, painfully obvious—and tragic for Ray Stern."

"What exactly do you think the sheriff should be doing?" The reporter was young, looked like he knew his way around a make-up kit.

"Well, I'm no detective," said Ellenberg. "But the first thing I'd do is find out who was in the valley that day and interview every one of them, one by one. Seems pretty basic. But even Dean Applegate here, he hasn't been quizzed. It's obvious they want to kiss it off. But there's a hunter up there who can't tell the difference between a 145-pound man dressed in a deerskin and a legitimate—

if you can even use that word—elk target. Someone pulled the trigger and it's the sheriff's job to figure out who it was."

The reporter turned to his cameraman and gave an invisible signal. They were done.

Ellenberg turned around as if she expected another reporter to be waiting.

"Hello," said Allison.

"And you're with . . .?" said Ellenberg.

"Nobody," said Allison. "Just me."

"Are you here to sign up?" said Ellenberg. "It looks as if you might be another convert like our friend Mr. Applegate. Are you a hunt*ress*?"

"A what?"

"A hunter."

"No, I've never killed an elk or a deer. You know, pulled the trigger. My name is Allison Coil and—"

"Why all the hunting attire then?"

"I work for a hunting outfitter. I'm a guide. I help the hunters. I know what you think about hunters and hunting, obviously, but that's not why I wanted to ask you . . ."

"What?"

The protesters slowly gathered around their leader. Dean Applegate moved in close and stood behind Ellenberg. They were more than comrades.

"I heard you were up near where they found Ray Stern's body."

"That's right," said Ellenberg.

"Excuse me."

The voice came from a man coming up behind Allison. It was Deputy Gerard.

"Dean Applegate?" the deputy inquired. "We'd like to ask you a few questions in private if you don't mind."

"Mind?" said Ellenberg. "Now? Right now?"

"Excuse me," said Gerard. "I'm talking to Mr. Applegate here."

Ellenberg and Applegate exchanged glances. If Allison knew anything about reading a face, she sensed a touch of fear beneath Applegate's wan, forced half smile. Applegate shuffled off with the deputy.

"Tell them everything," said Ellenberg, grabbing Applegate's FATE sweatshirt near the T. "Ask *them* why they haven't done more until now to figure out who killed Ray Stern."

"I guess you got their attention," Allison said to Ellenberg.

"We'll see," she said. "I'm not too impressed with your police authority talent up here."

"There are good people on the force," said Allison. "Maybe they're stretched thin."

Ellenberg's crew mingled closely around her, protecting the FATE queen bee.

"Hard to see the effort," said Ellenberg.

"But you were up there?" said Allison. "How close were you?"

"Close enough. I identified his body, right where that chicken hunter left him. Can you imagine? Making a mistake like that, making a huge mistake like that and then *leaving*?"

"No, I really can't," said Allison. "I have to agree with you on that."

"It's clear you don't agree with us on much else."

"How do you figure?" Allison wondered if this could turn confrontational. What was her exit strategy?

"Your whole hunting guide garb here," said Ellenberg. "And you already said you help the hunters with their slaughter."

The words dangled like bait. She tried not to nibble. Or, worse, swallow.

"I was wondering if you could show me on a map, maybe, where you were, where they found Ray Stern?"

"Why?" asked Ellenberg. "What's it to you? What difference does it make?"

"I was up there, the day he was shot. I saw someone dragging something, probably a body."

Ellenberg focused her gaze and cocked her head ever so slightly. If Ellenberg had learned the move by watching spaghetti westerns with Clint Eastwood, she was a poor mimic.

"Have you told the police?" said Ellenberg.

"Yes," said Allison. "Everything. The thing is someone else is missing, too. Another guide. He works for a different outfit than mine, but nobody has seen him. His friends are worried sick. They think he might have been up there too, at the top of Ripplecreek Canyon."

Ellenberg relaxed, sharpened her eye contact.

"What did you see?"

"A man dragging something. I was looking through a snowstorm. It was all fuzzy, like a TV with bad reception. The cops think I saw the man who shot Ray. I think they're dead wrong because it was further up the hill. Much further. I think I saw something else."

Allison scanned Ellenberg's crew: a few older women, a few earnest young men, some scruffy and some clean cut. One reminded her of Vic, the young stud she'd met at the camp on the day all of this started unraveling. He looked enough like Vic to be his brother. She glanced around the ring of Ellenberg supporters: FATE, FATE, FATE, FATE, FATE on their sweatshirts. As if Allison needed a reminder about the difference between one airplane seat and the next.

"I'm not much help," said Ellenberg. "I couldn't tell you with any degree of accuracy exactly where we were. Maybe the cops have GPS coordinates from the spot where Ray was murdered."

*Shot*, thought Allison. *Accidentally.*

"I don't know," said Allison. "They think I'm the one who's confused."

"Sorry," said Ellenberg. "But how exactly do you sit there and watch these beautiful animals being killed and carved up?"

Actually, I don't sit there, I show them exactly how to gut and quarter.

"Probably not a good idea to get into it," said Allison. "I think we can agree to disagree on that one."

"No, seriously," said Ellenberg. "These majestic, beautiful creatures. Slaughtered. And you think it's okay? You seem like a woman with a bit of a worldview, if I'm not mistaken. It's a hunch but you seem smarter than the average local up here."

Allison again looked over the FATE throng. They were waiting for an answer.

"I'm from the city, originally, it's true," said Allison. "I respect what you're doing and I respect your point of view. It's not mine. The fact of life today is that you can't let the elk and deer populations explode unchecked. There are too many. And hunting is older than the wheel. It's the way it is. You can't go back and undo the fact that human beings have the ability and the desire to hunt. It's an animal instinct."

Ellenberg shook her head slowly.

"You think people—societies, whatever—have no control over their future?"

"I think reality is reality," said Allison. "That's all."

*Some people die accidentally. Some people die because they are hunted and killed in war. They all end up in the same situation. Hunting is part of human nature.*

Allison took a tentative step back. She knew this was headed nowhere but ugly.

"I do wish you well in pressing the police to figure out who killed Ray Stern," said Allison. "All hunters are trained to identify what they are shooting before they pull the trigger."

Allison hoped the common ground would signal truce.

"But you enable the slaughter of deer and elk," said Ellenberg. "That's what you do. You helped put this moron in the situation where he *could* pull the trigger."

"Sorry," said Allison.

"You are?" said Ellenberg.

"No, I didn't mean sorry, sorry. I meant *sorry*, that's not the way I see it."

"Then there's blood on your hands, too. Animal blood."

The FATE bunch stirred and Allison could feel their stares.

If looks could kill, she thought.

\*\*\*\*

"You did what with your rifle?"

"I know it sounds crazy. And I shouldn't have littered. But first I whacked the barrel on a rock. I mean, it's not useable or anything, wherever it is."

Sheriff Jerry Sandstrom attended to his notebook. Applegate waited, going for his best relaxed and unconcerned look. He considered the notion that there would probably be a whole battery of folks interviewing him if Grumley had told Sandstrom what had really happened. On the other hand, they might be setting a trap. Either way, Applegate felt his eyes were too blurry and wondered if that was noticeable. He wondered, too, if there was any way Sandstrom could tell that a muscle high up on his cheekbone had begun to twitch.

"Do you know which cliff?"

"Can't remember. It was a spot where the rifle went a long ways down."

"And what type of rifle was it?"

"A Winchester."

"What model?"

"A .270 I think. I don't think hunting was in my blood, which is where it belongs if you can bring yourself to shoot—"

"No lectures, please," said Sandstrom.

Applegate sipped coffee from a Styrofoam cup, studied the creases in Sandstrom's pant legs. He concentrated on keeping his story straight. Ellenberg had offered to accompany him, but he decided it would look too protective, too paranoid.

"So when did you guys get word of Ray Stern's death?" said Sandstrom.

"The first day back down."

"And then you hiked with your rifle back up to some spot to throw it away? Isn't that going to a lot of work?"

"Maybe a bit impulsive," said Applegate. "But it seemed right."

"You didn't tell any of your old college buddies what you were doing?"

"No. I didn't think it would go over too well."

"Where, approximately, did you decide to heave it?"

Applegate shifted uncomfortably. What if they actually had the gun right now? And what if this was all a ruse? He had no choice but to keep the storyline up.

"There's a trail that leads up the next drainage east of Ripple-creek."

"An hour's hike, two?"

They weren't really going to look.

"Two or three is more like it."

"And where were you on the day Ray Stern was shot?"

"I took a walk."

"A walk as in hunt or a walk as in hike?"

"I think I had my rifle along, but it was a joke. We hadn't seen anything bigger than a marmot, bless their fuzzy little bodies, the whole two weeks. The others wanted to lie low, except Grumley."

He realized this was a subject he shouldn't have raised. It brought up all the sticky issues about time and place. Sandstrom didn't ask a question, so Applegate thought he would fill in the blank. "He didn't miss a chance to hunt. The rest of us were on our own."

"So, a hike. And you went—where?"

"Down the valley, if I remember right, even though I was kind of interested in seeing the protest and how it was going to work. I guess I had sympathies. Even then."

Enough, enough, Applegate told himself, although now it would be difficult to appear curt and cool after putting on a chatty demeanor. He was having difficulty imagining what Grumley might have told them. In a separate line of analysis, he wondered if Grumley had fed the cops enough stuff, perhaps anonymously, to put them on his tail.

"Draw me a line where you hiked—here," said Sandstrom, unfolding a topographic map.

"It's been so long."

"The best you can," said Sandstrom.

Applegate studied the map. He spotted the ridge where they had camped and he doodled a line from there in the opposite direction from where Ray Stern had taken his last steps.

"And where did you chuck your rifle?"

Applegate drew a line to a place where the contour lines were jammed closely together and it looked like it might be steep enough to toss something off.

"So you were up by Lizard's Tongue on your hike, the day you didn't expect to find anything?"

"In that area."

"But you didn't see anything else. Tracks? Nothing?"

"If I did, I'd tell you," said Applegate.

"And you returned to the camp at the end of the day?"

"No, I hiked out all the way when it started to snow."

In fact, Applegate had headed down as instructed by Grumley, but he was too afraid to start a fire or attempt to survive a night in the wilderness alone. So he had stumbled down the trail. He had managed to not lose the way. He snuck into one of the barns, where he had shivered and sobbed until dawn. At first light he walked to his car and went for a long enough drive to warm up. He found a café out by the interstate and ordered food but couldn't eat.

"It's not every day that a hunter suddenly changes his mind about hunting." Sandstrom put his hand by his right temple and turned an imaginary key.

"Now do you want the lecture?"

Applegate smiled; Sandstrom didn't.

"It's heart and mind in this case," said Applegate. "And the protest for me was that. His death, Mr. Stern's, made me think. But almost like there was no need for thought. It felt like I was living in the wrong camp—and perhaps I was. Never had that feeling? That gun of yours, it's a symbol of what's gone—"

"Please," said Sandstrom. "Really. How long will you be in Glenwood if we need anything else?"

"I don't know," said Applegate. "I think that's up to FATE."

\*\*\*\*

They seemed to be hovering. The frosty Flat Tops stood motionless below. The same headwind that was pushing the airplane back to Eagle was blowing giant puffs of white fizz off the ridge on the west edge of Ripplecreek Canyon. Grumley trimmed the nose down a notch as the Mooney bored into the teeth of a snarling, high-pressure howl at twelve thousand feet. The plane was grinding. Above, the sky was crackling blue.

Grumley dropped down with the sinking elevation, all the while asking lame questions about Dabney Yount's supposed exploits in other corners of the world. Yount paid cash up front and carried four customized Weatherbys. He oozed wealth. He hadn't made any amateur comments yet, hadn't shown an ounce of concern about the airplane's slow progress and didn't seem worried about the schedule.

But Yount also didn't mind being served. After the airplane landed, Yount watched as Grumley loaded their gear into an old Ford pickup. He let Grumley assemble a plate of food for lunch: gourmet bits of smoked sausage and sharp Gouda cheese with rye crackers, grapes and homemade soup from an oversized thermos. Grumley cracked caps off two bottles of German beer. They ate standing on the dirt strip next to the Mooney, which provided a break from the persistent wind.

The truck bounced over rutted dirt roads, which zigged and zagged at right angles back toward a cluster of hills to the north. Grumley followed directions scratched on the back of a used envelope. The envelope had been attached to the pickup's visor. The roads were unmarked but the distances between them served as a gauge. The few landmarks that existed—a mailbox, a telephone pole, a type of fence—matched up well with the scrawled directions. They truck followed the grade uphill and the structured grid of roads collapsed on the steeper terrain. The snow covering the road amounted to wind-blown patches at first and finally obliterated the hard-packed soil altogether.

They reached a north-south shelf that offered a panorama to the west, a hundred or so miles down an immobile ocean of forest and rangeland. The snow had piled high on the road in spots and Grumley dodged them where he could and gunned through the hubcap-high drifts where he couldn't. The road petered out. They stopped behind a pickup truck with a camper shell. Three horses stood silently nearby, two saddled and ready, the third with saddlebags, all hitched to the side mirrors on the front of the truck.

Yount turned down the offer of hot coffee in the camper and watched as Grumley organized the loading of the packhorse with their personal effects and weapons. Grumley and Yount dressed in heartier winter gear in the camper. Yount climbed up on Dozer, a large chestnut and white Appaloosa. Grumley took Flapjack, a smaller but surefooted quarter horse.

Two hours later, most of it spent climbing, the horses kicking through a foot and a half of snow, they arrived at a four-man canvas tent. A campfire burned outside. The tent sat in a clearing ringed on three sides by a tightly packed grove of blue spruce.

One of the guides heard them coming and stepped outside. Grumley introduced Yount, who gave off an air of impatience. The rifles were taken down, unpacked, checked and loaded. After hearing the herd was less than a mile away, up and over the ridge behind them and likely to be nestled down in scrub and heavy cover, Yount chose his .340 and 250-grain bullets. Grumley had a Savage 99. The other three of Yount's rifles would stay.

A guide produced a walkie-talkie, muttered something softly into it and waited for the response back. Ten seconds of silence preceded the whispered response. Grumley led Yount on foot, heading for a jagged knoll on top of the ridge. Yount tried to hide the fact that he was working. The slope required them to jab their toes into the grade for balance. Grumley set a steady pace, knowing it was harder to stop and start repeatedly than it was to keep plugging.

He could not take his mind off Applegate and Allison. Yesterday, Trudy had called him in from the garage where he had been welding a busted hinge on an incinerator. Trudy said they had teased a report on the evening news about a protest at the sheriff's office. She was pretty sure she had seen another picture of his "pal." Sure enough, the first report showed Applegate and the bitch, Ellenberg, stomping around the cops' parking lot, demanding action. Applegate must have stepped onto the train on one side and off on the other. The one thing he couldn't do was reach through the television and grab Applegate by the neck and use the microphone cord coming off the reporter's camera as a noose.

Grumley would have to track him down, again. This time would be the last.

"Last bit of full-blown daylight."

It was Yount.

"We're fine," said Grumley.

From the stone outcrop they spotted the guide, who was crouched low behind a boulder halfway down the slope on the other side. The guide spotted them and used both his arms to signal them to stay low. They did, hunching over as they walked down. The wind was in their faces, which helped.

"Three hundred yards," whispered the guide, using his thumb to point up and over the boulder. "Some beauties. Watch your step. A couple of stragglers have ventured over this way in the last hour or so."

Grumley led the way out, heading parallel with the ridge top to maintain the higher ground for as long as possible. The ridge was dotted with massive Douglas firs and lodgepoles, ringing an old burn. A red-tailed hawk circled silently in the dusk. Elk tracks wound through a stand of aspen. Grumley saw one pile of the distinctive, elongated scat and it was fresh. Yount spotted an elk first and emitted a soft cluck as he stopped and squatted slowly. He cocked his head to the left as a way to point. A long-necked cow was picking her way around the base of a lodgepole, chewing grass that poked up through the snow.

Yount shook his head *no*. Too small.

The elk munched, oblivious. Grumley signaled to stay put and still. The cow drifted off. Grumley led the way in behind it, using the trees and the steady breeze in his face as cover. The snow crunched a bit too much for his liking. The overnight freeze had created a crust on the surface that would make it difficult to sneak up on anything. Any attempt at forward progress could spook the cow and as a result the whole herd. Wherever it was. The good news was the snow depth, only a foot or so. The elk weren't having any trouble finding food to keep them satisfied. But the hunters' best bet was to stay put. Grumley figured twenty minutes of shooting light remained. Perhaps the herd would drift back in their line of fire.

Yount pointed in the direction he wanted to go. He was ten yards back, hanging low.

Grumley pointed to his boot, to the snow and his ear. *Too noisy,* he communicated with this pantomime.

Yount shook his head *no* and pointed ahead. Grumley put up his hand like a cop stopping traffic. But Yount started walking, bent at the waist. He headed straight for the close cover of the pines and skirted them, staring ahead. Every step came with a crunch, soft and audible, like a cannon shot to elk radar. Trying to avoid a pattern, Yount took three steps and waited, two steps and waited, four steps and waited. He crouched at the base of a tree.

Grumley took aim at the back of Yount's head, lining up the crosshairs on the spot where the top of his fleece collar touched his neon green cap. Through his scope, made for spotting the spine of an elk at three hundred yards, the back of Yount's head filled his field of vision. *Pop, pop, pop* said Grumley to himself. Why did some of 'em always think they knew better? He wanted Yount to turn around so he could catch him in the face.

Yount stepped around the tree out of sight. Grumley raised the rifle and propped the butt of it in the snow so he could lean on the barrel. He waited and listened, thinking he could hear Yount's steps, but it was his imagination. A black-backed woodpecker swooped through two nearby lodgepoles, landed on a third and chiseled for beetle grubs. The tops of the lodgepoles swayed, but the wind at ground level eased. Grumley waited fifteen minutes, figuring Yount had taken responsibility for his own hunt.

The bull strutted out between two trees and stood rock still. A gift. Grumley automatically took in the length of its antler beam, a cinch fifty-incher.

The bull dipped its head down to feed. The antler tips were as high as the top his shoulder. The rack was deeply curved with long brow points and nicely shaped sword points. The bull, giving Grumley a broadside view, looked up. Its ears jutted back. Grumley tried to keep his thoughts from moving. The bull took a step to its left and turned slightly, the ears going slack. Grumley lowered the sight until the crosshairs found the bull's shoulder. It was eighty yards to the elk, maybe a shade less. The spine would shatter easily. His brain and finger were considering the shot when he heard another crack, not far away. The report surprised him. He had nearly forgotten Yount. At the sound, the bull bounded off its hind legs. Grumley followed the target as it reared and followed the shot in the distance with one of his own. The bull pulled its rear legs in and sat down. It teetered and collapsed sideways. Grumley lowered the rifle and jogged toward his kill. The shot had shattered the bull's spine; no finishing shot was required.

It would take the whole crew to help quarter and pack out so much food. The horses and the help weren't far, but the gutting job would have to be done by campfire light.

He heard Yount before he saw him. He came running like a three-year-old who had discovered candy.

"Holy—" he said, half out of breath, taking in Grumley's kill. "I thought mine was—*Jesus*, look at this mother."

"Father," Grumley corrected. "You got one?"

"A cow, nothing to write home about."

Yount was breathing hard, whether from excitement or exercise Grumley couldn't tell. Some hunters were like that, the adrenaline pumped up at the idea of killing something.

"One shot," said Yount, inspecting the blood-caked hole in the bull's backbone.

"Yours?" said Grumley. "Where'd you hit her?"

"Rear quarters," said Yount. "She got about five paces and called it quits."

"I'll trade you," said Grumley.

Yount looked at him like he had spoken in another language.

"This baby is trophy class."

"Cow meat is sweeter. You tell your story, I'll tell mine. Switch the bodies."

"You have quite an accommodating guide service."

"Hey," said Grumley. "If you drop something better tomorrow, we'll switch back. If you don't, you hang this rack."

"Best damn outfit this side of the Mississippi."

"We like repeat business," said Grumley. "Let's go raise some boys to excavate all this meat and hang it up to cool. Unless you'd rather—"

"It's getting awfully dark," said Yount. "I'm not sure I could handle a sharp knife in these conditions. And I'm a mite thirsty from all the aggravation that goes along with this hunting business."

"Feeling tuckered?"

"Christ," said Yount. "The only way to have made it any quicker would have been to chain these suckers to a tree."

\*\*\*\*

Allison was stepping out of the shower, replaying the "conversation" with Ellenberg over and over in her mind, when she heard the horse snort. She grabbed a towel, yanked open the bathroom door, shouted "just a minute."

Underwear, socks, jeans and sweater were tossed on as quickly as possible, the jeans battling damp skin. She opened the door barefooted.

"Just waking up?"

Bobby Alvin, one of Grumley's hunting grunts.

"Making up for the hot water we all miss during season."

"No need to get dressed on my account."

Bobby Alvin had been a three-night fling many months ago. At first he came across as the cool, low-key, earthy sort whose every move and thought was born and bred in the backcountry soil. He had short hair and square but rugged good looks, with deep-set eyes. Her downfall. His attitudes were as natural, normal and relaxed as a cow grazing in a pasture. He was a big one, barrel chest over knobby, gnarled legs that flopped beyond the end of the bed. But Alvin's world didn't stretch much beyond horses and hunting. She realized she had been mistaken when he didn't seem to care about anything outside his shallow puddle. It was Allison's relationship with Alvin that made her realize her own interest in the rest of the world was not so easily squelched. The sex had been forgettable, coarse and abrupt. When The Boy Scout—Slater— showed up on her radar, Alvin hadn't put up much of a fight.

"Coffee?" she offered, heading to the pot to fill the tank with water.

"Got any bourbon?" said Alvin, plunking himself down at the table. He sat sideways in a chair, tilted it back so he was leaning against the wall.

"Most likely," she said, opening a kitchen cabinet to check the supply. She found a bottle of Wild Turkey. He poured himself an unhealthy portion.

"You called?" he said.

"I was wondering if you could tell me who camped last week with that guy Dean Applegate."

She was careful to put the focus on Applegate, not Alvin's boss, Grumley.

"The quiet one."

He knocked back his first drink and reached for the bottle.

"How's that?"

"I helped pack Grumley and his buddies up and down three years running and I never could figure out that guy."

She let it dangle. She wanted to poke around, but didn't want to sound like the FBI.

"Now I hear he's all over, talking like a raving madman," he said. "Go figure. I couldn't get ten words out of him. Not like the others."

"The others," said Allison. "The others were—"

"Pretty cool. Flatlanders, don't get me wrong, but they knew it. Applegate always had to have his camouflage."

"Do you know them?"

"By name?"

"Yeah."

"*Nick*names—two of 'em. 'Fishy' Marcovicci and 'Locks.' Oh, and another guy named Frank. And Grumley and Applegate. Why don't you ask George?"

This was the hard part, not knowing how secretive to be, not knowing how much she could trust Alvin. This was the part where she had hoped he would play stupid.

"He's a busy guy . . ."

"It has to do with Rocky, right?" he said. "Word is out that you're poking around. I've had questions myself. I mean it's been a long time now. Too long."

"The cops are petering out," said Allison, "and don't seem to care."

"And that's because—"

"They're too busy with the guy in the deer suit," she said.

"And what do you think these three have to do with anything? They're puppies, let me tell you, who could barely manage to survive for a day by themselves in a stocked hunting camp with a full-time maid."

"I'm curious if they know anything."

Alvin buried his nose in his drink and crossed his eyes to watch the fluid go down.

"You don't think the cops already got to 'em? Hell, they found me. One of the guys from one of our camps got pinned down on his way out, just because he was driving out from Grumley's barn. He tried to explain that they had been hunting eight miles north of Ripplecreek."

"You're probably right," said Allison.

"It's possible Rocky got caught, strayed from his camp. Maybe he couldn't find his way back. Froze or something."

"I suppose," said Allison. She said it with a touch of conviction, but didn't mean it.

"What you need is all the guns in the valley that day, test all the ones that could have handled the bullet that zipped into Mr. Deer Suit, get one stupid murder or accidental shooting or whatever it was off their minds." Alvin spoke like it was all a snap. "And get the cops to help find Rocky."

The phone rang.

"Allison?" It was Trudy.

"Yes. Hi."

They had been talking on the phone daily, but this was the first time Trudy had initiated the call.

"Do you have a second?" said Trudy.

Alvin took a drink, looked tense, but wasn't going anywhere. Allison turned away, toward her small kitchen.

"I need a second," said Trudy. "My airport friend called. I told you George took the plane out. He's coming back late this afternoon. Very quick trip. An overnight, which is unusual. And the jet that brought in one of his customers—well, the pilot is there now. They're prepping it. I guess it's one of those new corporate jets. A Gulf Something."

"Stream," said Allison. "A Gulfstream."

"Expensive," said Trudy.

"Very," said Allison.

Alvin looked at her and smiled.

"I thought I'd let you know."

"Interesting. Thanks," said Allison.

"Did you get your house back together?" said Trudy.

"For the most part. It looks okay. Look, I've gotta go now, but I'll stop by real soon. Thanks."

Allison hung up. Alvin's grin was gone; he was stone-faced.

"Was Rocky fighting with anyone?" said Allison.

"Cops asked that one eight ways from Sunday. No."

"You think he was up there working?"

"Sure."

"He wasn't doing anything—"

"Peculiar?" said Alvin.

"Yeah."

"Rocky Carnivitas? Maybe he smoked a joint now and then, maybe he drank too much in the shit-kicking joints, I don't know. You think you're concerned, go ask Trudy Grumley."

"Why her?" Allison played innocent.

"The Grumley crew, that was one of things we had to do, rotate in on 'Trudy Duty.' Woman's got a problem with her brain, it freezes up, I guess. I've never been there, thank God, when it's happened. Anyway, we've got to babysit her, take her places. She can't drive."

Alvin stopped as if that completed a loop of logic.

"And Rocky?"

"Was her favorite. He started picking up shifts, seemed like, to be with her. An A-1 hunting guide spending his days shuttling her around? I think she took a fancy to him. I bumped into them one day in the grocery store. Sick woman and her helper? I don't think so."

"But—"

"No, I don't think anyone would take the chance of playing

footsie with the boss' wife. Most likely, they were friends. Anyway, that was Rocky. He could get real sympathetic."

"George didn't notice?"

"Who's to say? Go talk to her, but bring your machete."

"Huh?"

"Her house is a jungle. Plants growing out of every nook and granny. I mean cranny." He started to laugh.

"Cats, too. Every shape and size, climbing on everything."

Alvin stopped. His face contorted like he suddenly solved the quadratic equation. "But maybe he saw a set of antlers, an unbelievable rack he couldn't resist and he set off after them. Got lost. It's happened. He was always after the prize, wanted to break all the records, get his picture plastered all over the paper. That boy was convinced the record rack was right here in the Flat Tops. Convinced."

"Really?"

"And velvet too. Rocky said he had a pipeline to get the velvet to Korea and China and places like that. Prize USA velvet or even fresh antler, all ground up and preserved. Like I said, Rocky always talked about a pipeline outta here, right under the export radar and off she goes, money coming right back."

"You believe that?" said Allison. Alvin was getting a faraway look in his eye but she still needed something from him.

"What, that it's some sort of Chinese Viagra?" said Alvin.

"Yeah, you believe it?"

"You mean, have I tried it?"

"Didn't ask that."

"Well, I would try it but I don't fucking need it, pardon the joke," he said. "Mind if I use the bathroom?"

"Before I forget, can you get me the names of the other three hunters? The full names?"

"Still onto that? Sure," said Alvin. "Of course. If you want to get your hands all dirty."

He wobbled a bit as he walked. He stood a moment before opening the bathroom door, getting his bearings. Allison started thinking of how to scoot him out, maybe pretend she was the one that had to leave. She'd rather be with Trudy. She wondered if Slater had the sources to find out which cop might have talked to Fishy, Frank and Locks.

She was lost in thought and didn't hear Alvin finish up. He came up behind her and put a hand on each shoulder, rubbing the muscles. His hands felt like steel clamps, stiff and indifferent. Built to grip, not to touch. She squirmed, leaning forward.

"Aw, the big brush-off."

He worked his way around to her chest. She stood up and turned around.

He held up his hands like an innocent and feigned surprise.

She leaned against the table, eyeing him and getting a whiff of the bourbon. He retrieved the bottle, took a drink and passed it to her like an invitation. She shook her head *no*.

He took a step forward, standing between her legs. He brushed his knuckles on her cheek.

"It's been a long time," he said.

"Bobby."

"Who's gonna know?"

"It's not going to happen."

"Going?" he mocked. "It *is* happening."

She gripped the table as he went for her arm.

"The girl from the big city. That's how they talk. *Going*. Is that how they tease, too?"

"I thought we could talk."

He reached around, grinding his pelvis against hers. He grabbed for the bottle. He knocked back a swig. "One little go 'round," he said. "Like the rodeo. A go 'round."

"No," said Allison, thinking that striking him might be like whipping a spooked horse.

She felt him hook a finger in the top button of her Wranglers. "Don't do this," she said.

"Animals do it and they don't even know why," he said. "You're not gonna deny a guy who's a bit down on his luck. One peek at that cute butt." He cracked a slick half smile, working to provide a glimpse of warmth. "How does such a petite thing like you learn how to ride them big ol' horses, anyway? Okay, let's pretend I'm the horse. Saddle me up, strap me on."

She turned her head slightly as he moved in for a kiss. He landed his desperate, dull mouth on her cheek. She kept her arms propped back against the table behind her and tried to look unconcerned. He rocked his pelvis, wanting her to feel his excitement.

He had already wormed his face around to the back of her neck, thinking it was irresistible. She resented his size and position and demands. The top button of her jeans popped loose. She put a hand on his hand, where it was searching for the next notch of hope and pulled it away.

"Stop," she said. She hit a tone point past firm but not quite angry. She put her hands on his cheeks. "Stop. You need to stop right now. This is not a re-start. I needed help and I thought you'd be willing to give it to me. That's it, that's all."

He stood slow as a bear after hibernation. He looked her in the eye.

"Jesus," he said. "Sorry. I thought maybe, thought we . . ."

"I know," said Allison.

"If you ever . . ."

"I know," she said.

"Yeah," he said. "I don't know what . . ."

She buttoned her jeans.

In the world of events, she thought, a romp with Alvin wouldn't have hurt. But it might have given him hope. And there was the complication. Pieces of the heart, once frozen over, should never be deiced.

# 8

Allison parked her Blazer beyond the perimeter fence of the airport and picked up her binoculars. There was no problem picking out the Gulfstream, a showroom-clean and bright white jet parked amid the smaller props. Four men were sorting gear and moving equipment around. George's Mooney was wingtip to wingtip with the Gulfstream. Trudy had given her the Mooney's tail number and Allison jotted down the Gulfstream's.

A small truck was parked nearby and even without its sign Allison would have recognized it: Ted's Taxidermy. The enclosed rear of the truck was refrigerated. It was not possible to pick out George until near the end of the fifteen-minute exchange of baggage. The last item moved was an elk or a deer. A sizable set of antlers poked out of the canvas wrap that held the skin. Elk. Two men shook hands and one headed to the steps that led up to the Gulfstream. The other man, who went back to his pickup, had to be George.

"Where's Rocky?" she said out loud. "Where's Rocky, George? Do you know?"

The staircase automatically folded up into the Gulfstream and the clutter of men and equipment vanished from the jet's skirts. Allison rolled down her window to listen to the engine's whistle. The machine lumbered out to the runway. Without stopping, and without an ounce of extra noise, the jet reached takeoff speed with no visible sign of struggle. It shot up into the clouds. Ninety-nine point nine nine nine nine percent of the time, she thought, aircraft function like they should.

Allison slumped low in the front seat of the Blazer until she heard George and the Ted's Taxidermy truck drive past. There was one road in and out of the airport. She could see enough to tell that George's truck was full. The taxidermist followed George and she slowly turned her Blazer around after they had left. There was no need to follow. Ted's destination wasn't a question.

\*\*\*\*

Slater's desk was one of four in a jumble that supported an apparently free-floating swamp of newspapers, newsletters, memos and junk. There was no trace of organization.

The rangers' district office was upstairs in a renovated old warehouse, overlooking the train station. The floor was the original bare wooden planks. The soft clomping of staffers and secretaries echoed and creaked at the slightest movement below the exposed-beam ceiling. Slater's desk and the three others were each propped over braided area rugs, as if this defined an office.

"Thought you were working," said Slater, hardly surprised at seeing her. In fact, he didn't even seem that interested or happy or much of anything about her arrival.

"Thought you were up-country," said Allison. "Stopped by on a whim."

"Just got back, changed at home and came here to do, uh, paperwork." He glanced at the menacing pile on his desk.

"Right," said Allison. "Hard to believe."

"And you?"

"Called in sick. Outright lied."

"So we can go back to your place?"

"And . . ." It dawned on her. "Yours is closer."

"Yours is more comfortable."

Slater lived in a trailer park south of town. She'd seen it twice.

It was a doublewide, neatly kept. He was saving money for something. But it was a trailer in a trailer park with trailer people. She wasn't that sound a sleeper. Nothing about his home setup said "Welcome, girlfriend." She never really thought about the place where he lived but chalked it up to his generally thrifty ways.

"What are you up to, if you're not in fact ill?"

"Trying to figure out a few things."

"Still," said Slater. It was more a statement than a question.

"Nobody's seen Rocky Carnivitas for a real long time." She walked him through a few details he'd missed the last few days, particularly the identity of Rocky and a few bits about Trudy. The rough picture. She did not want it to sound like a crusade. "So the missing Rocky is number one. I found parts of a matching GPS collar in Rocky's trailer—"

"Oh?"

"Trudy asked me to take a look and gave me a key. No Rocky. But I found a unit identical to the one we found up top with the dead elk."

"I meant to tell you," said Slater. "A team from CSU got a federal grant to study herd size or something, a five-year grant. Your taxpayer dollars at work. I should have told you sooner. They were supposed to notify us which herd they were going to track. But they've been working it all through the Meeker district office."

"So this is coincidence?"

"I'm saying there are biologists all around."

"And why the dead elk?"

"Shock? Overdose? I don't know." Slater studied a sheet of paper as if it was the last document on earth.

"Overdose?"

"I can't explain it, that's all."

"We should have taken a piece of the dead elk," said Allison, "and sent it to the lab for tests."

"To find out what?"

"How it died, maybe. Wouldn't you want to know if these biologists screwed up?"

"I should have taken a sample," said Slater.

"I'll get you one," said Allison. "I'll be up there soon, I'm sure."

Slater stood up, found a chair and brought it over. "What else?" he said. Finally, a hint of warmth. And a smile.

"I don't know. What was Rocky doing with GPS gear?"

"I don't know," said Slater. "We'll ask him."

"If he shows up."

"Rocky? He will. It's not like these people are on a schedule. You should know."

"I have a bad feeling. Plus, it pisses me off that Sandstrom thinks I don't know where I was."

"He said that?"

"I know where the heck I was," said Allison. "To the inch."

"Of course, of course," said Slater.

She told Slater about her place being ransacked, then reporting it to the cops and running into Sandstrom. In a genuinely concerned tone of voice Slater asked if she was frightened and if any valuables had been damaged or ruined.

"Can't you do something?" said Allison, knowing he couldn't. She didn't even want to go into the business at the airport. What business was it anyway? Just hunting and hunters, fancy style.

"What would I do? Declare stupid cops are banned from these parts? Or go find Rocky myself?"

"What if Rocky and his buddies use GPS to track game?"

"Then they'd be bad boys. We'd step right in, no question. But you need more than parts in his trailer. You'd still need Rocky, to ask him about stuff."

"You don't seem that concerned."

"Lots of speculation."

"About everything, including who shot JFK."

Slater threw her an eyebrow-popped glance. "At least there you had a body," he said.

"I know, I know. But you didn't hear the shot. I did. You didn't see this guy dragging a load. I did. It wasn't down the hill where they found the deer suit guy. It was right there in front of me, down a ways, but in front of me."

"Yes," said Slater. "But it took you a while to come off the pass. By then, you know, he—"

"Who?"

"He, whoever, could have covered lots of ground. Even in shock, from having killed this guy, he would have had his adrenaline pumping. He might have considered turning himself in and admitting to the accidental death. The adrenaline runs out, he's tired of carrying the body. He decides to hide it in the woods. And decides there's no way they can figure out who killed the guy. And so far, he's right—one hundred percent right."

"And the dead elk?"

"A fluke. A separate deal, but a fluke. Give Rocky a chance to turn up."

He's had a zillion chances, thought Allison, and hasn't taken one.

She stood up, hiding her exasperation, not wanting to challenge Slater's logic.

It made sense to a point, but it didn't connect with what she felt.

"I'm going home. Maybe I need a rest," she fibbed. "I'll be there later, if you want to swing by. Up to you."

She smiled.

"I'll see," said Slater. "I'm pooped myself."

She looked around and gave him a quick kiss.

"Any federal rules about that?" she said.

"If there are," he said, "I'm going to court."

****

Ted's Taxidermy took up all of a low-ceilinged barn that faced the Colorado River halfway between the interstate and the main road up Ripplecreek. The truck served as signage, always placed in the same strategic spot near the road for maximum impact.

Ted Slowik was tall, thin, graying and forever with a pipe in his teeth, whether or not the sangria-smelling tobacco was lit. He had a couple of helpers and had grown to know all the outfitters in the area. He was the best taxidermist in the county, the most meticulous. He really didn't need to advertise. From head mounts to full body mounts, Slowik prided himself on high-quality work.

Allison parked and walked into the barn, which was constantly heated by a pumping wood stove. Two German shepherds looked up from their naps and a black rabbit, Midnight, hopped over to greet her. Nobody new. The dogs went back to sleep; Midnight was quickly distracted by a stray wood chip. Allison picked up the bunny, found a pile of browning lettuce near her cage and offered nibbles by hand.

"Another one?" said Slowik, who was spreading a skin out on his workbench.

"Nope. Just stopped by. I wasn't sure if I'd given you the name and address for that doe I brought over yesterday."

"The head mount? Sure you did. Standard procedure for us. Let me check."

He pulled a file from a shelf above the bench. "Here it is. Trabowski, Oak Park, Illinois. Got it."

"Wow, that's a beauty," said Allison, admiring the bull and its enormous antlers.

"Biggest rack so far this season. Weighs forty pounds alone, bank on that."

"Whose?"

"Who else?"

"Again?"

"Well, Grumley's client, anyway," said Slowik.

"But George always brings 'em in. Who was the client?" It was an innocent question.

"Jeez, you should have seen this guy's jet. Huge. Brand new. Engines that burn more fuel in a minute than you and I use in a month. George introduced me, but damned if I remember the name. Not without looking it up." Back to the files. "Dabney Yount. Houston, Texas. Thought I smelled oil money out there at the airport."

Allison traced the antler rack with her hand, felt its sharp points and the smooth woody sensation. It was hard to believe blood flowed through the antlers like sap in a tree.

"Grumley's crews are lucky."

"Or good," said Slowik. "And rich. They bring in more full body mounts than any other outfitter, that's for sure. That one'll take time."

"Quite the gash," said Allison, eyeing the ripped skin near the spine.

"That's the easy part," said Slowik, putting a match to his pipe, making it puff. "Try finding the inside thing for this guy that brings him back to life."

"I've thought about that," said Allison. "If you had elk lungs, elk heart and elk innards, I'll bet you'd know where all the parts go. You better than anybody else."

"Maybe. All except the on-off switch," said Slowik. "That's the one funny one. I'm never sure where to put it."

\*\*\*\*

Applegate tried to stop fixating on what the cops were thinking and doing: whether they would burst through the door any day with the bloodhound sniffing a path to his heels. And if that happened this second, if they could get through the door unannounced, the dog's nose would be working overtime as it took in the lush, slightly acrid aroma of sex, minutes old. Or perhaps they didn't need the dog. Maybe there would be another incriminating scrap of evidence, a piece of fabric from one of his mittens they found at the scene. Or a cast of a bootprint. Maybe they had a new technique to identify bootprints even after a new snowfall. Was that possible? And they would ask to see his outdoor equipment and a wise old scientist would be standing by to confirm the match. The dog would wag its tail.

Applegate had days of unbridled fear, registered as a constant chatter that chewed on his other thoughts, the ones up front, the ones he was supposed to be concentrating on. He wanted to whack down the voice in the background, but the ideas it articulated were hard to ignore.

Ellenberg shifted on her side. Her naked breast grazed his chest and she sighed. In his book, which was a thin one, it had been a gangling, awkward half hour of tumbling. But it had also been satisfying.

Ellenberg had come to his room with a bottle of red wine. They sat on the bed cross-legged, facing each other. She poured and told him it was time to pack up and leave Glenwood Springs. And then one toast ended with a kiss, more like a tap on the lips, nothing deep, and that was that. She was a kindred spirit. He admired her spunk. The kiss made him think it was possible to wriggle free from his old snakeskin and put on a new layer.

She pushed him over on his back. They hugged and explored each other's mouths, her long brown hair creating a private pup tent. She smelled of Ivory Soap behind her ears. With the wine, the kisses carried a perpetual tingle. She did not object to a hand on her slender rear and he had worked his way up underneath her red-checked, flannel shirt. She buried a wet tongue in his ear, jammed her pelvis down on his and offered a throaty growl of approval before she stood by the side of the bed and stripped casually, displaying a bit of pride in her lean body, boyish hips and cone-shaped, high-set breasts.

Standing naked, she unlaced his shoes and pulled down his pants and underwear in one swoop, stopping to give his erection a red-wine smack of its own. She helped him off with his shirt and made him feel that being able to make love with him was the grand prize in a long-odds contest. She straddled his knees and licked him. He kneeled on the floor and tried his unskilled best to return the favor for a few minutes between her spread legs. She spun around on top of him and lowered herself down. She pumped slowly, her hair tickling his face to the rhythm. He tried to hold back for a minute, but couldn't. He bucked her wildly from below as she grabbed his chest, looking for a handhold.

"Eye yie yie," she said when he was done. Her hair had stuck to her warm cheeks. "Now that we've got the ice broken . . ." She let the thought dangle.

She rolled off and snuggled down alongside him, a hand returning to cup his crotch and give it a pat. Was this a deal, he wondered, that Ellenberg would want to take public? Perhaps she did a lot of the guys. Perhaps this had been a thank-you screw, a kind of sympathy fuck to put a cap on the protest.

"Dean?" She thought he was dozing. Actually, he was picturing the bloodhound leading troops to their motel. "You know it's not over," she said. "Your work with us, I mean."

"It's not?" he said. How do you hide a look of surprise? It wasn't easy.

"We don't worry a whole lot about titles, but everyone would like to see you come on board and keep doing what you do, plus a lot more. You won't believe the projects we have in mind. The spring bear hunt, the new aquarium in Denver. We're getting information about nasty experiments with rats at the university."

"Rats?"

"There's so much to do. Besides, you can't crawl back in a hole. Not now."

"What would I do exactly?"

"We tend to let the roles evolve. It's more natural than making up a job title and job description and then wedging people into them. You start hanging around, we'll find stuff for you to do. Don't worry."

"Manager of stuff."

"Now there's a spiffy title."

She rolled back over on top of him for a hug. Her skin was warm. He ran his hands down her back as she buried her nose in his neck. Relax, he told himself. Enjoy it.

\*\*\*\*

"She's very curious. Enough for a whole cat house."

"Yeah?"

"Nosy. Lots of questions. Wondering about Rocky."

Grumley shifted in the squeaky swivel chair behind his desk. Alvin looked nervous, perhaps half unsure why he was telling his boss any of this. Boyles sat on the couch, running his fingernails over the tip of a pocketknife.

"Wondering what?" said Grumley.

"When he's going to turn up, stuff like that. She thinks the cops need to talk to your other buddies, the ones besides Applegate."

"And why not him?"

"I suppose she figures they've already grilled him, I don't know."

"You told her who was who?"

"I told her it was none of her damn business, that she oughta let the cops do their thing." Alvin looked proud of what he'd said, like it was a difficult message to send.

Jesus, Allison Coil was a pain. First with his own damn wife, right there in his own house, then questioning Boyles. And now this.

"Thought you'd like to know whenever your name is being mentioned behind your back," said Alvin. "Especially in connection with—"

"With what? I've talked to the cops and I don't care if you're working for the fucking cops or you are a fucking cop yourself, it doesn't have much to do with me."

Alvin studied his mucky boots. Boyles stopped fiddling with the knife.

"I suppose Miss Coil has theories about the death of the jerk in the elk suit?" said Grumley.

"No," said Alvin.

"But I do," said Boyles.

"Care to fill us in?" said Grumley.

"It was an animal hugger that pulled the trigger—had to be. No real hunter would've mistaken a 120-pound man wrapped in a brown cape for the real McCoy. So they staged the whole thing and tried to hang it on the hunters. They even had a plan for destroying the gun. It's a fucking ruse."

"I like it," said Alvin.

"Best one I've heard," said Grumley.

"Cops said they talked to all the protester types, too, but let's be serious, okay?" said Boyles. "What would the chances be—that on that day they would have run up against a hunter with the IQ of a brick? They had to do it themselves, trust me on that one."

"So they killed a human being to prove a point about killing animals. Makes sense to me," said Grumley. "Allison Coil comes snooping around again, holler, okay?"

"Will do," he said.

Alvin muttered something about mucking a stall and headed off.

"Some people can't leave well enough alone," said Grumley.

"Sure seems that way," said Boyles, standing up and sliding his knife into a sheath on his belt. "What's next?"

"I don't know," said Grumley. "I got a business to run. I need these headaches?"

Boyles knew better than to answer.

"So what is Miss Allison doing?"

"Trying to get the authorities curious."

"So what do we do?"

"Keep close tabs on her—and Trudy."

"And what are we looking for?" said Boyles.

"See if she's just fucking around or trying to fuck us."

# 9

A firm midwinter breeze bore down as Allison walked to her lawyer's office. The wind gained strength from the empty, cold caverns of a city on a weekend.

The office was near the top of Denver's tallest building. She rode the elevator admiring the sheer trust involved in letting cables and pulleys and motors and switches boost you hundreds of feet in the sky. Were there any parts in this machinery that could freeze up? Would she freeze up? Could she pull the trigger and sue the bastards? Were they really bastards? Weren't people doing their jobs? Doing their best? And now she would be given money in exchange. In exchange for what, exactly? In exchange for surviving? Really?

Ambivalence was the word of the day. Her guts and heart were filled with unadulterated ambivalence, garnished with a few drips of creeping dread. Mostly, she wanted out of the elevating steel cube and the skyscraper. Perhaps at the top of the tower she could hop on a zip line back to a place where her blue jeans would be on a horse, not in a lawyer's leather office chair.

The reception area featured a staggering view of the mountains, from Mount Evans to the west and north to the Wyoming border. Pollution? The wind today made it someone else's problem. A too-pleasant receptionist asked her if she needed coffee or water and Allison half expected to be asked to leave her beat-up cowgirl boots at the entryway and off the polished floor. No request surfaced.

"Allison."

Even on a Saturday, Paul Reitano was all business in his button-down collar and silk tie.

"You guys have moved up in the world. Literally."

They shook hands.

"Corporate merger. We picked up a few accounting firms, clean ones not tainted by the accounting scandal meltdowns. Well, *charged*." He smiled. "But not tainted. It makes for pleasant surroundings, anyway. And right now we're running six days a week, no casual Fridays, no casual Saturdays either."

He was sixty-ish and soft-spoken. He came across like a kindly professor who could scorn a set of bad grades with a look of deep dismay, one that carried weight. He had piercing blue eyes, puffy bits of unkempt white hair and the weathered skin of a lifelong skier.

Reitano led her down halls lined with contemporary art to his small office.

"Thanks for making the trip down. They've had a test-run trial in New York. It was a real trial, but it's used as a means for determining who pays what amount. It's like dividing the check at a restaurant: determining who ate more, drank more and therefore who gets to pay more. The two major parties were the airline and the airplane manufacturer. The airline tried to find something mechanical that went wrong. And they failed."

She listened as if it had just happened, as if she was still dripping and crouching awkwardly on a rock near the water in the harbor. The water continued to chop and churn. There were bits of stuff everywhere—jackets and magazines, suitcases and those under-sized airline pillows. And there were people, struggling and flopping around in the water, not seeming real at all, more like actors in a bad movie. Shock coated their pain, bewilderment covered their agony. Some were making it to shore. Some didn't move at all. And one or two peered down into the black water, floating lifelessly.

Reitano talked about deicing and how long an airplane is airworthy, once it has been hosed down, until the glycol solution loses its battle with the elements. He mentioned that they could have opted for a second kind of solution that was an anti-icing agent as opposed to a deicing one. He talked about how the pilot asked the co-pilot to check the wings thirty minutes after they had been through the deicing station and the co-pilot, according to the tapes they pulled from the wreckage, came back with the all-clear. Only deicing solution on an airplane wing has an "effective window" of twenty-five minutes, no more.

She remembered someone in uniform coming down the aisle, peering out the windows a few rows back. Everybody watched him study the wing. The "everybody" included a few people who were in their last few minutes of life, the co-pilot among them. He could have seen something, even made it up. Why not squirt your windshield one more time when it's being splattered with rain and snow and crud? Why not put the jet through for another swab of pink goo, to hit it again before takeoff? It had been twenty-four minutes, said Reitano, when the jet was given clearance to head for Denver. But what good was thinking of Denver when you might not make it off the runway?

"Your injuries were major. But, in the end, you recovered your life. The settlement they are offering is nine hundred thousand dollars. I could go into the strange ways an actuarial table can change, how emotional distress factors in . . .?"

"That's an offer?"

"No trial. Terms to remain confidential. There's a group of survivors and the families of others who think the suit has gone far enough," said Reitano, "who don't want to take it another step. They are the ones involved in the mock trials. It looks like the airline and its insurance companies will be asked to compensate victims moderately, as these things go. But there's another group that wants the government to pay their share, too."

"The government?"

"It's a delicate balance: regulating the industry and running it. If the airline doesn't follow the recommended safety standards set by the glycol manufacturer, the government wants to be able to say that it's none of their business, that it's a cut-and-dried decision on the part of the airline and its pilots. Twenty-four minutes? That must be okay. They think their air traffic controllers should have no monitoring function, no oversight. It's not that hard a thing to track the time and the weather. But the tapes recovered from the airline conversation with the tower show there wasn't a lick of concern from the tower about how long your jet had been parked and waiting. To put it another way, the government thinks that if they post sixty-five on the highway and you go sixty-six, it might not be their fault if the asphalt is poor quality, maybe a stretch of bad road popped your tire and you wound up in the ditch."

Reitano paused and spun gently in his chair.

"We want to keep pressing this lawsuit. There are only eight of us left. It's a bit of a risk, not taking what they are offering at this, uh, juncture."

"Nine *hundred* thousand?"

"Less my fees and taxes."

Allison couldn't imagine what it would be like to be responsible for, or think responsibly about, a pot of money that size. Or maybe larger. Was it possible to grasp this as having any connection to swimming in the sound when she should have been flying?

"But is it greedy to seek more?"

"It's not greedy. It's a risk. Lawyers in my end of the business have a saying we borrowed from investment bankers: *Pigs get fed, hogs get slaughtered.* You're looking to get fed, trust me, no more."

"But wasn't the government doing its best, or trying to?"

Reitano leaned up on his desk, coupled his hands together so the middle knuckles interlocked neatly.

"On that basis, so were the pilots. So was the glycol manufacturer. But the government is another thing we can challenge."

"How much more could we . . . win?" It was a difficult word to use.

"Hard to say. And there's more to it than financial value. It's a matter of proving a point, cleaning it up for others. Someone once said that the government is both a dangerous servant and a fearful master. The government is us. It's all of us. Watching and monitoring. Providing checks—and balances. It's little people pointing out problems and being rewarded for their suffering. Suing your government doesn't mean you hate them. It means you respect your fellow citizens. It means you want to make the world a better place."

"More than nine hundred thousand dollars? That's hard to grasp."

His demeanor was too steady to be troubling, his reasoning too solid. She pictured the deicer trying to work beyond its limits, as if it had a brain to know how important it was to keep the wings from freezing.

"I'll take your lead on this," she told him.

"The principle is with us, on our side. Remember, it's not the individual people we're going after. It's the system, the way they do things."

"Do I have to decide now?"

"No. We have a few weeks to notify the airline if we'll settle at this stage. You want to think about it; I understand."

"I like the idea of having it over with, that's all. Tying up all the loose ends."

"The money is tempting," said Reitano. "Don't think I don't realize that."

The whole conversation, its premise, was far removed from her world on the Flat Tops. Or maybe it was the steel and glass setting that gave the discussion an unreal quality. How could you make such a decision? On what basis? What was nine hundred thousand dollars *worth*?

After staring off for a moment, Allison stood up. Reitano also began to get up but politely sat back down as Allison did.

"I've got a favor to ask."

"Shoot," he said.

"Different matter," said Allison. "Isn't there a state system that keeps track of debts? Posts them?"

"The UCC. Uniform Commercial Code. It's a registry in the secretary of state's office. Invaluable."

"Can you show me how to access it? And, if you're online, I was wondering if I might spend on hour or so on the Internet? There's a big spender in Texas. I want to see how many cattle come with his big hat."

Reitano smiled. "We have a spare office," he said. "Right this way."

****

Allison flopped on her unmade hotel bed, a half acre of cushion. It was so large she had barely messed one corner of it. She wished Slater could come help her tangle the rest of the sheets. After she got back from her meeting with Reitano that afternoon, she made a phone call to Slater.

"Why in the world would these men talk with me?" she said. She studied the list in her hand. Bobby Alvin had called back with the names she had asked about: Sal Marcovicci, Frank Cassell and Darrell Lockwood, known as "Locks."

She tucked the telephone between her tired head and the pillow.

"Because you want to know," said Slater. "If you think not being a cop is a disadvantage, you're wrong."

"They don't have to talk to me."

"Of course not. When people talk to cops, though, their lips might be flapping but they don't always say very much. Or they make it up. Like Applegate."

"What did he have to say?"

"Sandstrom gave an update at a summit meeting today. Applegate said he gave the rifle the old heave-ho off a cliff, after hiking back up through three feet of snow. I don't think so. If any of those guys can give us an idea of what Applegate was up to, it would shed serious light."

"Sounds like you're dubious."

"Ask any of 'em if they know where Applegate's rifle might be and find out if they saw Applegate anywhere the day that guy Ray Stern went down. I'm not dubious. I am trying to imagine it all, trying to get pictures in my head that make sense. And I want you to be careful because if they do know something, they might not appreciate having to lie constantly about what they know. And they might get a little edgy, do something stupid."

"Really?"

"Sure. This could be an intricate cover-up. Be careful."

"Gee, I feel like a deputy, but don't you have to come down here and officially deputize me?"

She would spring for the best bottle of champagne the hotel could muster and maybe tell him about the nine hundred thousand dollars, seed money for their lives together.

"I would if I could," said Slater. "That official ceremony will have to wait."

"I still feel nervous—and alone."

"Nobody's forcing you to do anything."

"Could be we're barking up the wrong tree," she said, "or even poking around in the wrong forest."

She wanted Ray Stern's killer caught more than anyone other than Stern's mother. She imagined a conversation with Stern's killer, Sandstrom right there to hear it all. Every delicious word from Stern's killer, recounting his day of stupidity, would disprove Sandstrom's assertion that she didn't know where she had been when she heard the shot. Besides exonerating her memory, finding Stern's killer would mean they had found the stupidest hunter in the country. It was one thing to mistake a moose for an elk or a doe for a buck, but a human? It was beyond the pale.

"Then come on back," said Slater. "Sandstrom claims it's a full-court press. Somebody's going to feel the pressure and crack. Count on it."

"So you want me to talk with these guys or not?"

It didn't seem as if Slater was really interested in absorbing and analyzing information that might be related to the whole snarl of events up on Ripplecreek. Whether or not her information was related, his general attitude was starting to piss her off.

"I think you should leave it to the pros but I also think, from what I know, that it doesn't matter much what I think."

"Don't leave me feeling worried," said Allison. "Say something to make me think you'd rather be right here."

There was a slight pause and Allison imagined Slater staring at the ceiling, hoping for inspiration.

"Be careful," said Slater. "I know you'll be smart, but be careful too. I'd prefer you head home."

"That's not exactly doing the trick," said Allison.

"I know," said Slater, "but it's the best I can do."

\*\*\*\*

Sal Marcovicci lived in an old Victorian that overlooked a small lake on Denver's west side. Canada geese pecked at the yellow-green grass on the park that rimmed the lake. She had picked up the phone to call Marcovicci as soon as she finished talking to Slater, allowing no time to brood on Slater's words of caution.

Marcovicci was the closest, so he got the first call.

Was this hard—asking questions? No.

Maybe a touch awkward? Definitely.

Was she out of her element? For sure.

Her head kept up the mantra.

Nine hundred thousand dollars. Nine hundred thousand. Nine hundred. Thousand.

The door opened before she could ring the bell.

"That was quick." Marcovicci was a short stub of a man.

"Nice view of the lake and mountains," said Allison.

"Denver would be Kansas City without the mountains. So y'all may as well look at 'em. Come on in. You said you live in Ripplecreek?"

She followed his chubby, molded-butter walk inside to a living room that dripped leather and absorbed light. Lots of ginger teak and black trim.

He was all blobby roundness. The puffy, reddish orbs of his nostrils looked like miniature versions of his cheeks, which were surely stuffed with tissue. He offered her coffee, which she declined, and water, which she accepted.

"I was up on top of Ripplecreek Valley, coming down, the day that protester was shot."

"I notice the cops can't figure it out." He clearly had no problem getting down to business.

"Everybody notices the cops can't figure it out. Haven't so far, anyway. Your friend Dean Applegate—"

"Haven't talked to him since his switcheroo. None of us except Grumley really ever understood that dude."

"Us?"

"Lockwood and Cassell and me. When Applegate took off that last day to go hunting, we kicked back and relaxed, played poker and listened to the wind howl. With the protesters, the best thing to do was to lay low, stay out of trouble. Who needed the hassle? Next thing we know, Applegate is on television or sprawled across the newspaper every time you turn around, talking about hunters being the animals. Now there's a twist, coming from a guy who painted camouflage on his face like icing on a wedding cake." Marcovicci patted his cheeks with both hands. "Excuse me, but what a weirdo."

"But Grumley liked him?"

"They got along. Applegate might have had the stamina, but not a lick of technique."

"You're a big hunter, too?" said Allison.

"Come here, I'll show you something."

Marcovicci led her around through the kitchen and down the back stairs.

"I overhauled the basement three years ago, dug out the old cement floor and built myself the room I've always wanted."

Marcovicci snapped on a light.

The room was a rainbow of browns—walls of tan paneling, animal heads mounted in various shades of brown, picture frames dark and woody, a long brown couch and an old mahogany desk. Dark bookshelves were filled with magazines and books that didn't require a filing system to separate the subject matter. There was only one topic: hunting. One whole shelf of *Field And Stream*. Another of *Sports Afield*. There were books on tracking, camping, rifles and ammunition. And dozens of personal hunting pictures were mounted on the walls. One picture was in a frame made of wooden, hand-carved pistols.

"My palace," said Marcovicci.

"You don't seem like the hard-boiled hunter."

"Just something I love: the sport of it, the search and the science. And, of course, bringing home a winter's worth of venison or elk steaks or whatever it might be. Hunters aren't monsters; they're mostly decent people following centuries-old urges. Think hunters do more damage to the countryside than skiers? What about all the ripped-up forests? What about hikers and mountain bikes, with all the trash and all the permanent trails? They turn hiking paths into bald highways. Applegate and his band of merry protesters haven't a clue. Applegate should know better. It's all so silly."

Allison sat down in the chair behind the desk and admired the shrine.

"It's always seemed to me, when I'm up there spending time with hunters, that there's an awful lot of wilderness, a ton of animals. Most people who like to hunt also provide a service—thinning herds, being careful with the meat, the whole bit."

"Bingo," said Marcovicci.

"What about Applegate's rifle?"

"Maybe he sold it."

"He says he didn't."

"Oh, really? You talked to him?"

"Cops did. Glenwood Springs is a small town," said Allison, anticipating the question. "Said he walked it back up into the mountains and tossed it off a cliff."

"Bullshit," said Marcovicci. "One hundred percent pure. Look, let's cut to the heart of the matter here."

"We need to know where Applegate was, where Grumley was and where Applegate's rifle might be found, if anybody knows."

"You used the old 'we' thing."

"Sorry. *I*." She smiled.

"Why you?"

"I've been asking myself the same question. I heard a shot up top by Black Squirrel Pass—"

"Nothing unusual."

"And saw a man dragging something. Or somebody. By the time I got down and around to the spot, they were both gone.

The man, that is, and whatever he was dragging. Except there was a dead elk right there, but the elk was too big to have been dragged anywhere. All this happened in the first hour or so of the storm. I'd love to turn this all over to the cops, but they don't believe much of what I say and I know I don't have any real trouble to point to."

Marcovicci took her story in with a stoic face, studying her.

"Have you talked to Applegate?"

"Haven't yet," he said.

"You plan to?"

"At some point. It makes sense. And what if I know something? Why would I tell you?"

"Because I asked."

Was that enough?

It didn't take a detective to read his nervousness or a book to interpret the body language.

"So if I come up with the rifle, you might be able to figure it out if that rifle's in trouble?" he asked.

"I'd get it to the proper authorities."

"Have you talked to Grumley or the others?"

"No," she said firmly.

"But you know Grumley?"

"Small valley. He's a big name."

"But you haven't talked to him?"

"Like I said."

"Is he the issue?"

"Doubtful," she said. "Maybe. Who knows?"

"Whatever, look. I don't have to be connected to any of this? Identified as a source?"

"About the rifle, I wouldn't think so. Cops need a witness about Applegate's movements—"

"He wasn't up near Lizard's Tongue, or anywhere up by Black Squirrel."

"When did you last see his rifle?" she said.

"A good question that I'm not going to answer," he said.

"If you change your mind about that, do you know where to reach me?"

"Write down your information, in case I need it."

She scratched out her name and the main number at Pete Weaver's.

"Couple of days, do you think?" she said.

"Maybe."

They shook hands at the door. His grip was warm and soft like fresh marshmallows.

"Did you really see something?"

"Yes," she said, "and it wasn't pretty."

"And you think this will help, even though there's no way Applegate was up there?"

"I don't know," she said. "I'm following my nose. Seeing if the pieces will come back together."

\*\*\*\*

It was a long way from the straight lines, white carpet and contemporary furniture in his suburban townhouse.

The ceiling rafters at headquarters were exposed. The office was wide open, democratic. It was filled with men and women who believed in the earth. Within minutes of starting work, Dean Applegate realized he would need a few scruffy edges if he was going to blend in with the scene. Unshaved armpits were popular with the women. They even wore dresses that advertised this preference. In a political sense, they had organized a commune with their own code for dress, manner, attitude, diet, lingo and scent. Everything tended toward natural. That meant, of course, unpleasant at times. Teams rotated providing lunch, which was a time for airing complaints or shooting the shit. There was a camp of workers who looked for the publicity angle in every wisp of an issue. There was another, smaller group who sought to wage this war on a more intellectual level. The publicity hounds were always looking to mount an event dramatic enough that news directors and reporters couldn't resist. Applegate had never realized how the news could be so easily controlled. Anything "visual" did the trick. Applegate was often asked for an opinion on this strategy or that issue, but it was more to make conversation than anything else. Ellenberg made the final decisions.

A few members of the FATE fold trusted him completely. Others seemed less certain about his conversion. Every national interview he conducted routinely attracted thousands of dollars in contributions, so they couldn't ignore him. But he wasn't one of them. It was all heart for them, especially for the young women. The cement in their foundations was still setting. There was lots of talk about cross-country skiing and vegetarian cooking. It was all subject to change, thought Applegate, on the whims of the right guy.

He helped install new computer programs to track donations and pump out newsletters. He installed some of his own software in the organization's computers: better word processing systems, a more sophisticated spreadsheet program, an income tax program. He worked on their network. He took over design and construction of their website and made it more interactive. He bounced from project to project, discussion to discussion.

The hardest day, his third back in the city, was when Ellenberg came back from a photo studio with a long cardboard tube tucked under her arm. After lunch she gathered the staff around. She removed the tube's contents gingerly, as if it were a centuries-old treasure map. She rolled out a life-size photograph of Ray Stern.

It was a candid shot. Ray Stern looked like he'd been caught off guard. The backdrop was solid grass. He was leaning back on his arms, content. Black and chocolate puppies crawled all over his stomach and legs. Labradors, Applegate guessed. One had scampered up on Ray Stern's chest and was busy licking his cheek.

The staff gasped as she held it up.

"His brother sent me the image," Ellenberg announced. "Thought we'd hang it on the wall where you get off the elevator. Any objections?"

"Of course not," said one idealistic, herb-tea type. Nobody else spoke.

"Dean," said Ellenberg, "could you help frame it and get it hung up?"

There was a black cloud in his head. Some days it floated off to the edge of the horizon and he didn't even notice it. From time to time it rushed back, blown by a curiously quick wind.

"Sure," he said.

# 10

Allison was unsure of the idea from the moment it occurred to her—but how would Trudy Grumley say no? Politely, if at all.

The horses, Bear and Stingray, a gray Arabian, were hitched to the outside of the trailer, saddled and ready. It had been only fifteen minutes since she left the horses along the riverside and drove the rest of the way up to Trudy's. Allison didn't mention anything to Trudy about the idea until she stopped her truck next to the trailer, which was parked in a wide spot on the road.

"Yours?" said Trudy.

"Ours, at least for a couple hours," said Allison. "Game?"

"I haven't ridden since high school."

"Then you know there's nothing to it. I've already told Bear to be especially gentle. He's a rock anyway and hard to fluster. There's a trail that leads up along the banks of the river. It's a bit chilly, especially with the wind, but I brought an extra coat that Weaver loaned me."

She held it up: full length, brown, leather.

"I'm—"

"Nervous? Don't be."

"This is so . . . I don't know. Either I'm at home or in the car with somebody else driving."

"But you're game."

"Sort of."

"Okay then."

Allison helped Trudy up on the saddle. Trudy smiled. "Whew," she said, "the view."

"What's for lunch?" said Allison, loading Trudy's Tupperware into Bear's saddlebags.

"Tuna and pickle sandwiches with sprouts on sourdough, yogurt-covered raisins, fresh mango slices, cranberry-almond muffins and whole-wheat Fig Newtons."

"Fig Newtons?"

"Like 'em?"

"God's gift to guides. A staple."

"I hope it doesn't remind you of work."

"Not a chance."

Allison led them down a gentle path to the river's edge. They waited for a few minutes while the horses dipped their snouts in a calm eddy. The river bubbled cold and white and blue, rippling around snowcapped stones.

"Warm enough?" said Allison.

"Like a summer day," said Trudy, the cool wind flipping her long hair off her shoulder.

They rode slowly along the river, heading downstream. Allison watched as Trudy turned her head to the sun, closed her eyes and basked in the fresh air. It was Allison who had called and said they needed to talk, but there was no hurry, no reason to press things. It was all too unsettling.

The path dipped down along the river, far enough below the road that for a half mile or so they were alone in the wilderness, like explorers. The lone signs of civilization were a distant set of power lines and the well- trampled trail. They watched a fly fisherman working a pool, aiming his hook at one particular spot over and over, his concentration so intense that he didn't notice them coming up alongside him. When the fly finally landed, a plump trout exploded up from beneath the surface and snagged the bait.

"Woolly booger?" said Allison.

"Works every time," said the fisherman.

"Beautiful," said Trudy.

The fisherman held up his catch for them to study. Sunlight glinted off the multi-colored skin for a flash. Gently, the fisherman held the prize underwater and let it go.

Trudy clucked Bear along, clearly getting used to this. Allison took a moment to stretch and look back upstream and to the west, checking the skies. A man sat on the guardrails high above them. Allison could barely make out the top of a brown pickup behind him. For a second Allison thought the man was simply shielding his eyes from the sun. Light reflected off a small pair of binoculars. The man was not wearing a coat; he hadn't been outside long. Allison stared back. Trudy had gone ahead around a corner and out of sight. It was probably nothing. Allison trotted to catch up.

They walked the horses for an hour in silence. Finally they found a spot where a good-sized boulder shielded the wind and nature had built a dry, grassy embankment a few feet above the water's surface. They weren't too far below the road. They could hear the occasional car or truck overhead, but it was an easy trade-off for the windbreak. Allison tied the horses to a scrub oak a few yards further downstream, huddled down with Trudy next to the warm rock and cracked each of them a split of wine.

"Screw-top. Sorry," said Allison.

"Like I'm complaining," said Trudy with a broad smile.

"Chilean merlot," said Allison. "Here's to mountain rivers."

They clinked glasses and took a sip. Trudy let out a small, satisfying sigh.

Trudy picked at her food casually, unhurriedly, as Allison started talking about the Gulfstream. Allison eventually got to the point of this meeting by telling Trudy about the information she had gathered off the Internet at Reitano's office. She described pulling the state records that listed public debts, which documented the money Trudy's husband had borrowed at the outset to buy his plane and to launch his sporting goods store.

"His plane alone was worth $350,000 new," said Allison. "He probably needed to or wanted to stay liquid."

"Liquid?"

"Cash-wise liquid. So he borrowed it, or most of it. The debt gets registered with the state."

"I didn't know about any of this," said Trudy.

"When my friend, this lawyer I know, saw what I was doing, he took me over to another computer in his office that has a hard line straight into the computer database for the courts. All the records and filings are there."

"There was a piece on a news show about those databases, public records at your fingertips," said Trudy.

"Type in his name, boom. Seems your husband isn't a huge fan of the federal government and its pesky IRS."

"I can vouch for that," said Trudy.

"Three years ago, he was audited," said Allison.

"I remember an auditor who came to the house to look at the books. She looked like your typical suburban housewife mom. Hardly what you'd expect."

"A dispute surfaced. It was minor at first, but according to the transcript of the trial your husband came this close to being thrown in jail for contempt of court. Once we had his name and the case number it was easy to pull the records of what happened. Anyway, he didn't show up for the first day of the trial. Then he insisted that he be allowed to claim the house, your house, as a deduction for his business operation."

"It's a house, like any other."

"Claimed he entertained clients there. He apparently didn't think there was any difference between home and going out to a restaurant."

"Never saw anybody," said Trudy. "Or very few clients."

"A few facts spilled over the falls in the trial. My friend called again this morning. He was helping me put some things together. Want to know your husband's net worth?"

"Please," said Trudy, closing her eyes.

"We figure it's about five million. This was five years ago. It's been a while. Interest on that alone would add up considerably."

Trudy slumped at the news. She put her sandwich down.

"Your husband has been successful for quite some time. But that much profit from the store alone? It's hard to figure. And outfitting? He only has a dozen camps under his special-use permit with the Forest Service. And it's not like he doesn't have expenses."

"He could pay for my operation in a blink."

"Yes. He could pay for your operation in cash and let you stay the entire time, before and after, in the finest hotel in Denver."

"Incomprehensible," said Trudy.

Five million, thought Allison, was no more difficult to imagine than nine hundred thousand.

"I know a guy who was the nephew of the guy who invented the grocery cart," said Allison. "The grocery cart. It was a big deal when he did it. Everybody started buying more in the stores because they could carry everything at once and really load up. It changed the design of grocery stores. The guy inherited a fair chunk. He says it's like discovering a secret room in your house that's chock full of money, stuffed to the living gills. You go in there and take out ten, fifteen grand and go spend it, just a handful. The day you go back for more though, the empty space has filled up where you took money. The pile of cash has taken over a small closet. Must be nice."

"There must be an explanation," said Trudy. "Maybe he's lost it since?"

Allison let Trudy answer her own question, let her struggle with it.

"He was so kind, built that beautiful house, seemed so sure of the world and his role in it. Always did," said Trudy. "You must think I'm a fool."

"Hardly," said Allison.

"What now?"

"I don't know."

"It all points in one direction. The GPS gear and everything. And especially what you said about Slowik, about how often George comes through with kills."

"Prime kills every time—or nearly every time," said Allison. "They've gotta be rigged."

"What about Rocky?"

"That's what I'd like to know."

"It can't be good."

"Don't say that," said Allison. "You can't think that."

"I can sense it."

"But we don't know for sure."

Bear snorted. Scrub oak rustled above their horses. Allison looked up. The side of a four-door dark pickup had pulled up tight with the roadside. The diesel engine idled noisily. Popeye Boyles stood next to the cab, smoking a stubby cigar, one hand on the rearview mirror.

Grumley came around from behind Bear, striding hard.

"Trudy," he said. "You know this is dangerous."

"No, wait," said Allison.

"You wait," said Grumley. "She's not well."

Grumley grabbed Trudy by the arm, pulling her up.

"Give her the coat back," said Grumley.

"No, really," said Allison. "I'll take her back—"

"You'll do nothing. Got it? *Nothing.*"

Grumley was directly in her face. Allison caught a nasty whiff of old sweat and rank grime.

"George, really," said Trudy.

But George dragged her off. Allison snuck a glance at Boyles, who had the door to the pickup swung wide open.

They loaded Trudy in the back seat. Boyles rode shotgun up front. The truck peeled out. Trudy stared straight ahead.

\*\*\*\*

A day later, the bank of gray clouds overhead was so thick that it was as if the Federal Reserve had stuffed the sun in its darkest vault. The humidity soaked Allison's cheeks, her only exposed skin.

She thought constantly of Trudy, of what Grumley might have said, of what Trudy would've said in reply and how ugly the day must have been after Trudy had been snatched away. She wondered how much Trudy might or might not have said. Allison's hunch was, not much.

Bear stopped in a boulder field on the southern flank of the butte, a spot where they usually lingered to drink in the vistas. The packhorse ambled to a stop beside them. Bear relieved himself as if on command. Allison climbed down and stepped a few paces off the trail to do the same. As she stood up, buttoning her jeans, she heard a distant snort. Horse. Ahead or behind, she couldn't tell. She stood next to Bear and stroked his snout, looking and waiting for a horse to materialize. Nothing.

"Weird," she said. "I could have sworn—"

They picked their way through the boulders and headed over to the western face of the butte where the trail plunged down through a section of krummholz, belly high to the horses. Her chaps strummed snow from the stubby branches as they rode. The smothering thickets opened up and gave way to a clutch of aspen. She took a deep breath, consciously filling her lungs to capacity with the damp air and she praised the fact that the world wasn't all urban jungle. A Northern Flicker tapped the bark on an old lodgepole pine and darted low, swooping down at ground level, powered only by the intermittent flaps of its wings.

The trail maintained its heading back to the north, gradually descending for a mile or so until it hit the bottom of the drainage before winding more steeply back uphill toward a high, lake-dotted plateau thick with aspen, a thriving undergrowth and every critter known to Colorado. Allison spotted the camp as the sun briefly threatened to define itself in the haze. She caught a wisp of shadow, her own, before it evaporated.

"Hello!" she called from thirty yards out. "Anybody home?"

"Hello!"

The return call came from one of the canvas wall tents. A metal chimney puffed gray smoke into the drab sky.

Allison hitched the horses. A man and woman draped in over-sized parkas emerged from the tent, smiles at the ready.

"Nice day, huh?" said Allison.

"If you like the inside of a walk-in freezer at night," said the man.

They all shook hands. Bill and Cindy Pearls, Scottsbluff, Nebraska. Outfitted as though enough catalog camping gear would take care of everything, including sneaking up on a big fat mule deer. They huddled in the tent, the neatest and most im-maculate indoor space Allison had ever seen this far from indoor plumbing. Somebody, she guessed, wasn't doing much hunting. One of the other guides had set them up four days ago, but it looked like they had been airlifted in straight from a Martha Stewart hunting camp.

"On the first day we got close to a couple of deer, two small bucks. You couldn't have paid me to pull the trigger," said Bill, laughing. "I love to eat meat and think venison is God's gift to taste buds. Next to elk medallions, that is. But no way could I have been responsible for destroying one of those beautiful, beautiful creatures."

Bill had the tough-guy features of an ex-Marine or a football fullback: moose-like chest, zero neck and shoulders designed to absorb punishment in a variety of forms.

"It was so cute," said Cindy. "Thousands of dollars for all of this, months of preparation, even shooting practice, and he didn't care."

"But I'm doing some serious reading," he said, pointing to a stack of paperbacks. "And when it's been clear, we've gone for hikes to look for the deer or elk."

"The other two hunters?" said Allison.

"They went back out this morning to finish dressing a deer they dropped at dusk last night," said Bill.

"Close enough that we could hear the shot," said Cindy, as if that made it more exciting.

They unloaded Allison's packhorse and Allison followed Cindy on foot to the spot where the others were supposed to be, less than half a mile from camp.

"They weren't quite sure about this part," said Cindy. "But they said they wanted to get it strung up for the night."

The carcass was on the ground in a small clearing next to a frozen lake. The clearing had been charred and stripped of life by a spot fire not too many years ago.

"Professional help at last," said the woman as they approached. The woman's job was to keep her hands tucked in her pockets and serve as head cheerleader. The man stood up, his hunting clothes bearing splotches of goo and red.

"I think you would need to do this once or twice," he said, "in order to avoid making a nasty mess. The video made it look easy."

Cindy introduced them around. Steve and Martha Ellis. She

shook hands. He waved at first, removed his goopy glove for a handshake.

"You had him hung up pretty soon after you shot him?"

"Within an hour," he said. "Tried to get most of the viscera out of the cavity before night fell and propped it open with a branch, but we didn't get all the upper guts, the heart and lungs. We wanted to skin him and get the hide salted, but it was too damn dark."

Steve was compact and stout with a square head, black mustache and rounded red cheeks. Martha was a couple of inches taller. She looked more capable and more rugged, but only by a matter of degrees.

Allison helped them skin and quarter the animal as Cindy and Martha chatted away, saying things like "yuck" at appropriate times, such as when Steve sawed through the eyeballs to save the skull and antlers.

Allison stayed for a late lunch at the camp. Cindy whipped up tuna salad that was one part fish and two parts mayonnaise. More goo. It followed her around. Trudy's tuna was vastly superior, with a gourmet's touch.

Bear and the packhorse munched oats as she loaded them up. Because of the quartered deer, she would have to return to the barn rather than make a stop at another camp up over Black Squirrel Pass. She had been half hoping to go back that way again and look from the same spot where she had seen the man dragging something, to see if it would help her recall anything useful. She'd also wanted to bring down a good chunk of the dead elk for tests.

"Somebody will come pack you out the day after tomorrow," she said, climbing up on Bear. The four of them stood around kicking at the snow.

"So if we happen to get another deer down today or tomorrow and if you know I've already filled my tag and if you know old tough guy Bill here didn't do the shooting . . .?"

"What?" said Allison.

"You think that's okay?"

"Two licenses, two guns, two hunters, two deer. No biggie."

"Just checking," said Steve.

It wasn't hard to imagine their mini-mansions in the suburbs, with the hand-waxed automobiles, plush carpeting and fixed routines. Another Friday night, another pan of lasagna or whatever it said on the schedule. She wondered what it must be like to go through life on a static ride, safe and beyond trouble, outside fate's scrutiny, with a steady stream of income, untormented by nine-hundred-thousand-dollar windfalls and decisions over whether or not to sue your own government. She once knew that world. But she couldn't recall how it had felt, probably because she hadn't seen the need to feel it or define it. Minutes ago she had sanctioned the death of another deer. The pilot didn't want to die. Ray Stern did—so why care about his killer? Was it better to let it be? Better for whom?

Bear was content with the idea of following his tracks back to the barn. His steps were brisk. But they wouldn't make it back before dark.

"Whoa," said Allison. Bear looked around like he was wondering what she had forgotten this time.

A set of unfamiliar horse tracks headed off the trail and up the ridge on a diagonal line. Not tracks, really, but snow kicked up and disturbed. Distinctively horse. They were only a quarter mile from the camp. She slipped off Bear and walked ahead, down the slushy trail bed. Her packhorse followed Bear's line closely. The tracks were clear. She studied the set, a wider arc on the horseshoe itself. Perhaps a much bigger horse or mule. The gait was long too. Back at Bear's side, she peered up the slope and back behind her. She stood up in the saddle and looked down the hill. The woods were empty.

Three hours to dusk. Five hours to the barn. Night temperatures headed for the low teens. The footing around the front of the butte, through the boulder field, wasn't ideal in daylight. They would go until an hour before dusk and stop. "You're going to be mad at me when you see me break out the tent," she told Bear. "It's for the best, though."

The thick woods gobbled up what light the heavy clouds did not. A cool breeze cut across her face and started loosening the treetops from a frozen slumber. The weather might be starting to pack its bags, having already stayed beyond its invitation.

Two hours later, Allison spotted a small, flat clearing down off the trail. A forest floor coated with pine needles in mid-July, now it held a foot of snow. A ring of towering lodgepole pines guarded the space.

She took the packs off the packhorse and the saddle off Bear. She tied the deer quarters together and hoisted them up on a rope, ten feet off the ground. She set up the pup tent in a patch of snow after digging out a square so she could stake it in frozen soil, using a hammer. Her hands shook as she tried to hold the stakes steady. She tossed her sleeping bag inside with a small roll of extra clothes. She would fashion a pillow out of a combination of clothes. She scouted for firewood, retrieving dead limbs from what she could reach. She made a fifty-yard sweep in four directions before there was a pile that matched the tent's height and width. A hatchet turned one branch into wood shavings. She made four more piles of successively larger twigs, sticks and smaller limbs. A dry exterior was the key, dry enough so she could fool the fire into thinking that it wasn't winter, that all the fuel was premium stuff.

She needed green limbs that could serve as a platform for the fire. Two perfect branches, both slender and clean, would have been reachable if she'd been able to stand on top of the snow. If she was, say, weightless. To reach another good candidate, she had to shimmy up a trunk a bit thicker than a telephone pole and whack away with the hatchet. "You'll survive," she said. "I'm a bee. This is my stinger." Ten more chops and she was through. She made six pieces out of the limb closer to her tent. She lined the six up side by side, wedged together by the snow. She built a teepee of the smallest twigs in the middle of her platform.

The first match blew out. The flames from the second leapt into her vented stack of miniature lumber like they recognized good fuel by smell. A soft crackle went up within a minute. She fed the wood down the fire's gullet. Every taste became another, larger bite. And then nothing, as if someone had covered the fire with an invisible glass hood. The flames shriveled up and died. Screw it. She went to Bear's saddlebags for a packet of liquid napalm, a plastic tube like a frozen ice pop. She always brought a few spares along. Bear probably knew she was cheating. She dribbled the goo on the wood and lit another match to the glob.

"Hey, okay, big deal," she said to Bear. "Turn me in."

The fire sputtered for a second and burst into full-bloom.

Dinner would be beef jerky, an apple, slices of yellow cheddar. The fire roared. The earth around it started to soften. She went to check on the horses and give them the last of the oats. She sat by the fire warming her hands and toes. The orange furnace was the only thing to watch. The flickering light danced to an irregular but busy beat.

The horses whinnied sharply and Allison stood up abruptly out of instinct, except the ground rushed up from the side and whacked her shoulder and head. She yelped with surprise and grunted as she smacked the earth.

Her feet didn't move and she looked up, groggy from the tackle. She tasted the residue of seawater, its stinging bitterness and slimy texture filling her mouth.

Why couldn't she move?

His body squashed her legs. He flipped her over. He shoved her head down in the snow, all his weight and strength pounding into her. She didn't want to exhale in case that last lungful was all that kept her rib cage from collapsing. Her cheek on the snow started to freeze. The hand on her butt felt enormous. Her left arm was tucked tightly underneath. Not for long. He jerked it around and tied her arms together behind her back. He had come a long way if this was going to be rape. The idea flashed and was gone. He was sitting on her butt, yanking the knot together.

She risked a breath, inhaled snow, spit it out.

"What the—" brought a whack across the back of her head.

"You're fucking around where you don't belong."

The voice was gritty and old. Anger filled Allison's mouth with panic and determination.

"You don't—"

Another whack.

She wriggled and kept struggling. He groped for control on top of her, crunching her hands.

"My arms—"

He was fiddling with her ankles, which snapped together.

Rope flew and her ankles went up with a jerk. She was off the ground, upside down. The world spun. She made out a hulking shape. She twisted slowly as she dangled, blurry shots of him in each rotation. He was heading away.

Was he gone? For good?

Her left shoulder throbbed and burned. It felt loose and wobbly.

She did half a sit-up, holding that position for a few seconds to study the knots and rope. The pain was searing. Her knife sat in its sheath on her belt, all tucked in. With her arms behind her and with the knife sealed behind a flap of Velcro, the blade may as well have been resting on the Sea of Tranquility. She uncurled and dangled back down, eyeing the snow far below.

\*\*\*\*

"Trouble," said Grumley.

The voice grated in Applegate's ear. He held the phone away for a second, realized Ellenberg might hear it. He pressed it back tightly.

"What?" said Applegate, eyeing the clock.

12:15 a.m.

"Who is it?" said Ellenberg.

"It's okay," said Applegate.

"What the fuck?" said Grumley. "Are you listening? You got trouble."

"What kind?"

"The kind of trouble that comes from fucking with me. But that ain't nothing. This Allison Coil number. She's getting so close to you she's about to smell what a true asshole is."

"What do you mean?"

"You gotta get your butt back up here and deal with her," said Grumley. "I sure as hell ain't doing your dirty work. You gotta put a scare into her or she's going to nail your ass. That is, unless you want it to get nailed."

"Who is it?" said Ellenberg again, a hand gently stroking his back.

"It's okay," said Applegate again, feeling torn. What could he do? If he did *anything* he might expose himself to the police. "I can't," he said to Grumley.

"I'm sitting here looking at your rifle. Nice one. Maybe the cops will enjoy a peek, too."

Fucker, thought Applegate. "She can't have anything worthwhile, can't put anything together."

"You haven't seen nosy until you've seen this bitch."

Grumley hung up without any good-byes.

It had been such a great evening. The spaghetti hadn't turned out that badly and they had plowed through a bottle and a half of red wine before making love next to the gas-fired fireplace on the white carpet in his townhouse living room. They had watched a thriller on the cable and Ellenberg had made mental notes during one section where a horse was forced to dive off a high cliff. The movie studio was not one of the majors. Ellenberg wanted to pass a note along to the national organizations, to see if the studio had signed any agreements about not abusing animals. There was no disclaimer with the credits.

"What was it?" said Ellenberg.

"Nothing," said Applegate. "At first, I thought it was somebody I knew. But I was wrong. Wrong number."

\*\*\*\*

The rapidly dimming orange dot of fire was Allison's reference point. She focused on it as she spun.

Her ankles were tightly lashed. She could manage a half sit-up but the position didn't accomplish much.

The surreal aftershock of her attacker's departure was settling in. The cold was getting a grip on her insides.

She shimmied up again. She wanted to howl, but the fear demanded quiet. She couldn't see the knots that bound her ankles.

Her back creaked. She needed energy to keep her arms upright, behind her.

The orange dot of fire was right side up as she peered off. She shook the rope with her body gyrating. She ignored the pang of her complaining shoulder and inched up, her body like a high diver tucked in a jackknife, hands around her knees. She searched for the strength to lift up above the knots that gained the cinching power of her own weight.

Up. An inch.

Endure the pain.

Her toes wiggled. The bottoms of her heels came up—down—from the inside of her boots. He had lashed her boots, not her legs. There was room to wiggle but no bootjack for good leverage.

She clawed up using her hands, her right foot finding more leeway. Her right foot popped loose and then her left but she stayed in her boots for a moment, keeping her toes curled, holding her in place.

She looked at the snow below. She slowly pointed her toes and fell out her boots, beginning a flip as she felt gravity take over, hoping for a soft landing and wondering if she should come up swimming or taste salt water.

# 11

Pete Weaver had wrapped her in a colorful serape. She sat on a floral-pattern couch in his huge farmhouse, a hundred yards from the barn where she had arrived, obviously injured. She sipped tea and stared into the huge fireplace, roaring full bore.

"I called Sandstrom," said Weaver. Either he or someone else will meet you in his office late this afternoon."

She stared at the fire, looking for answers.

Why hadn't the assailant killed her? Had he meant to give her a chance to survive? If so, why?

"You've got to report it," said Weaver, his kindly old eyes unwavering. "I've never heard of anything like this."

"There's not much they can do," said Allison.

"Hell there isn't," said Weaver.

"There's nothing to look at, the camp site is trampled all over. I'll report it, but don't think it'll exactly fire 'em up."

"What about Mr. Forest Service?"

The thought of repeating the story more than once was agony. She wanted to tell Slater and maybe Trudy, then sleep the whole thing off.

"I'll tell him. I'm sure Sandstrom will play Bigfoot on it, keep all the other forms of government footprints away."

"They still oughta be told."

"It's not like they need to warn everybody who goes into the backcountry. It was me he was after."

"This whole business, I don't know," said Weaver.

"It seemed like everything was fine in this valley until the mother of all protests," said Allison.

"That's not—"

"What?"

"What I meant. But you're right. Everyone in the valley is on edge. This won't help."

"It doesn't have to get out."

"Doesn't *have* to. It just *does*."

"How much tranquilizer would it take to kill an elk?"

Weaver, who had taken up a cozy spot on a recliner and started to light a pipe, stopped and gave her a funny look.

"Excuse me?" he said.

"Would two shots do it?"

"I have no idea," said Weaver.

As soon as she talked to Sandstrom and grabbed a good night's sleep, she'd go get answers to her own questions.

Why hadn't he killed her?

"I'll need a couple days' R&R."

"It's okay," said Weaver. "We'll make do."

\*\*\*\*

"Big like football-linebacker big . . . or was it somebody bigger than your petite self?"

A few flecks of spit flew as Sandstrom hammered the t's in *puh-teet.*

Allison lowered her tender left arm onto the sheriff's steel desk. It wasn't her whole arm that stung, but the throbbing strain in the bicep made the entire limb flash messages of anger every time she moved it.

"Big, strong. Lumberjack. Paul Bunyan."

"You didn't get a good look at his face?"

"No."

"Didn't hear or see anything else all day?"

"At one point, I thought I heard a horse off in the distance. That was in the morning. Maybe behind me."

Slater, who had escorted her over, sat on the couch in Sandstrom's office. He was busy taking notes as if she'd come in off the street and they had never met. In fact, Slater had her run it down several times and asked lots of good questions.

"No other indications?" said Sandstrom. "That someone was following you?"

"Another time I had seen tracks, heading up the trail and then splitting off. I didn't think much—"

"Obviously you were being watched," said Slater, cutting to the quick.

Sandstrom cast a look at Slater that said kids in college calculus classes shouldn't demonstrate their ability with adding fractions.

"But no visual contact?"

"No. Oh, this," said Allison. "I almost forgot." She pulled a long length of rope from a plastic bag and plopped it on his desk.

"Standard issue," said Sandstrom. "Hardware store variety. Plus, this one's already served a lifetime. But that's appreciated and quite smart of you." Sandstrom put the rope on a shelf next to him, as if it was something she was returning.

"And your assailant said, again, the part about fucking around."

"Where I don't belong," said Allison. "Fucking around where I don't belong."

Allison slid another glance at Slater, who looked like he had his mind on the backside of a distant planet. There wasn't much Slater could do now. This was her pickle.

"So a guy comes and strings you up upside down in the middle of nowhere because you've been doing nothing, asking around about *nothing*."

She had seen this slightly difficult problem before deciding to report the incident, but hadn't resolved how to deal with it. Slater had urged her to get it on the record, at the very least, and she softly dodged questions about her level of involvement.

"Any particular individuals you'd care to mention who might have had their feathers ruffled?" said Sandstrom.

"I was simply reporting the assault. I really didn't think there was much you could do about it, unless I had more of an idea who did it."

"Then consider it reported," said Sandstrom. "But that doesn't mean we're not interested. We'll need you to show us where this happened."

"There's nothing there."

"He might have dropped something."

"Doubt it."

"We'd like to see."

"Take the east trail to Buffalo Peak. Halfway to Wall Lake, you'll see the remnants of my camp. If you get to one of our campsites, you've gone too far by about a mile and a half. There are two couples staying there now. The tracks around should explain everything."

"I know where it is," said Slater. "Our people can show you."

Standing up, Allison winced as her arm again came under its own weight.

"You know, whatever it was I saw—originally . . ."

Allison let the thought hang, to see if Sandstrom bit.

"Yes?"

". . . is connected with this."

Slater took a breath and cocked his head as if his neck had a painful kink.

"You've stirred the bees off the honey pot, if that's what you mean. Although I don't think you've come clean with me, young lady. Speaking for myself and not the official government record, I believe one thing. When we find the brainless piece of particulate matter that killed Ray Stern and if we get a confession, you'll discover that what you saw was Ray Stern's killer, trying to hide things away. I don't think you were exactly where you thought you were, with all due respect for your guide skills. I think you saw the spineless idiot who killed Ray Stern. Maybe he was cleaning up his mess. You were, after all, a city girl until recently, were you not? Those mountains, I mean, really. How many varieties of shapes, bowls, peaks and ridges can there be? Don't they all look alike after a while?"

"Then where the hell is Rocky Carnivitas?" she said sharply.

"Whoa," said Slater, standing up, reaching out. Allison stepped away, but kept staring at Sandstrom.

"Off following oversized hoof prints in the next county. There was nothing tying him down, nothing. Talk about your transient business, guiding is one fleeting way of life."

"Find him," said Allison. "Put out the word. Ask why his truck's been parked at George Grumley's barn in the same spot for a couple weeks now. I drive by it all the time."

"It was a huge storm. He could have been trapped," said Slater. "It's possible."

Allison shot Slater a stare, upset that he'd derail her train. "Me or you," said Allison. "Not Rocky, no way."

Slater offered back a weak smile. Allison felt her heart begin to thump hard, felt a bit of confusion clog her throat.

"Track Rocky," said Allison. Although he won't be much use when you find him, she thought. She did the one thing she'd been sure she wouldn't do; she wiped a sobless tear from her cheek. At least neither one of them came to comfort her. That would really have pissed her off.

"We'll see what we can do," said Sandstrom.

"Thanks," said Allison and stood to leave without saying good-bye. "If you don't find him, I will."

Allison waited for Slater in her Blazer, thinking of spending a day scrubbing the cabin down within an inch of its life or giving Bear a thorough groom for the heck of it. But both activities involved her shoulder. She wouldn't mind a day of not thinking about it, of not forcing the puzzle together. The view through the binoculars had seemed, at first, like it would remain clear forever. When had the image started to wobble? Who was responsible for that? Could the moment she heard the shot really have coincided with the last moments of a human being's life? One she knew? Was that possible?

Slater ambled out and stood by her rolled-down window.

"You think the report amounts to anything, really? Telling Sandstrom?"

"A chance for him to talk in football lingo," said Slater.

"It's the season," said Allison.

"You hit a nerve, anyway. Someone went to a whole lot of trouble up there, chasing you around. But when you get a minute, think about it. It might have been the protesters."

"What?"

"Whoa now. A thought. This guy was suicidal."

"So?"

"So maybe he had help with his wish and now, because of what you saw, maybe it wouldn't look so good anymore. I'm saying it may not be the obvious."

The idea was hollow, offered no substance as she unwrapped it in her head. It was a strange world—but not that strange. Not worth debating.

"Do you think Sandstrom will do anything?"

"Depending on what there is to do, yeah, he'll take a look. Maybe someone else saw this guy, can give them a description."

"Maybe," said Allison.

He leaned down, kissed her briskly and headed to his own truck at a slow jog.

Out on the highway, Glenwood Canyon was draped in its late-fall garb. The canyon's cliffs were dressed in their finest, butterscotch brown. Here and there, daubs of gold from the late-season aspens. She let her eyes go soft-focus. The scene looked as if a painter had come through with a brush full of water that forced the colors to run together. A long freight train picked its way along the opposite bank and she briefly thought she spotted a hobo poking his head out of an empty green boxcar. But the road veered sharply in front of her and by the time she flicked her eyes back he was gone, even though she could now see deep inside the boxcar. She sped up to see if she had the right car, but there were no other green ones on that whole section of the train.

There was no giving up.

Now, as she headed home, the thought of being alone wasn't unpleasant. Her arm and shoulder still stung. Her mind swirled between Sandstrom's odd interview style, which was too carefree, and the snapshots of sounds and images—snorts and strange horse tracks—leading up to the assault by the fire.

How long would it have taken for somebody to find her body hanging from a tree? Her brain zipped through the events like a mental mobius strip that forced her to relive each moment again and again, sometimes in slow motion.

After freeing herself from the rope, she had lain awake in her sleeping bag, gingerly avoiding putting any weight on her stinging arm. Fear turned every creak of a tree branch into the return of her attacker. She had fed the fire every hour. At dawn she'd hopped over to Bear in her socks, her feet in frozen agony. Climbing up on the saddle, she had guided him around and stood on his back to retrieve her boots, still stuck in the rope. She had warmed the boots and her feet by the fire. She had stared into the flames, replaying the attack as if it had been a movie. She had to watch the movie over and over. It was the only theater in town. There was only one person in the audience. There was nowhere else to go.

∗∗∗∗

It was the same space. Same cats, same plants, same everything. But Trudy felt shaky. She could not adjust to the sensation of being a prisoner. Her mind ran wild with theories and speculation. She kicked herself for giving in to George and leaving Allison there on the riverbank, for only putting up a minor fuss.

Trudy tackled chores and routines, letting the small stuff soak her up. She repotted plants and cooked a bit, but nothing freed her mind, let her relax. She made a game out making nice with her half-hearted captors, those switched temporarily out of "Trudy Duty" to "Jail Guard." Every morning they passed the baton. Once or twice they had even overlapped for a few hours. She could hear them both in the living room, laughing and shooting the breeze while they ate their coffee cake and worked their way through a pot of good French roast, not that they knew the difference. It was all very civilized.

George hadn't said much of anything. The point was clearly to stay put and mind her business, but how was that possible? Her mind tried to slash its way through a thicket of anger and uncertainty. She felt trapped by the facts from Allison. It all made sense except for the sheer scale of the hole George had dug for her, a hole from which she hadn't been able to see much of anything but a pinprick-size glimpse of his whole dealings. Rocky must have gotten caught up in the tangle of money and illegal junk. Trudy half wondered if it was something she had said that might have given Rocky the feeling that he could be more bold confronting George. She wondered what Allison would do with the information, where it all might lead. She knew that it wouldn't work to sit back and wait. Someone had to make a move.

****

The trail was trampled, mucky in spots. The snow was beginning to yield to the steady power of the sun. The dead elk had been gnawed and picked over by more than a few predators. They had picked their favorite parts. It was not a cheerful sight. Nature's version of an autopsy wasn't attractive.

The landscape was lifeless, as she had feared. She didn't want to go another step, but she climbed off Bear gingerly, cautious with her tender arm. She took in the sounds of wind and air and her own breathing.

"Rocky?" She said his name out loud. "Where are you?"

She had seen Rocky and Grumley confronting each other, in her mind, over and over. Maybe it was over Grumley's wife. Or the business. Or both. Poor Rocky, standing up to a gruff boss and at the same time soft enough to want to care for Trudy.

It was Rocky, more than anyone except Weaver, who had accepted the city girl into the fold, showed her the ropes, literally. He never let on that he expected her to fail.

Failure. An interesting word. Wings fail to provide lift and the result is a flying machine in the cold, salty drink. And dead bodies bobbing all around. Whose failure? And why? And why did it happen when it did? Failure? Or nature? Meant to be? A matter of fact? Just deal with it? Which question led to the best chance of your brain accepting what it was being asked to absorb—and live with it forever? Would blame ease things? Could you really assign it to the winds of fate? Did that make it any easier?

Human beings can be propped up and strapped down in rows six seats across with an aisle down the middle one second and then tumble, through external forces and events way beyond their control, into mess and fury the next. She had learned that from personal experience. One moment, events are calm and peaceful and the world functions in an orderly fashion. The next moment, life—right down to the molecules—comes unglued. You cannot reach out with your hands and put any of it back together, even though you want to and think you can. Once the egg starts cracking, it cannot be made whole again. Since the airplane flopped into the water, in fact, she realized that a thin, fragile shell bubble-wrapped each waking moment. Life, for people or animals, could be shattered apart at any moment. And here it was again, that feeling, now more distinct than ever in the stark, snowy landscape. The plastic bubbles were right there, all around her, and they were starting to pop, one at a time.

You're here on the side of the mountain, Allison thought, breathing fresh air. And somebody else is long gone—simply because of a seat number. There was no time to prepare for the lifeless bodies in the water next to her. They were all so recently alive. And there really was no good way, no surefire way, to absorb the loss after it was over, after the survivors had been rounded up and counted, after the dead had been lined up and counted, after the crash had been folded into the wrinkles and warps of history.

"Stay here, Bear," she said, eyeing an out-of-place lump, down off the steep slope, up against a tree. She trudged down, but once her angle had changed she lost track of which tree she thought displayed something irregular. At the bottom, she had trouble re-setting her bearings. The trees were all similar in size, build and stature. The snow was packed, less conducive to wading. It was like gooey gelatin, not yet set. She picked a tree and headed for it. Whatever had been semi-clear from the trail was murky here down at snow level. Allison stepped slowly. The base of one tree was smooth, ordinary. So was the second. Should she go north or south? She glanced back at Bear, who wasn't even watching.

Her heart went for a brief sprint in her chest, looking for a safe rhythm to run a marathon.

From a few paces away, the shape suddenly revealed itself, a snow-covered, sitting-up shape. Her chest tightened. She gulped for air.

There was nothing to fear, nothing that could hurt her, only acres of snow and mute trees. But her brain wasn't finding a way to connect up and get in gear. Allison kneeled down and dug through the snow at the top of the sizable lump where no rock should be.

She brushed at the snow and instantly something non-white appeared, something light brown. A hat.

Her stomach had time to register its opinion by slamming itself up inside the back of her throat and trying to crawl out on its own. She buckled, spit slime. She scooped a glove full of snow and patted it on her cheeks and stumbled off a few yards and stood up. Deep, long drags of the mountain air filled her lungs.

"Rocky," she said. "Shit."

She scraped more snow and thought of all the times Slater and Sandstrom had dismissed what she had seen and heard.

There was a side to his face that was normal, except the awful pallor, and another that hardly existed. The bad side was shattered bone and muscle and a blown-out eye socket.

There was no need to dig any further. There would be no lifting him up to the slope and then to the trail, no way to flop him over the back of Bear, no way to budge him more than a few feet.

She reached for his hat, every bit as good as fingerprints, but stopped. This was a crime scene and she had to leave everything intact.

Everything had fallen into place, as she'd hoped it wouldn't.

****

"Hey, why would I be worried about the gun?"

"If I was you, I'd make sure it really disappeared."

"I've told you three times what I told them; I hiked it back up into the mountains and gave it a good heave."

"She's onto something. Sniffing hard."

There was always a good steady background buzz of clatter and chat and bustle at FATE headquarters, so agreeing to meet at the office with a Grumley pal, in this case Sal "Fishy" Marcovicci, seemed at first like a low-risk proposition, especially in the partitioned cubicle which served as his office.

"You think she's onto something?" said Applegate. "There's nothing to be on to."

"Earnest kid, I must say. Lot of experience in a meager frame. Although she's got a sweet rack on her."

"Please," said Applegate.

"Oh, Mr. Sensitive now. Sorry."

"So what did you do?"

"I called George, of course."

"And—"

"He didn't like the idea of getting tangled up in all this mess any more than I did. And that's why I called you, because she was mentioning your name quite a bit too."

"Thanks. She's wasting her time, whatever it is she's trying to do."

Suddenly Applegate realized that he didn't want any more contact with the people who knew him as his previous self.

"So this anti-hunting thing," said Marcovicci, "it's real?"

"Of course."

"What I mean is, you believe this stuff? It's got you on television and in every newspaper from here to Podunk, but—"

"But what? I changed my mind. It's about as simple as that."

There was an unbending silence in the space between them.

"Excuse me?"

Marcovicci cranked his head at the sound of the female voice at the opening to Applegate's partition. Ellenberg stepped in, not waiting for permission. The office was like that, free flowing. Applegate had grown to like its loose feel. Applegate introduced them but only mentioned Marcovicci's profession: nothing to do with the hunting. Ellenberg didn't seem interested in small talk.

"Pleasure to meet you," she said curtly.

"We need to talk schedule when you get a minute," said Ellenberg. "Local morning show here wants you to debate the author of that new, disgusting book that says hunting is in our genes and can't be suppressed."

"The guy that says hunting is like loving yourself," said Marcovicci. "Interesting premise. Yeah, what's the title? *Born To Gather, Dying To Hunt.*"

"Gives me the creeps," said Ellenberg.

"Actually," said Marcovicci, "he's a reputable scientist, or theorist."

"Like how our brains can't possibly control an impulse stuck in our genes," said Ellenberg.

"Stuck—or built up, developed over the centuries," said Marcovicci.

"Perhaps you'd like to debate your friend here," Ellenberg said to Applegate.

"He'd eat me alive," said Applegate. "So to speak."

"Yeah," said Marcovicci. "Bet the cannibalism metaphors don't go too far around here."

Ellenberg gave Marcovicci a faint sneer, nothing he could have detected. It was in her eyes, the hint of disdain.

"We've got a big fundraiser and everyone wants you there for a few words. The next weekend we have a stunt up our sleeves for the people breaking ground on that new aquarium. So when you get a chance . . ."

Ellenberg smiled and was gone, casting a curt glance in Marcovicci's direction.

"You're doing the horizontal bop with the queen bitch," said Marcovicci.

"What do you mean?"

"What do you mean what do I mean?"

"Jesus—"

"Jesus, what? Christ, Applegate, you're a fucking mess. War paint camouflage and looking for a big elk one week, boinking Mrs. Fucking Doolittle the next. And I mean *do little* but make a fuss and raise a stink for her goddamn political purposes. She'll probably run for Congress or mayor and all her minions will have laid the groundwork. And you, you ride in like Mr. Cowboy who suddenly decides to engineer the fucking peace train. I hope you're getting plenty and I hope it's good, but there's nobody out there who believes a blessed word of what you're saying."

Two pulsing veins flanked Marcovicci's throat. Applegate thought he felt the cubicles nearby go hush. He wanted to signal Fishy to cool it.

"You got problems or a rifle or whatever you left behind up in the mountains, then I'm sorry I even bothered. Christ, screwing her."

"Wait, Fishy, it isn't that simple."

"Then what's complicated about you standing in the middle of FATE headquarters like the last great talking head? You guys and Operation Rescue and all the strident one-issue groups. It must be nice to see the world in such black and white terms. Later," said Marcovicci, turning to leave. "Or maybe never. One thing for sure, more room in the tent next year."

"Fishy, look."

What was there to say?

It might not matter. There was plenty to do.

The rifle. He'd need to drop things for a few days and get back with Grumley. He'd have to go up there and do with the rifle what he'd said he'd already done.

Fishy was gone. What excuse would he give Dawn?

He couldn't afford to let things wait. The rifle. Maybe Grumley had destroyed it. Maybe he needed to make a phone call to find out. Could he risk a phone call? Life was confusing, just when he was starting to believe in something.

✳✳✳✳

"You can't honestly think," said Trudy, "that I'm really and seriously a threat."

Popeye Boyles sat at the kitchen table, gun propped precariously over his knee.

"Like physical threat? No, I don't suppose," he said.

"You're letting me fix us a decent lunch, perhaps we can at least be civil about this prison thing."

"Just following orders."

Trudy stirred the homemade clam chowder in her cast iron pot, added some milk and set the flame on low. She wanted to stretch things out.

"Clam chowder. Don't ask where a Colorado mountain girl comes up with a taste for slimy old seafood, but it's possible. Always made me feel kind of warm and cozy."

"Only chowder we got in the U.S. Navy was corn with canned ham. A side of baking soda biscuits. Surrounded by an ocean and never clam chowder—well, maybe twice a year. Go figure."

She half wondered if this leathery old man had an eye for her. It crossed her mind that if she couldn't go through with the mushroom plan, which had kept her awake most of the night— the idea emerging crystal clear and foolproof—she might at least

196

make herself available for something physical. The age difference between them was fifteen years. She could live with that. And his gruff way of talking didn't bother her as much as his dull musty odor. It was like the back of a damp basement closet. She wasn't sure what might be growing there.

"There's no ham in the house. But I do have tomatoes and cucumbers and this wonderful seven-grain bread. With a bit of Dijon and a pinch of mayo, not the imitation stuff, you'll never crave a pork product again in your life."

"Sounds veggie," said Boyles.

"And we mustn't forget my secret zing."

Boyles stood up as Trudy skipped quickly into the greenhouse and pushed aside the massive glass top that covered her own private piece of forest floor. She had thought about secretly pocketing a couple of the fly agarics or orange Clitocybes, which studded the loamy bottom of her terrarium along with the dependable chanterelles and yummy oyster mushrooms. But she couldn't imagine being sly enough to slip them into the sandwich. The rich, humid, mossy and slightly lemony air filled her nostrils. She took a moment to savor it.

"Whoa, whoa, whoa," said Boyles, right behind her. "I ain't eating nothing out of there."

"I suppose you like all your food wrapped in plastic and shipped half way around the country for a couple of weeks before you take a bite." Trudy pushed back ferns. The irregular, vise-like mushrooms looked healthy and prime, the salmon-orange caps giving way to a brown base.

"Mushrooms?" said Boyles.

"You've never tasted a mushroom until you've had a chanterelle fried in butter with a dash of nutmeg."

She grabbed the impostor Clitocybe by the base, the fattest of the six, and pulled the root free. The Clitocybes also had gills that extended far down the stalk, but the chanterelle's trunk was stubbier. The cap on this Clitocybe was puffy and full blown, but the whole thing barely created any weight in her palm.

Boyles took a step backward.

"They grow from dead things, dead things that have energy." She spoke calmly. She wanted to hold the Clitocybe up for Boyles' inspection but realized her hand might betray her fear.

"A dead insect, rotting wood, anything with left-over energy. The mushroom is the fruit. But it doesn't need chlorophyll to capture energy from the sun. Mushrooms mostly avoid the sun. People pay top dollar for chanterelles in hot-shot grocery stores and we've got our own right here."

"Curse of the Navy right there. If you know your history. Disaster for oak-hulled ships up until the American Civil War. The mushrooms were packing a punch—dry rot. Nothing but a headache that meant constant repair. Couple of ships, I think with the British Royal, even had their hulls rotted clear through. At sea. Entire crews gone."

"I think we need two," said Trudy. "I wasn't aware they were such a problem." She plucked another mushroom, this one a nutritious chanterelle.

She built the sandwiches, sliced each mushroom neatly into two separate piles on her cutting board.

Think ahead. Keys to the car. Grab his gun. Slit open a 20-pound bag of cat food, good for a couple of weeks, perhaps. Pack clothes. He might writhe and gasp; he might not go all the way out.

"Cut diagonal or straight across?" she said.

"What?" he said.

"Your sandwich."

"Whole's fine," said Boyles.

She spooned the soup into a bowl, thinking a broth base might have been better because all the thick milk might coat his stomach if he ate the chowder first and the mushroom might not as easily find his bloodstream. Maybe he'd get sick. She started on her own sandwich while he peppered the hell out of his soup, stirred it around and peppered it again.

He tested the soup and backed away because it was too hot. He packed his mouth with a bite from the sandwich.

Her heart fluttered and went light.

And then another bite. And three more.

"Beer to go with that?" she offered, wanting to be out of reach when it hit.

"Sure," he said, through a mouthful.

She spent longer than she needed, digging in the refrigerator. She couldn't turn around. How could she look? She listened for sounds of anything behind her, the clink of a spoon on the soup bowl. Nothing.

She pulled out two cans of Coors as the kitchen table careened up and crashed down. She scampered for the far corner of the kitchen and crouched by the garbage can and the bowls for cat water. One of the cats gave a howl like its tail had been squashed. A bundle of black fur flew as the table came to rest on its side, followed by a gagging sound like his guts were on fire. He was moving, crawling toward her. She stood up, thinking she should have planned to head the other way, because now she had to go around him and through the mess. And she would probably have to look. Slowly she went along the counter, her back to the cabinets, keeping an eye on the table that shielded her view of him. Maybe he was pretending. Maybe he had tasted the poison. One of the two Siamese, Pookette, lapped peacefully at a pool of clam chowder on the floor. Bliss.

She scrambled across a thrown chair. His arm came flailing from behind the table. She screamed and scrambled free, not looking back.

Put the clothes in a suitcase, especially the heavy stuff, she thought. Her heart beat wildly. Why wouldn't her hands calm down? How long did she have? She'd have to drive, at least a few miles down the road. She needed his gun and realized she should have grabbed it first, right away. Put the suitcase in George's old 4Runner. God, did she even know how to work the clutch? Could she? Don't forget her purse and credit cards. Anything else? The table moved; it sounded like the table moving. Did the table move? Cat stares everywhere. Take a big winter coat, the wool one. The gun. She couldn't look. She covered her eyes so there was only a small gap to see.

Bless her brain, it was hanging in there.

She stepped to the kitchen and tried not to see too much. The gun. The evidence! Down the disposal? The telephone—911? She would make that the last thing. The gun, where was the gun? Boyles was keeled over sideways and wrapped around a chair, hugging its legs. He wasn't moving, but his chest heaved. The gun—it had to be here. There it was—the barrel underneath his leg. She squatted down, giving up on the idea of not looking. She reached around to where the grip should be and dug for it under his grimy jeans.

A hand clasped her forearm, locked on and dug for blood. She grabbed the gun by the muzzle and whacked the knuckles hard. The hand bounced off and she sprang away, shuddering.

She and the gun sat in the front seat of the 4Runner. Now make that 911 call. Two rings. She spewed out just enough information and gave directions, let the phone dangle off the hook after saying she was heading out to look for help.

The clutch went in too fast the first time and she killed the engine. She concentrated on being smooth, deliberate. The second time the engine snapped off with such authority she thought she might have done damage. The third pop with the clutch, the 4Runner jerked backward but kept rolling. She cranked the wheel after the car was outside to turn it around. With the clutch down, she practiced finding the four gears, keeping a nervous eye on the door to the house.

First gear. A lurch and she was off, down the driveway hill. She would get better at it. She was free.

"Meow." It was a high-pitched whine but most likely an echo in her head.

She took the main road back to the interstate. Third gear, fourth. Keeping her mind alert, supple, focused, relaxed. Relaxed? Impossible. The world was vivid and alive and coming at her in a Technicolor rush.

"*Meow.*"

Even more demanding. She risked a look around.

"Good Lord, Fossil. What are you doing?"

Two yellow eyes peeked out from a ball of black fur that had found a bed on her big winter coat. The cat didn't move, but answered politely with the only word it knew.

# 12

Allison's A-Frame looked friendless and neglected, an untended orphan, in the dusk-lit clearing. But she wouldn't be alone.

A boxy station wagon was parked off to the side of her house. The car was broadside to her view from the top of the road leading down. She couldn't make out the car's color, only the shape and its odd parking place off to the side as if it knew it didn't belong.

A figure moved from her front stoop to the car.

She stood with Bear for a second in the road, kept an eye peeled on the car and headed down.

The man drifted back to her front porch. Something about his gait and build looked familiar, but she couldn't connect her gut with good or bad.

Flame from a match made a gentle arc from waist-high up to his face and then was gone, replaced by a hot red dot that repeated the arc in reverse. There was a quick glimpse of skin, no meaning to it, even though she was much closer now.

One gentle turn remained in the road to the A-Frame. Now at least she knew he wanted to be seen. Bear snorted on cue.

The man was tucked half in the shadows. The orange cigarette tip bounced down her front steps and suddenly she recognized his froggy frame and pug-like profile.

Fishy Marcovicci was dressed in full winter padding and stood off to the side of her porch.

"I was going to give you another ten minutes. I've about had it, listening to my toes go pop, pop, pop," he said.

"It's supposed to be five below zero by dawn," said Allison, hitching Bear up to the porch. "Something that couldn't wait, I suppose?"

"Damn right about that," said Marcovicci.

His puffy white cheeks were locked up tightly. He shifted his weight on the gravel driveway and the noise from underfoot, the only sound in the deadly cold, crunched like it was hooked to an amplifier.

She realized that the over-sized shadow with the rope had materialized at her campsite shortly after her chat with Marcovicci.

So, Allison thought, the assailant might still be sniffing around, chasing a trail. Working both sides.

"Are you still after Applegate's rifle?" he said.

"Nothing has changed," she said. Except finding a team to extract Rocky's body and bring him down, she thought. But she didn't want to go into it.

"Tomorrow," he said. "You and me. Let's go find it."

His look was maniacal and cock-sure.

"Do you know where it is?" she said.

"I didn't say that."

"Then why are you suggesting it's possible?"

"I know we can get it. Just as long as there's no—what might be the appropriate word?—involvement of those parties that now, um, possess it."

"You mean I can't squeal on whoever has it now," she said.

"Precisely."

"But I get the rifle?"

"You get it."

"But you can't tell me where it is?"

"Can't," he said.

"You have to show me?"

Marcovicci thought this over.

"It'd be like looking for a chunk of fool's gold in Fort Knox. You'll need help."

"Just a personal favor to me?" she said.

"Something like that," he said.

"Where are you staying?"

She couldn't reveal any slight mistrust, not if what he was promising was true.

"Man," he said, already stepping off into the darkness toward his own car. "I thought you'd never ask."

"I gotta make a few calls," she said. "I found something. Uh, somebody."

"Body?" said Marcovicci, pronouncing it like buddy, not the street word for corpse.

She opened the door for Marcovicci, headed for the phone. Sometime soon she'd have to take Bear back to the barn.

"Yes," said Allison. "Now there are two."

＊＊＊＊

"You two were eating lunch. Cozy."

"She offered. It seemed—"

"Don't tell me. Harmless."

"Yeah. I suppose."

"A sentimental jailer," said Grumley. "Just what I needed."

Boyles' face was sunken. It carried a gold, unhealthy sheen. Grumley wondered if there was a plug he could pull, make the face turn the color of death.

"Felt like my innards were on fucking fire."

A nurse giving a sponge bath to an old guy in the next bed glanced over.

"I gotta find Trudy," said Grumley.

"I'll bet she's long gone."

"I doubt it."

"Because she doesn't have any friends."

"This is the part of the country she knows best."

George stewed. Should he make a beeline to Alaska, right now? File a flight plan for Alamagordo but head to Juneau?

He had every refueling stop planned out. He had a friend of a friend who would trade him for a Mooney with a rebuilt engine outside of Spokane. For years the images in his mind about the day he'd disappear were all calm: an ordinary day in the summer, chatting with all the usual people, doing all the usual things; cash from the private and quiet sale of the store; cash from the private and quiet sale of the outfitting business; cash from the routine sale of his car and horses. That fantasy was dead.

He had never decided what to do about the house. He supposed in his head and heart he had always pictured leaving it to Trudy, so she could decide if she wanted to liquidate it, or part of it, to pay for her operation. Now it might be possible to sell the house if Trudy truly disappeared.

There'd be another couple hundred grand. If Trudy truly disappeared. Another couple hundred grand, minimum a hundred and a half if he was in a hurry to cut a deal. If she truly disappeared.

\*\*\*\*

The Sulphur Inn carried CNN free of charge. The inn with its neon steam rising off the sign was tucked between a new Wal-Mart and a lumberyard out on the road to Carbondale, south of Glenwood Springs. The road provided a plateau of commerce in the otherwise steep canyon formed by the Crystal River.

The motel was laid out like a sideways H. Trudy asked the grandmotherly clerk for a room around in the back. She hadn't even bothered to unpack before checking the cable. The sign out front had said "Vacancy, Free Cable, No Pets," but she smuggled in Fossil when they weren't looking. She had bought cat food, kitty litter and air freshener at Wal-Mart. She hid the litter box under her suitcase during the day, until after the maid finished her rounds.

She timed her brief trips to the grocery store to coincide with local news on the radio, but there had been no mention of the authorities finding a dead man at their house. A good sign. Perhaps Boyles had regained consciousness before the ambulance made it out there. Finally it dawned on her to call the medical center and ask for Boyles by name. The operator patched her through without a verbal blink. He was alive.

She wanted to drive back home and feed the cats, but she couldn't work up the courage and couldn't imagine what would happen if she ran into trouble like, say, George. In the rush she had forgotten the plan of slitting open a bag of cat food. Maybe she'd call into the barn and ask one of George's helpers to swing by and look after them. It wasn't as if they could trace her call or even know if she was nearby.

Everything pointed to going to the cops, but now there was an obvious problem. They would first want to talk to her about Boyles' trip to the medical center and about why his stomach had to be pumped. She supposed if Boyles pressed charges, it would not be too difficult for any prosecutor to show that she should know, given all her plants, what ground vegetation to throw into a sandwich. There was a possibility the cops had already scooped up a few slivers or scraps from the kitchen counter. She wanted to try Allison Coil: ring her up. But she had probably asked too much already, then had given in so easily when George had shown up at the riverbank. She didn't feel she had any right to lean on her again, to ask any favors.

Maybe in a day or two, but not right away.

****

Marcovicci cleared his throat, sipped his coffee.

"We had a deal, remember? You don't get to care who owns the gun now."

"Grumley."

"So you're a genius. You think of the crew up there hunting and you figure I'm here, in Ripplecreek. There's not many other possibilities."

"It's Grumley."

Marcovicci took a long slurp of coffee and bit off a chunk of bagel to slop around in his mouth. Allison, standing by the sink, imagined a sponge in a warm bucket.

Marcovicci had slept on the spare bed, snoring deeply off and on all night. Allison had stayed awake for an hour, wide-eyed. She worked on figuring out why George Grumley would have destroyed Applegate's rifle. She spent a minute imagining how Rocky died. That was followed by a minute of picturing Slater, relaying the news she'd given him over the phone to Sandstrom. And back around again.

How soon would they head up and get Rocky off the mountain?

She wanted to tell Sandstrom herself, to rub it in, but she'd let the "Boy Scout" handle it. Perhaps they were already putting a team together, to be ready at daylight. A red bandanna stuck on a stick off the trail indicated Rocky's body. Her footprints would lead them the rest of the way. And what would Marcovicci say? After chewing on that question for a half-hour, it was back again to Rocky. She imagined Trudy being told and it wasn't hard to picture Trudy weeping. And so she cried, too.

Marcovicci's mention of the "arsenal" had clicked. She remembered her job interview and the racks of rifles that lined his room in the barn, the definition of overkill.

"You think your pal Applegate could have slipped up?"

"Let's put it this way. Now Applegate's another one of the millions in this country looking for the fastest route up Moral Mountain to stake out a big piece of turf on one issue or another and to point accusing fingers down the slope at anybody who dares to disagree. Makes me sick."

"Agreed," said Allison. "But he's your buddy."

"Sort of. Are you trying to talk me out of helping you?" said Marcovicci.

Allison sat down next to him.

"Not at all. Who else did you tell that I had come asking around?"

"What's the difference? You're leaving him out of this. The deal, you know?"

"A few days after you and I talked down in Denver, I was up with a couple horses doing my rounds, checking on our camps. Coming down at dusk, I pitched a tent and built a fire in the snow. Nobody around, right? Out in the middle of nowhere. Except this guy shows up out of nowhere, jams my face in the snow, tells me to mind my own business. And strings me upside down from a tree."

Marcovicci winced.

"So Grumley has Applegate's rifle," said Allison.

"I didn't say that. I said I'd help find it."

"Okay. You assume he's got it."

"If a guy shoots somebody, I think he should be a man and step forward. Confess. Can you imagine walking away from a person dying in the snow? A person you shot accidentally? Leaving him to die?"

"You don't need to go with me," said Allison. "I can poke around over there. I've got a friend or two if it comes to that. Tell me what I'm looking for."

Marcovicci focused on a distant planet, then came all the way back.

"What am I looking for?" she repeated.

"It's a Sako. The sight is chipped in spots underneath, around the trigger housing. On the butt of the rifle, my initials. S.M. Engraved. It's one of a kind."

"Your rifle?"

"Yeah," said Marcovicci. "Four years back, Applegate said he liked it. We were out target shooting. I had bought myself a new one, so I sold it to him."

\*\*\*\*

Applegate's chest trembled from the cold and fear as he approached the barn, a dull hulk in the pre-dawn starlight. It was twenty or thirty steps across the compacted, frozen snow to the side entry, a people-sized door within a horse-sized door. He gripped the door handle and tugged it open.

The barn was cold, too. The air was rich with the smell of animals. Horse heads hung with sleep, worry free. They made him nervous.

Flapping wings bore down on him and Applegate ducked away, something bigger and nastier than a barn swallow. The hard fluttering was gone but his heart matched the rhythm. A light flashed through the window next to the door and he bounced back out of the way. He watched the beam flicker across horse heads, climb the far wall and switch off. A car flew up the road and was gone. Applegate slumped against the inside of the door, mentally wracked. The cavernous, imposing interior of the barn, packed with that cold quiet, taunted him: *you'll find nothing here.*

Fishy's voice drove him on. Among all the things he couldn't imagine, having the rifle linked to him was the last. The world would laugh in unison.

To the office. He had seen Grumley dozens of times dig for the key in a saddlebag hanging in the tack room, near the front. Why would he have changed the location? The saddlebag was there. So was the key. The lock snapped open and Applegate returned the key back.

Flick on the light.

A few rifles? Maybe fifty. Maybe a hundred. Maybe more. All lined up neatly, stock down, side by side around the walls in racks. He scanned them all up close at trigger level. He picked up a few and held them to his shoulder, looking for a feel. One and another and five more, ten more. Back to the first. Different but similar. One felt close; they all felt the same. The weight? The length? All were within a narrow range. It was too subtle.

Finally one felt right. He flipped the rifle around in his hands. He sighted the rifle again and forced himself to touch each of the others in the racks. The process was like trouble-shooting a computer program. You had to scrutinize each comma and parenthesis. Study them: each barrel, each trigger.

Suddenly a thud and a slow whine of a door hinge. A shuffle of boots followed by a soft snort from a horse. The doorframe filled back up.

"Whoa Jesus, thought I heard something."

The kid had his hands stuffed in his jean-jacket pockets.

"Who the hell? Christ. I know you."

Applegate recognized the kid, one of Grumley's helpers. Bobby Alvin.

"You've been on TV. What the fuck you doing?"

"Looking for George," said Applegate.

"A bit early to be rousting him."

"Don't bother," said Applegate, wondering if by any chance the kid might know one rifle from the next.

"You're the one that's working for all them animal groups. I remember you."

"Grumley is a friend, for Chrissakes."

"Some pretty weird shit going on here lately. Boyles in the hospital with his stomach all ripped apart. That Allison babe asking all those questions. You ain't supposed to be here. I can smell it. The fuck . . . I will wake up George."

Alvin headed for the desk.

"Don't," said Applegate, stepping between Alvin and the telephone.

"Get the fuck outta my way," said Alvin, giving him a shove.

Applegate pushed him back. Alvin stumbled, rattling a couple of rifles as he reached for a grip to break his fall.

"Asshole," said Alvin as he charged back.

Applegate's fist connected on the fuzzy and freckled jaw. Falling to his knees, Alvin spit blood from his low-slung head.

Applegate grabbed Alvin off the floor and shoved him against the desk, body-checked him against the wall. He pounded his fists fly into Alvin's stomach and around his head, frustration and anger pouring from his whole being and his knuckles growing raw. His arms grew weak but the rage kept coming. Alvin was reduced to a sputtering mass of self-protection.

Applegate stumbled from the barn, Alvin's moans far behind. The cold didn't register. The seats in his car were blocks of ice— no spring, no give, just cold. The engine turned over with a snarl.

\*\*\*\*

The solid whack had been flesh on flesh, followed by coughing and gagging. Allison stepped back into the stall, the horse's stiff belly wedging her against the wall. She hoped the animal didn't spook. She stroked his flank with one hand and patted his cheek with the other.

One of the two had headed out. She recognized Bobby Alvin's

posture as much as his voice, but the shadowy shape that drifted past, inches away, had been too tall to be Bobby.

The door slammed shut. Her adopted horse shook its head like a dog with fleas, stretched out its neck, shifted around as if to see, in the dark, what person was crowding his space without giving him the benefit of a brush. The car revved up and took off.

Allison squeezed alongside the horse to the front of the stall. Light poured from the office but it wasn't making much of a dent in the barn's central cavern. She waited a moment. Two. Three.

She picked up a faint scraping noise, like something being dragged, accompanied by a low moan and a wet cough. Distant and muted, but there.

And a voice. Bobby's. She thought for a second she had badly miscalculated, that there was a third person, too.

"It's Bobby . . ."

Allison moved out into the broad open space, halfway to the office, stepping lightly. No protection. She stopped to listen.

" . . . It was him . . ."

And moved closer, smack behind the open door.

" . . . Him. One of your old buddies . . ."

Bobby coughed, struggled to speak.

She peered through the crack between the door and the jamb. He was on his knees, clutching the desk with one hand, propping up the telephone with the other.

" . . . The one that joined up with what's-her-name, the animal queen . . ."

Bobby's voice shook, his tone was weak. His hand was bloody.

"Applegate . . . at the barn, going through your stuff."

Applegate?

" . . . Took off . . ."

Long pause. Bobby listening, touching his jaw, making his face red.

" . . . Couple minutes ago. Didn't have nothing when he left here . . ."

Allison back-pedaled. She waited. Bobby mumbled something, cried out in pain.

She counted to twenty like a careful kindergartener, reached behind her, opened the door and slammed it shut again. Nice and loud, with purpose.

There was no decent excuse for being here. It was not her barn and it wasn't the time of year to go chit-chatting. Casual visits were for summer on break days when the creeks gurgled and the sun baked the Flat Tops. She tried to generated extra noise as she walked, but it didn't amount to much.

Bobby Alvin stepped out of the office, holding the door for stability.

"Hey, it's me," she said. "Allison."

"Christ," said Alvin. He turned back inside the office.

"Holy crap, are you okay?" she said. Alvin let himself collapse on the couch, a streak of blood across his cheek.

"Are you alright?" she said.

"Christ, yes," said Alvin. "Caught me off guard."

"Who did?"

"Better question," said Alvin. "What are you doing here?"

"Looking for someone who knows the trails south to Deep Lake, the ones that cut up over McKenna's Ridge."

"Christ, that's the only way to go, on horseback anyway. The only other decent route from this end turns into all scree at the top." The words came slow. Bobby sighed and moaned. "You're going there now? God it hurts to talk."

"Later today," she said, in case he ended up seeing Bear, who was packed for nothing better than a stroll around a corral in one of those "horse ride" rip-offs by the interstate.

"You okay? Your jaw?"

He rubbed it, rolled it around and winced. She blinked and suddenly the rifles came into view.

All the rifles.

In their racks.

At arm's reach.

"I've gotta meet George back at his cabin," said Alvin, standing up to leave. "We're gonna track that pesky little mother down."

"Who?" said Allison.

"One of his used-to-be friends."

"I think he has more than a couple."

"Probably true."

He wasn't going to say.

"Business friends?" said Allison.

"Not exactly."

But he wanted to say. He wanted to spill it.

"Old buddy?" said Allison.

"Say 'former.' "

"Not that guy who flopped over with the animal nuts?"

"Bingo," said Alvin.

"Applegate," said Allison, as if it was no big deal.

She kept thinking about the rifles, sneaking a glance. She wanted to avoid looking too interested, too studious.

"Surprised the heck out of me," said Alvin.

"No shit," said Allison. "But I thought he's not supposed to be doing any fighting. Bad boy."

"Guy was fucking desperate."

Now Allison needed to drop it, before it got to be too obvious.

"You don't need help?"

"How do you tell if a jaw is broken?"

"X-rays," said Allison. She sat down next to him. He recoiled at her closeness and sat up straight. She pressed two fingers along his chin.

"Ouch," he said when she reached a spot near his ear. "Fuck."

"There's a doctor in your future," said Allison. "Of course, there's nothing they can do for a broken jaw other than give you a bottle of pain pills and a box of straws."

Alvin shook his head in disgust. "Fuck," he said. "I'm going to get that fucker."

"So where do I pick up the trail?"

She stood up as if to leave and hoped Alvin would take her cue.

He stood too, describing where to find the trail. She half-listened, working to spot the Sako, thinking it might jump out. Alvin locked the door before she had time to spot anything useful. He slipped the key into the saddlebag and led the way out.

"Thanks," she said, climbing onto Bear. "Hope you find him. You really oughta get that checked out." Alvin was headed to his pick-up.

Allison thought she heard him mumble another "fucker," oblivious to her concern. He climbed into his truck and didn't even look around.

She circled Bear around, listening to Alvin's truck rumble away. On the opposite side of the barn, she tied up Bear loosely.

Key from the saddlebag, door open and she was back inside.

It took a second to lift each rifle out of the rack, drop it down and look, hoping and praying that the next one was it. She kept her ears dialed in on outside noises, anything.

She worked her way down the first rack. Nothing. She turned the corner at the wall and kept working.

Down, flip, look, return the rifle.

Balancing speed with quiet.

And finally in the second row, waiting patiently for its turn, initials just as Fishy had said: S.M.

Lights off. Lock on. The horses were watching, but she was otherwise alone.

The rifle felt good in her hands as she reached the door where Bear was parked and she turned around to look things over. It was her sixth grade math teacher who made a big deal out of reading through problems twice. That's what this was: one big word problem—things so obvious you could skip over them.

Like the key in the lock. It was still in her hand.

She propped the Sako by the door and scooted back, eyes focused on the padlock and thinking she should have kept going, what difference did it really make? The sun was up and she certainly wouldn't be alone much longer. Why was the office so far away?

A truck came to a quick-skid stop right on cue.

Five steps from the lock, so close, her momentum and brain following through.

Why bother?

She hurled the slim slice of metal into a high-arcing orbit that carried it up to the loft above the stalls next to her. The piles of loose hay swallowed the key with a silent gulp.

She was halfway back to the rifle when the door clattered open behind her, two guys talking or arguing, the sound muffled by the size of the barn and her inability to listen for detail and run at the same time.

Allison scooped Fishy's Sako up in her hands, the shouting growing in her head. She worked to keep her mind from sinking into the swamp of chaos and panic, where her heart had already gone.

"Christ!" The blurt was loud, urgent.

She looked back. Alvin. And another figure next to him, extending a gun at shoulder height.

*Boom.*

The bullet smacked the wood by her head and she wondered when she might first feel the pain and how bad the wound would be. She yanked on the door and ducked through.

Bear looked like an impatient dad waiting for the teenagers to come home.

Rifle in the scabbard.

Ties off.

Turning Bear before she climbed up, she kicked him into gear as the door crashed open behind her.

She was already weaving Bear around trees that lined the road in the direction she didn't want to go, away from her house. Bear was at a dead sprint before she had both boots in the stirrups.

Fishy's rifle was in reach where she could touch it for reassurance.

# 13

Applegate sat on the banks of the river at the Grizzly Creek rest area, deep in the heart of the canyon. He choked and sobbed, replaying the tangle with Alvin. He half wished he had wiped out the little fucker. He should have stayed to keep looking for the rifle. So close to the rifle, so damn close. His salvation was so close. And so far away.

Earlier, he had gone out of his way to the closest spot to fill his gas tank. He used the station's pay phone to leave an upbeat everything-is-fine message on Ellenberg's voice mail. Said he'd be back in Denver for lunch and was sorry he'd missed a night with her.

He fidgeted in the downtown pool. He had sat in the steamier section with all the morning regulars, the locals, who avoided the mid-day tourists and late-day skiers. His puffy toes floated off in the distance through the fog. He hid his celebrity in the steam. Nobody said a lick, but he felt disoriented, constantly watching each thought.

He drove back through the canyon and spotted the rest-stop pullout, realized he needed to get his head screwed back on right before driving back. He needed to think things through as an important player in the FATE camp, not as Dean Applegate, loser.

He sat and watched the white caps churn. He stared at the cliff tops. He tried to figure out what impulse had overtaken him to mix it up with Alvin and to allow his anger to boil.

It occurred to him out of the fucking blue.

The rifle was Marcovicci's.

Fishy's.

Why had it taken so long to realize that the rifle, if it was found and turned over, would lead straight to the guy who had been trying to get him alarmed? Fishy was the one saving his own fat-laden skin.

A smile percolated through his brain, subjecting all other clouds in his head to a bit of sunshine. Whose word against whose? Fishy would say he had sold the rifle to him. Where's the paperwork? Fishy would say he wasn't hunting the day Ray Stern was killed. He might have an alibi. But between naps and drinking, were the others rock sure of every single minute and who was where on the day Ray Stern strapped on his suit of felt? Applegate would say he'd gone for a hike. Besides, he was known among them as the least likely to hunt alone.

Bobby Alvin was a problem. He'd already thought of that. Alvin, at a trumped-up trial, saying Applegate had come looking for the rifle, would be a big problem. Maybe he could blame Fishy for spooking him, getting him all worked up. It sounded good in his head. It was a detail to be sorted out. There had to be a rational blip of logic that would make everything clear.

In the meantime, forget the brick wall. Think of the distant vista.

Fishy's rifle. His initials were even on it, for Chrissakes.

Applegate leaned back on the cold grass next to the river and stared up again at the steep canyon walls, flipping his mind back around to the struggles of Ellenberg's crew to follow through on the success of their anti-hunting protest. And another idea began to grow in his head. By the time it was fully developed, he was back behind the wheel of his car and he was driving back to Denver with a growing smile on his face.

****

Allison looked behind her, straight down several hundred yards of Bear's tracks. The grade was steep and the vegetation was thick. Somebody on horseback could easily be scampering up that section right now and she wouldn't know it. But beyond that was a long slow incline where the trail she had followed hugged the edge of an aspen grove, surrounded on three sides by snow-draped field. The field was empty.

Bear steamed hard, his chest white and wet.

She didn't think she knew the valley any better than George Grumley. Did she have a five-minute start? Ten? They would have had to get saddles. Maybe fifteen.

Glenwood Springs was too far, in snow, on horseback. On a good day in summer, it might have been within reach. But today it was the cold woods and finding a way back home, or anywhere safe. She had no food, no water.

"Stay in your own tracks," she told Bear, doubling-back. It was an old trick, but it might work.

The snow was light and fluffy. Bear's first set of tracks looked more the damage from an ineffective snowplow and not the work of an animal. It would take a careful eye to see the snow had been re-churned on the double back. It was a hundred yards across the clearing and she kept Bear at the same steady gallop as the first time. But the distance could have been a mile as she kept her eye on the horizon. She expected her view to be filled at any second with Grumley or Alvin or both, a killing look on their faces.

She stopped Bear stock-still in his tracks at the base of a towering fir, the bows draped low. She walked him slowly around its base. Eight steps. Ten. Twelve. Around to the other side of the tree, tied him loosely. She dismounted and stepped her way back to the junction of Bear's tracks, wiped out and smoothed-over the first few prints. She back-pedaled and listened for the clank of a harness, the crack of a rein. She brushed away her own tracks as she moved back. If her work paid off, the scene would look like Bear had been on a beeline to the ridge top. And by the time one or two more horses chewed up Bear's original tracks and they realized the trail flat-out ended . . .

She climbed back on Bear. They made a straight shot up the ridge, at a right angle to her old heading. She tapped Fishy's rifle to check again, wondering if she had wasted five minutes too many.

Up, bouncing on her feet in the stirrups as Bear climbed and crested a ridge, the wind smacked her in the face as quickly as she realized Bear was standing on grass. They were making tracks, but they wouldn't be visible to someone in a hurry.

A gift.

Allison headed to the top of the ridge. She didn't dare linger on a high spot too long. She feared throwing her own silhouette against the sluggish winter sun.

Allison guided Bear in a dance along the edge of the snow line until they ran out of rocks, and the barren, snow-free stuff came to an unceremonious end.

****

"I tell you she was asking about how to get to Deep Lake. Seemed innocent enough."

"Seemed," said Grumley.

"Hard to believe she circled back," said Alvin.

"Fuck it," said Grumley.

The tracks that dead-ended had set them back fifteen minutes. All the while Alvin hadn't stopped with his endless theorizing, whining and complaining about his jaw. Alvin was coughing up globs of bloody crud. Grumley hoped a chunk would harden and make him choke. Now, up on the ridge top where she could have taken any direction back down, he was at it again. It was small minds like Alvin's that made it difficult to trust anyone.

There had been one other set of headlights on the road before he reached the barn. Now he knew, after Alvin's eleventh monologue about the sequence of events, that the first headlights must have belonged to Applegate. Grumley had flashed his high beams at the second set of lights, Alvin's, and the two of them had headed back to the barn. At the time, he was thinking nobody should see how desperate he was to make sure Applegate's rifle was still in place.

What Grumley couldn't figure out was how Allison knew to lift the Sako, the only one missing from the rack. They had to shoot the lock off the office to get inside. What a mess.

"Maybe you gave her the rifle," said Grumley. "Maybe you want into her pants."

"Right," said Alvin. "I'm sure."

"The second you get off the phone with me, she happens along."

"Like I said."

"Yeah, yeah, the bit about Deep Lake."

"That's what she told me."

"Casual conversation at six fucking thirty. She strolls up."

Alvin thought for a second. Maybe it was now clicking together.

"That's what happened," he said.

They were walking the long perimeter of the windblown ridge top, looking for tracks. Every minute it was more of a joke.

"We're cooked," said Grumley.

"She has to be around here," said Alvin. "We'll find her, come on. Let's do another circuit of the ridge top, only in the snow, say thirty or forty yards down off the top here. You go one way, I'll go the other."

"How the fuck we going to find each other if one of us sniffs her drawers?"

"Together then."

"It'll take twice as long. Meantime, she's making tracks."

"One nosy bitch," said Alvin. His fake sympathy.

"How the fucking hell did she know which rifle?"

Alvin paused too long. A flinch.

"Not me, no way," he said. The words came out in a funny, splattered jumble.

"You screwin' her?"

"She wouldn't have me."

There was a touch of fear in the kid's voice now, sensing that this line of questions might keep up.

Who really cared about Bobby Alvin either? Would he be missed? Grumley couldn't stop thinking of the rifle in Allison's hands, how soon she might get it in the hands of the cops. Would they believe her story that it might have something to do with Mr. Elk Suit? With Trudy gone and that whole mess too and fucking Applegate on the loose?

Too many problems, too much to sort out.

He had given Trudy's trail to Popeye, but the guy spent a few hours driving around, grew queasy and gave it up. Still suffering the effects, he said. More likely he was too overwhelmed with the fucking prospect of not being able to find something he shouldn't have lost in the first fucking place.

Why did he suffer losers?

Grumley's mind swirled, but he couldn't figure the advantage now of leaving Alvin here to think about his mistakes forever.

"Where we going?" said Alvin.

Grumley turned his horse around and headed down.

On the other hand . . .

He pictured a bullet in Bobby's forehead.

"Are you okay?" said Bobby.

"Never better," said Grumley. He pulled out his pistol, the '58 New Army Texas, a .44. A replica. It should do the job.

"Hey," said Alvin, as he started to dive. But it wasn't a dive. An invisible force separated him from his saddle. He landed in the snow on his side.

The sound of the shot echoed in Grumley's head. There was something satisfying about making a decision.

****

A week after her taste of the harbor, Allison had been in decent enough shape to ask for the newspapers that covered the accident. Her parents had flown in and her dad, a chronic newspaper hound, brought the stack of past issues of *The New York Times*. She glanced at the pictures and scanned the copy, grating at the notion that a see-it-all-writer looking down from above could use the verb "flopped," as if the jet was a human form that could choose between a cannonball or a headfirst dive on its entry into the water. "Flopped" wasn't what had happened inside the cabin. "Flopped" had a fun and frolicking tone to it. There was nothing frolicking about the crash. The newspaper headline was the first time she had known how many had died, but she certainly hadn't needed to be told that many had, in fact, perished.

Walking now with Bear, she thought of Peter McBride, one of those naturally open, relaxed people who were always seconds away from a comfortable smile. He wore round wire-rims, sported short but tousled hair, and was about her size—compact, trim and lean. He had bright, clear eyes, like blueberries in a pool of milk. They were talking like good, old friends in the terminal long before they boarded. Their flight was late departing because the plane hadn't even left Baltimore at boarding time. Within a few minutes, she recalled, he had mentioned Zen. And she had pressed him a bit, discovering he had spent a week in the equivalent of a closet, meditating on the trouble his life and his being had caused his parents and others around him. He told her they were asked to break their lives down into three-year blocks and consider all the ways their mere existence had impacted the lives of those around them, right down to the nitty-gritty details of contemplating the number of diapers their parents had to change, no questions asked, before they could deal with their own shit.

Her mind had jumped at the exercise. Even as they continued to chat, her mind had gone busy scouring the memory banks. She scraped together bits and pieces of things she hadn't thought about in years. At four, she had pretended that a neighbor girl-friend had fallen from the roof of the house. They had poured ketchup around where she had "fallen" to give her mother a jolt, at least from a distance. She recalled old tantrums, battles with her mom over not wanting to waste time in the stupid grocery store and fights with her brothers over who knew what.

When she had the stack of newspapers, she felt it before she read it. And her parents probably assumed, when she started to bawl, that it was the overwhelming reality of reading about the accident that had caught up with her. But it was the name in newspaper ink. Too real. Too painful. *PETER McBRIDE, 28, Boulder, Colo.*

It didn't seem possible at the time, it didn't seem possible now. Time hadn't fixed that one. Bear picked his way in the general direction that would dump them out on the road, perhaps a mile or two down from her A-Frame. It was three o'clock and going on dusk in the ravines. They had slurped water from creek beds. She had found an old granola bar in the otherwise empty saddle-bag. Bear won the snack. She felt hungry, but couldn't imagine depriving him of a morsel.

Working on Peter's problem, she thought of the rooms in the houses where she had lived and how memories were mostly place. Nothing could happen without a place for it to occur. She remembered Peter tapping her on the shoulder. He boarded last, a stand-by. He could have been in this place, this space, this airplane. Or inside the terminal, bumped from the flight. What if each city had a dozen more good jobs for traveling businessmen, through a slightly better economy, and what if there had been no room for stand-bys on that flight? Peter would have stayed behind, safe and dry.

The woods thinned out. The grade turned gentle. The day's light was being given a brief reprieve as they moved out and away from the darkened north face of the ridge and through an expanse of aspens, spaced like they had been purposely planted a horse-width apart. They wound their way to the edge of a broad clearing that fell away, not so gently. The pitch was dotted with bush-size evergreens and scrub oak. The ravine ended a few hundred yards down, but so steeply she couldn't see the bottom. The other side climbed as quickly, but was topped by a small section of familiar looking guardrail. A stretch of no more than a few dozen feet was all she could see. And down to the right, to the east, a cherry-red house, a farmhouse, basked in the soft glow of the setting sun. It was a mile off, maybe more.

Behind her, someone followed.

She dug her heels into Bear. No coaxing, no time to be choosy. Bear lowered himself down on his hindquarters as his front legs paddled and scraped and pranced, hoping for footing and braking when they started to slide. She tapped Fishy's rifle, scooted low in the saddle and kept her weight back to help Bear stabilize. The guardrail disappeared and so did the farmhouse as they burrowed down in the hole, too steep. Bear angled off on his own compass, sensing an extra degree or two of grade that was beyond his capabilities.

She risked a glance back up. He was a big man, Grumley-size, but all she had was the three-quarter silhouette of him, on horseback. He watched her, standing where Bear had stood.

Bear was halfway down. The far side of the ravine was better lit. And it didn't climb fast enough to do her much good, provide any cover. Nobody would think twice about a couple of gunshots, if there was anything left to hear after the ravine swallowed up the noise.

She turned her head around to look back up the hill as Bear reached the bottom. Her pursuer was halfway down, making it look easy. She let Bear take a few strides in the relatively gentle pitch of the ravine bottom. There was no creek but it was rocky and uneven under the snow. Bear balked and hesitated, shot forward when he reached the far bank and found better footing, heading up. She worked to keep a straight line and hoped the cherry farmhouse would come into view when they crested the top.

The sound of the rifle shot had been in her head all along. She flinched at the crack and waited. Bear kept his stride, what was left of it. She took a second to find her breath again and wished she could meld into the saddle. She couldn't find a clear thought. She hoped for the farmhouse.

*Boom.*

Bear's nose plunged into the snow. She waited for her own flick of pain as Bear's front legs buckled and his rear rolled sideways and the snow came up to whack her. Suddenly, the background of farmhouse and dog pens and sky tumbled. Bear struggled to bounce back up, worked to right himself out of instinct, snorted and growled at his own frustration. And agony. Allison found herself splayed across his neck staring into his skyward eye. She rolled off and buried herself behind his shoulders, already starting to mourn before she saw the wound and the blood gushing from his haunch. Bear's head settled down onto the cool snow.

She tried to think of what to say, anything. His eyes turned milky and distant.

The rifle. She slid the rifle from the scabbard, thinking it had been fifty-fifty that she would have been able to reach it at all. If it had wound up under Bear, no way. She held it up to show the bastard what she had, in case that alone would make him scram. She propped it on Bear's sweaty chest and lined up the man's—was it Grumley's?—frame in her sights. She turned the rifle over, found the safety, hoped for ammunition, and put him back in her sights. He stood there.

She aimed at his head and moved it off a barrel's width to the west, her finger still hesitating.

The blast of her rifle spun the man around on the spot as he realized he was the wide-open target and she was the one with cover. He kicked his horse around and scampered off. Her ears rang. She stood and placed the rifle at the back of Bear's skull, between the ears, wasting no time for a good-bye with the next shot. Her heart cried as Bear sank another inch lower and she turned and ran through the calf-deep snow toward the dogs.

Her legs churned on an untapped source of power and fear. Two large pens flanked the farmhouse. A dozen or more dog-houses were scattered around both pens and each dog was linked by rope to its own house. The dogs howled and scraped the dirt, desperate for a ringside seat. She dashed up between the house and the pens, followed a beaten-down path along the side of the house and around to the front.

A woman stood on the front steps, holding a bundled-up toddler in her arms. An older girl stood wide-eyed next to her mom. Long red hair poked out from the hood of the toddler's jacket. A sack of groceries stood in the driveway, plunked down in the mud. There were more groceries in the back of a Subaru station wagon, the rear door open.

"Oh my," said the woman, clutching her daughter more tightly.

"No, no. Don't worry," said Allison. She held up her free hand like she was stopping traffic. "It's over. I think. I hope."

"What? Who are…?"

"I was being chased," said Allison. "Shots. My horse."

"They were shooting at you?"

"My horse," she said, but barely this time. The two words took forever to utter. "Shot my horse."

*Bear.* Could it be?

Her breath was a draining search for oxygen.

"Oh my, oh my," said the woman, pulling the toddler closer, panic on her face. "Come in the house—now."

Allison stood inside the massive farmhouse with its woodplank floors and bright braided rugs. Stacy Burnett introduced herself, her older daughter Valerie and toddler, Kirsten.

"But you're okay?" said Stacy.

"I need a phone," said Allison.

"Of course, this way."

Stacy showed her to a telephone on the wall next to the kitchen table. Valerie tracked every move.

Allison dialed Slater's number. Her world wobbled crazily, off-kilter. Her breathing was deep and unsettled. From the kitchen window, she scanned the wide field that swooped down toward the ravine. She could make out Bear's inert, prone hulk in the snow. She wiped tears from her cheeks.

Slater was out, checking on a few stray buffalo that came from a farm up toward Craig. She didn't feel like telling anyone else.

Should she call Sandstrom? Or Trudy? Or Weaver—to tell him about Bear?

Sandstrom. The female receptionist on the phone took notes. She was composed and maddeningly cool. She decided after a minute to relay her to a deputy, who took another set of notes for a minute and put Allison on hold while he tried to patch her through to Sandstrom in his sheriff's car.

"Ms. Allison," said Sandstrom, when he came on. "What's this—a shooting?"

"At me," she said.

"Jesus H.," said Sandstrom. "You staying put for a few minutes? Never mind the question. You are staying put."

"Cops are on their way up," Allison said to Stacy, cupping the mouthpiece.

"No problem," said Stacy. "They have to come."

Allison relayed the address; Sandstrom said he knew the kennels.

Stacy brought homemade chicken soup and wheatberry bread while they waited. Connecting with the authorities offered a touch of calm, along with the steaming broth. She found her focus. She concentrated on everything but Bear. She tried Trudy's number while she waited. No answer. It was a strange no answer, one she didn't expect. She tried Slater's trailer, in case he was home. His voice mail answered but she didn't know what to say except, "Call me when you resurface, there's a lot going on." She tried Trudy's number again and still it rang on and on, into the void.

Sandstrom and two deputies arrived more quickly than she'd expected, in three separate cars. Gerard, who gave her a wink, followed her boot prints down to Bear, after she pointed him out. The other one, a green-looking kid, Sandstrom sat in the living room with Sandstrom, her going over it all. The kid took the notes.

"I don't get why someone tracked you down clear over here," said Sandstrom, after she had finished.

"May I show you something? In private?"

The deputy and Sandstrom exchanged glances. Stacy said they could use the kitchen, she'd keep Valerie out of the way, or even better, they could use the walk-in pantry. Allison picked up Fishy's rifle from the kitchen, where she had left it, and led Sandstrom to the well-stocked food closet, shutting the door behind her.

"Dramatic," said Sandstrom.

"Necessary," said Allison.

"Whose is this?" he said.

"You got Rocky down yet?"

"We're getting to it, we're getting to it. Jesus . . . I'm not into tricks."

Sandstrom stared at the rifle.

"Then I'm here to cut a deal."

"Everybody always is. That's life. What's yours?"

"First, I wanna hear you say I wasn't crazy."

"We get the body down, I'll give you that."

"It's there."

"If it is, you're not."

Allison found that a bit of steam and energy were mixing in naturally with her anger over Bear and Grumley and Rocky. She hadn't mentioned Grumley yet by name, and couldn't. She wanted to light a fire that would jack-up all the issues at once.

"What's with the rifle?"

"I stole the rifle. As a kid, though, we used to call it 'borrowing back.' I went over to get route and trail information from Grumley's place. I was talking to Bobby Alvin. He'll tell you all of this." The words were coming easily. She could also clearly see the spot where she could nail Sandstrom. "I spotted this Sako. I took it, and a couple of men chased me. I have a pretty good idea who, but I'm not sure, so I'm not saying. This rifle's a bit unusual, I think you'll agree. But check the initials here. A guy named Sal Marcovicci sold it to Dean Applegate."

"Mr. Turncoat."

"Correct. A few years back. Chances are it'll match up like a bad recurring nightmare with the bullet you pulled from Ray Stern."

She waited a second to see if Sandstrom could soak this up.

"Now you can decide if you want to book me on a theft charge, make a nuisance out of that. Or, if you agree to let it go, and if you agree to make a very concerted effort to find out who shot Rocky Carnivitas, then I'll give you the rifle, and you can do experiments and see if you can solve this nasty migraine called the media that's been tormenting you for weeks."

Allison decided she would hold the Sako until Sandstrom made his choice clear.

"Theft?" he said.

His jowls quivered and he stared her down.

"Hey, I'll return it, through you. Unless you want to test it first."

"How do you know this is the one?" said Sandstrom.

Allison thought for a few seconds, wondered if there was any chance that she'd been set up, that Fishy was in on something, that this was all a fancy charade to make her feel better.

"Call it a hunch," she said. "Call it one big, fat hunch."

# 14

"What loose ends?"

"Things I had to deal with—there's no point in boring you with the details."

"We don't like you gone. I missed you, you big lug. Plus, secrets. They make me queasy."

"It's over, done with. History," said Applegate.

It was early evening. They strolled the cool, wet streets of lower downtown Denver after dinner. There had been waves of food with hummus and eggplant, all laced with garlic. And two bottles of wine had been safely tucked away as stew for their brains. The alcohol had erased any chance Applegate had of connecting all the dots from his bizarre journey.

"Another circle-the-parking-lot protest isn't going to cut it," said Ellenberg. "Makes us both look unimaginative, anyway."

"What you need is a major non-violent disruption, right?"

"Sure."

"You need a surprise attack, get national attention. And you need something soon."

"Tomorrow would do."

She sat down on a street bench, pulling him down with her to snuggle for warmth. He walked through the idea slowly.

"Caravan goes up the interstate. Say twenty cars, unmarked. No banners, no nothing. Not obviously together. Maybe there's a news crew with you—one, so it's not that obvious. You drive into the canyon two across, ten deep, maybe a hundred deep. All going the same speed. The cars come to a halt, cap the breakdown lanes too, and then pull out the banners and stuff. March down the highway, do whatever you want. Fifteen minutes. Thirty. However long it might take to draw a heavy response, make the point, make sure there's good video and one helluva long traffic jam behind you. That's what you want, a heavy response. As many cops as they got, bring 'em on. For a half hour you clog the only major east-west artery in the state and give old Sandstrom another stroke."

"It's brilliant," she gushed. "I love it."

The scheme made her giddy. They ran it through a few times to test for trouble spots, but it was foolproof. Nothing could go wrong.

"Maybe we should cut off the highway in both directions at the same point."

"You'll make it too difficult for the sheriff to reach you," countered Applegate. "And then he'll be really pissed. Plus, you want the cops, lots of 'em, to make for a confrontation."

A fine mist of snow had begun. Breathing felt like drinking. She hugged him around the chest as they walked and she buried her head against his coat. They weaved through a crowd of kids hanging out around a late-night dance club, but otherwise the streets and sidewalks were nearly empty. Applegate felt the solid buzz from the wine as they negotiated their way back to her place.

Ellenberg jumped on the phone, starting to spread the idea around, her face lighting up at the response. The word came back quickly: tomorrow. He heard her say "Dean's idea" and "Dean thought it up." Applegate poked around her brick loft, feeling useless as she chatted on the phone. Suddenly he felt very sober.

People would take the day off from work and would do whatever it took to make a difference. Mention doing something in the name of Ray Stern and an instant army was at your disposal.

They all wanted to get it going immediately. No questions asked. Ellenberg had a news editor friend who was sympathetic and the friend checked the advance log for the following day's scheduled news. It was a slow news day. That cinched it. The phone tree, dry timber, was on fire.

When she was done and when the phone stopped ringing, Ellenberg lit a dozen candles. Applegate had to stop and think if it was still the same day he'd wailed on Bobby Alvin. It was.

"Come here," said Ellenberg. She stood in the glow she'd created, unbuttoning her white cotton blouse, the one with the red and blue flowers embroidered on the pockets. Braless. She hooked her pants down, pulled back the quilt comforter and stood there in her powder blue short-cut panties, trim and lean.

"You going to stand there?"

"Enjoying it," said Applegate.

"Hurry up and get naked," she said. "We gotta get to sleep. Tomorrow's a big day."

****

The garage door was open and so was the door that led from the garage into the house. She heard one soft meow off in the distance and another, lower pitched and more like a siren. She shut the door behind her, stepped over a chair lying on its side and sprayed the room with the beam from her flashlight.

"Trudy?" she called out. Allison's heart fluttered. Scampering cat feet everywhere made it worse. Add trespassing to the list of charges, thought Allison, as if the cops don't have enough to worry about. This last piece, finding Trudy, was simply a matter of closing the loop with the only other person who cared about Rocky. And now she was beginning to wonder if anything was simple.

Allison stood in a ransacked kitchen. The table was turned over, there were smashed plates and a skid of food or slime covered the floor. Bits of broken glass and a bottle of mustard had smashed and exploded, leaving brown-yellow shrapnel everywhere. The light caught a pair of green eyes staring back at her from the floor. Another feline, this one jet black, crouched low in the middle of the mess. Careful of putting her footprints in any gobs of food, she picked her way around the clutter and upended table to the other side of the kitchen.

More meows. More cat eyes, pairs by the dozen.

She took the stairs up to the bedrooms. One bed was a mess, with squirming balls of fur in the middle of it. A mother and her new brood, hours old at most.

A bathroom was empty; a second bedroom empty, too.

Allison went to the greenhouse. Nothing. She poked her flashlight down the basement stairs. The chorus of meows grew in strength as she stepped down, with one cat doing a figure eight between her feet. She found the light switch and snapped it on. A cat sprinted up as she cautiously descended.

Allison found the tub of cat food and slipped the plastic cover off the giant vat. It didn't seem to make much of a sound, but the stairs behind her were quickly cluttered with cats. They pounded their way down and assembled at her feet like an alluvial fan of bubbling fur. They rubbed their chins on her ankles. There were five bowls, all licked clean. The cats jostled for position, spreading out and around until every munching station was full and the pecking order established.

"Knock yourselves out," she told them. And sneezed.

She went back upstairs. The house was clearly empty, but the mess didn't look good. Finding Trudy would depend upon how far she had decided to go and how long ago she'd left. Allison found herself standing next to a leafy fern-like plant in the living room. She jabbed a finger into the potting soil, to the first knuckle. The surface was dry, but the dirt below stuck to her skin. No more than a few days without water, she guessed. Trudy wouldn't have gone too far, wouldn't have left her cats and plants to the winds.

****

The motel room bugged her. There was so little room to move that it felt like a cell. All the surfaces were hard. There was nothing green. The only activity was on the TV. Worse than that, there was no news. CNN, sure, but no real news or developments. There was nothing on the local channels, either. The media needed a real slice of something meaty now for the next chapter to begin; anything but another loosely hinged sidebar about a remote aspect of animal rights, creative suicide, or the history of Ray Stern.

She needed Allison but wondered if she would still want to help. There hadn't been any answer at Allison's house the few times she had called. She left a message at Pete Weaver's barn, but the mumbling guide who worked for Pete was unreliable, at best. She decided to go right to the top. If anybody could find Allison Coil, it was Pete Weaver himself. The phone at his farmhouse rang uselessly the first four times she tried it, on the hour, until after dusk.

"Weaver."

The fifth time was the charm.

"Hi, Peter. It's Trudy Grumley," she said. The Grumley-Weaver tension had always been polite, but real. They were competitors after the same market in the same valley showing off the same wilderness, hunting the same herds.

"What can I do for you?" said Weaver.

"I'm looking for one of your guides. Allison Coil."

"Popular girl," said Weaver. "Been plenty busy, anyway. I'll leave her a note on the message board down at the barn. You tried her home?"

"Yes. No answer."

"Probably up on her routes," said Weaver. "How about her boyfriend? The ranger?"

"Don't know him."

"David Slater. Forest Service ranger. Lives down in Glenwood Springs or down that way."

Trudy said goodbye quickly, checked the directory for Slater, found a D Slater, no address, and dialed the number. She let it ring until she heard the message machine start. She hung up.

She had moved from one stuck place to another stuck place.

But she hadn't left her house, taken such a risk, only to lie low.

There was nothing that said she couldn't find the Forest Service office, ask around, or even drive out to Slater's place for a look. It was a matter of working up the nerve.

****

Slater was waiting for Allison at the Waffle Hut, not too far from downtown. He was deep into his third or fourth cup of coffee, judging by the disheveled newspaper in the booth. During the drive down from Ripplecreek, fatigue had briefly unbundled itself from her fears, but it was all back together now in a troublesome cocktail. Her mind was trapped in a box where the name George Grumley echoed with more and more volume.

"Hi," Allison said, having snuck up behind him, a fearless man with his back to the door. "Breakfast for supper?"

"First meal of the day," said Slater. "Got trapped dealing with unlicensed hunters from Indiana."

"You mean poachers."

"They hadn't shot anything. Yet. Fine line. We talked. And talked. Aren't you joining me?"

"I can't decide."

"Why?"

"I don't want to sit still."

"I can imagine, but now you're with me. Besides, I want to hear it all again from start to finish."

Over coffee and waffles? She wanted his undivided attention in a private place where she could be held. It was like being back in the harbor, floating and bobbing with airplane parts and everything the broken airplane coughed up. She'd never forget the bear hug clutch of the anonymous firefighter as he wrapped her in a blanket. Slater took a sip of coffee and urged her to sit down on the same bench with him. Not quite the same, but . . .

"No idea who it was? Chasing you?"

Slater looked cool, unmoved.

"Yeah. But nothing I could prove."

"Nonetheless, who?"

"Saying it would make it real in your head too. And I might be wrong."

"So?" He paused, stared.

"It looked a helluva lot like George Grumley."

"The guy who owns the barn where you picked up the rifle?" said Slater.

"You don't have to add two and two so quickly."

"Comes up four every time," said Slater. "Cops take good care of you?"

"More thorough than I had the patience for."

"What kind of rifle was it?"

"Which?" said Allison.

"The one you lifted."

"A Sako."

A waitress drifted by with a pot of coffee. Slater ordered waffles; Allison asked for juice.

"Finnish," said Slater.

"Huh?"

"The rifle. Made in Finland. Good precision. Should be easy to match up."

"Especially with Marcovicci's initials," said Allison.

"They'll need proof of ownership. Or they can pick up Applegate, pretend they've got the goods, tell him they found the rifle and get him to confess on the guarantee of a lesser charge? Have the rifle right there, see if he flinches, see if he does a good, solid double take and then spews it all out. No lab work needed."

"How about photographs of Applegate holding the Sako over the last few years?"

"If they're available. And very clear. Still have to be the same rifle, with the telling detail."

"Or maybe there's somebody who witnessed the sale. That would do, too."

"Jesus," said Slater. "You don't give up."

"What was I supposed to do?"

"I'm not sure."

"Nobody believed me. And now there's Rocky. I never saw anything that had to do with Ray Stern. Trudy Grumley calls and says Rocky is missing. All I did was a favor, running by his place. Speaking of which, now Trudy is missing. I went up to look for her, tell her what I knew, and her place was trashed. Tables turned over, mess on the floor."

Slater cocked an eye. "Not good," he said.

"Tell me," said Allison.

"But that would explain the name on the message on my desk," said Slater. "It was only the first name, Trudy, and a phone number."

"Did you call?"

"No, I didn't know there was any need or rush. It's on my desk."

"Can you call and get it?" said Allison.

"Closed up for the night. But we can go back when we're done. Or it can wait."

"Tonight."

"Fine," said Slater, a slight hint of irritation on his face.

Allison put a hand on his thigh underneath the table and slumped into his shoulder, letting weariness take another run at her. She drank her juice in a few long gulps and tried to suppress her desire to get going, to at least talk with Trudy.

"Do you know if they got Rocky down yet?"

"Don't," said Slater. "I've been out of the loop. Or out on the loop, depending on your point of view."

"You don't think that the dead elk and finding the GPS, meant . . . ?"

"Researchers?"

"Yeah."

"Not likely. I've already talked to Bridgers. We're putting a task force together to investigate this one, interview all the appropriate people that Rocky worked with and worked for. Should get going here in a day or two. We want to bring in folks from other districts who don't know all the players, to make it as fair as possible."

Slater wolfed down his waffles, whipped cream and a scoop of sticky blueberry compote. Allison tried not to gag.

They walked three blocks to Slater's office as a freight train lumbered through downtown. Slater unlocked the front door and led her upstairs in the dark to his desk, where he found the message slip among a bunch of others.

Allison dialed the number and asked for the room.

"It's Allison. Are you all right, Trudy?"

"Sort of. I'm fine, yeah. Thanks for calling. You got my message?"

"Yes. Your place, what happened?"

"You went there?"

"Of course, when there was no answer."

Slater took a seat and plowed into his paperwork as if it was high noon. He moved letters, files and memos one at a time from his inbox to the center of his desk and either to a metal, vertical sorter or to the circular file.

"There was a bit of a scrap," said Trudy. "I had to get out."

"Where are you?"

"Sulphur Inn, south of downtown."

Allison knew the place, with its fake neon steam on the sign. In fact, Trudy was only a mile away. She didn't want to tell Trudy what she had to tell her over the phone. Since Trudy hadn't brought it up yet, it was entirely possible she didn't know about Rocky, especially if the cops hadn't retrieved his body or released any information. But Allison could not imagine staying awake any longer than the twenty minutes or so that it would require to drive to Slater's trailer.

"You're okay for the night?" said Allison. "Can we meet first thing tomorrow?"

She'd have to talk with Weaver. It was hard to imagine going back to routine chores right away. But it was high season. Weaver's team was thin to begin with.

"I'm okay," said Trudy unconvincingly. "I'll be here. Room 141. Look for the 4Runner."

"First thing," said Allison. "Count on it." She said good-bye and hung up.

"She's okay?"

"Just," said Allison. "Lonesome and scared, for sure."

"Are we done?" said Slater, looking up from his now-clean desk. Only a stapler, tape dispenser, and pencil cup stood guard.

"Except the crashing part. Your place okay?"

"Alas, no," said Slater. "I have to head over to Grand Junction tonight, big pooh-bah from Washington is in town for a regional meeting pep talk thing at o-dark thirty in the a.m. I'm afraid you're on your own."

"Again," said Allison.

"Sorry," said Slater. "We're part of the show. Gotta lick boots."

"That's okay," said Allison. "I expect to be conked out for hours to come."

But already her mind stirred, imagining ahead the conversation with Trudy and thinking how she'd find the way to tell her. Trudy's airplane had crashed, too, only she didn't know it yet. How in the hell did you give somebody that kind of news? She would play the role of co-pilot, drift down the aisle, sport a matter-of-fact tone of voice and tell everyone: "Thought you all would like to know. We're going down."

\*\*\*\*

It was a soft knock, three quick raps, unassuming and weak, no demand involved. Trudy responded instantly.

"Just a minute," she said, looking for her new Wal-Mart robe and feeling her heart start to pump on a bit of adrenaline generated by the steep climb from parked to flying. It was still dark out.

It was only 5:30: too early for Allison, she thought.

"Yes?" she said at the door in a half whisper. Probably too soft.

"Miss Trudy."

It was the housekeeper, Mariela. They had chatted twice. Mariela had spotted the cat but didn't mind covering for the violation of house rules. She was a hard-working immigrant from Guadalajara who had taken the time to learn English.

"Miss Trudy." Another trio of knocks.

Trudy unfastened the chain, braced for a blast of cool air. She opened the door.

"Miss Trudy. I . . ."

Mariela stepped inside without being invited and stumbled awkwardly to the bedside chair, challenging Trudy's sense of decorum and hospitality. A worried, fearful look had gripped Mariela's face, only she wasn't looking Trudy in the eye, but at the door.

George Grumley. Gun in hand, filling the doorway. He was pointing the gun at Mariela, but he was looking at Trudy.

"Nice place," he said. "Good help."

"George, what the—she's not involved."

"She is now."

Trudy stayed standing, the back of her knees against the edge of the bed.

"Besides," said George. "I'm no trouble. This here is sort of a glorified key, that's all. Harmless."

George put the gun down gently on the table, grabbed Mariela by the hand, brought her up like a small child. He whisked her out the door, a fake smile plastered on his face. Trudy found herself on the other side of the bed, unsure how all this came to be—this moment and all its bare-bones reality. Did the bathroom lock from the inside? Was it worth a try?

"How did you . . . ?" she started to ask.

"Hell," said George. "You left your number all over the valley. Little thing called a reverse directory. Simple."

He was stepping around her, one hand out and palm up, inviting her to dance.

Trudy kept her own hands pressed between her butt and the wall, flattening herself into the paint.

He put a hand around her forearm and squeezed his fingers down between muscle and bone into a painful spot she didn't know existed. He flipped her onto the bed.

"What the fuck you doin'?" he said.

He was straddling her hips now, his face in hers.

There was no need to answer.

"You almost killed Popeye, know that?"

Fossil watched from a chair by the bedside table. Do something, she thought.

"You fuckin' bitch," said George.

His breath was sour, rotten. He reeked of bourbon.

Hand on her breast, he was mauling her. God no, she thought.

"Husband and wife," said George. "Motel room. No laws against it. Or maybe you know of one? Just a last fuck. A good-bye fuck. A fuck-you fuck."

She turned her head away as far as was possible.

"Try to show a little affection," he said. "It's me. Your fucking husband."

He yanked open her robe and leaned up a bit to undo his pants. "You pushed way too hard. But now you have nothing to push against. Nothing. Nothing. Because I'm outta here."

Trudy kept her head cranked to the side, feeling the powerful clamp on her legs, caught between deciding whether to struggle, or to lie still and disassociate from what was happening.

"Husband and wife," said George. "Been a long time since we did it in a motel room."

He jerked down her underwear. Trudy started to shake and buck. George smiled. "Please," he said. "Husband and wife."

He lay down on top of her, smothering her, and what effort she had mounted was of no consequence. He jammed his stinky head against her neck, pawed her breasts.

Laughing? Yes, a goofy laugh.

George was making so much noise he didn't hear the door open. Trudy watched Mariela step inside the room and in one smooth motion she grabbed the telephone off the bedside table and brought it crashing down on George's head.

George bellowed, went limp. Trudy shoved him to the floor.

"Mariela!" said Trudy.

"*Vamanos*," said Mariela. "I mean—"

"I know, I know."

Trudy climbed out of bed, looked around like she might need something.

"You can come back later," said Mariela. "No time now."

George started to stir.

What about the gun? Trudy picked it up with a bundle of sweaters, jeans and Fossil. Mariela scampered outside to the 4Runner. Trudy followed, digging into the pocket of the jeans she was holding, searching for the ignition key. She climbed in and started the engine, still wearing her robe.

She stared straight ahead. A thick coat of frost was caked on the windshield. It was the worst kind—thick and crusty.

"Drive with your head out the window," said Mariela.

"Come with me," said Trudy.

"I can't."

"He'll—"

"He won't find me," said Mariela.

Trudy closed the door, opened the side window.

"Do you know him?" said Mariela.

"*Mi esposo,*" said Trudy. The Spanish words came out of the blue, last used in a high school language class and long, she thought, forgotten.

Mariela's eyes widened as the door to Trudy's room opened. George stumbled through. Mariela ducked into the dark and was gone. Trudy backed up, jammed the truck in gear and drove away with her head out the window, freezing air blowing into her face.

****

Room 141. Look for the 4Runner.

Allison had etched the room number in her weary head, but the knock went unanswered. It was after nine. The whole world was awake. No 4Runner. None parked at any of the motel room doors. She circled the parking lot twice. Should she bother going to the office? What if Trudy hadn't checked in under her own name? Allison sat in her Blazer and waited, radio and heater on, engine running, antenna up. How long should she give her?

A maid pushed a cart along between the rooms. She had a pleasant face, youngish. Not trouble-free, not burdenless, but simple and uncomplicated. Wrapped in a down vest, she left the door open to room 140 so she could come and go with her supplies from the cart.

The images kept coming back to Allison: Rocky, Stern, Bear. She pictured each one going down. Rocky was still the puzzle. She saw the elk, whole and unblemished, the shell that held life in the combination of parts. She imagined vessels, organs, veins and muscles that needed to work together to keep each other functioning, to provide the host animal with the ability to breathe. Who had brought the elk down?

And what did Rocky really know?

There was a knock on her window. It was the maid. She was younger than Allison had thought.

"Excuse me," she said. Good English, but clearly a second language.

Allison smiled; the maid didn't.

"I'm waiting, is that okay?"

"Yes, of course. For the woman in this room?" Pointing to 141.

"Yes."

"Is your name Allison?"

"Yes." How did this woman . . .?

"Trudy told me you could find her in the parking lot at City Market."

"Is Trudy okay?"

"Okay."

The drive was a half mile, two stoplights' worth. Both lights were red, both urged patience she couldn't locate. She wouldn't even know where to begin to look. It felt as if connections in the whole business were beyond her grasp, slippery and odd, a world where putting one foot in front of the other meant going zigzag. The rest hadn't been rest at all, only fitful blips of snoozing with intermittent bouts of insomnia that neither chamomile tea nor rye whiskey could snap.

The parking lot was half full. Most were SUVs—Cherokees and Explorers. Allison figured she would find Trudy either on the perimeter of the lot where she could watch everything, or in the middle where she could hide. She spotted a 4Runner in a pack of cars near the center row. Allison parked a few slots away.

Trudy was seated behind the wheel, eyes flicking nervously about. Allison tapped on the window.

"My God," said Trudy, rolling down the window and reaching over to unlock the passenger-side door.

"Mariela found you?" said Trudy as Allison hopped in.

"It wasn't difficult," said Allison. "I was parked right there. How long have you been waiting?"

"Couple hours. Two cups of tea from the bakery. Mariela saved me, literally. George tracked me down to the motel." A kitten hopped up on Trudy's shoulder. "Fossil. The refugee."

"Tracked you down?"

"George said something about a reverse directory. Dumb me."

"What happened?"

"He crashed in, stinking drunk. He was all over me. Mariela came in, whacked him on the head with a telephone and helped me get away. I think he's leaving, as in really leaving."

"What do you mean?"

"Alaska. Some godforsaken place like that."

"He's bailing out?"

"He called it his trapdoor. Liquidate everything and go. He never wanted to be on any government record anywhere. This was always too much, dealing with permits and wilderness regulations."

"Apparently," said Allison.

"He always wanted to go live where nobody knew his name and nobody could easily track him down. I think he means it this time."

"The pressure's on," said Allison.

"What do you mean?" said Trudy.

Allison started off by telling her about Sal Marcovicci in Denver. She wound through most of the highlights of the days during which she and Trudy had been separated. When it came to telling about finding Rocky, she needed to pause for breath. She cracked the window and let her own tears flow in advance, anticipating Trudy's, which came before Allison said Rocky's name. They hugged. Trudy said it confirmed what she already knew, asked a few questions about whether they had moved the body. She cried some more. Allison went into the store for a box of Kleenex and cold sodas, keeping her eyes open for Grumley.

"It's all too weird," said Trudy when Allison returned to the 4Runner. "I can't make sense of it."

"It's all tied together," said Allison. "What if George stumbled across Applegate? The trail down from the spot where Rocky ended up would put him in the same area. Applegate is dazed and a mess from having killed Ray Stern. George gets him squared away, maybe even takes his rifle, but tells Applegate to keep quiet about them seeing each other on the mountain. Now the police have Applegate's rifle. And George knows it."

"The Mooney," said Trudy.

"I don't follow."

"We need to keep him here," said Trudy. "His plane. He would be stuck without it."

"What are we going to do, fly it away and hide it?"

"No," said Trudy. "But maybe we can clip its wings."

# 15

Three hundred cars were strung out behind them. Ellenberg drove with a giddy sensation of power, staying right at the speed limit. She sported a confident grin, nodding her head.

"Oh yeah," she said. "Oh yeah. We are going to shut this sucker down."

The mouth of the canyon lay ahead around a wide curve.

"Here we go," said Ellenberg.

The caravan was tightly bunched behind them. Applegate channeled their conviction, their purpose. The plan was working to a T. They jammed up both lanes. The highway hugged the north side of The Colorado River, swooped through tunnels, cut across the river on a graceful bridge, plunged through a long snaking tunnel on the south side of the river and dumped them back out on the north. They were cruising. Ellenberg stayed in the left lane and held her speed steady. An old station wagon matched their speed in the right. The driver, a woman with long blonde braids, flashed a V with her fingers and smiled, gave the air a fist pump. An old red Volkswagen pulled up in the breakdown lane on the right. Applegate looked back. The highway was thick with cars, trucks and vans. Of course it was impossible to tell if every car was one of theirs, but any innocent travelers had no choice in what was going to happen next.

Heading west, the No Name tunnels were the last in a series of bores that cut through a canyon wall. A half mile past the tunnels, in the long straightaway before Glenwood Springs and as the city itself came into view, Ellenberg brought her car to a crawl.

Applegate signaled to the station wagon driver and the station wagon driver signaled to the red VW. It was all prearranged. And working beautifully.

The crawl grew slower, to walking pace, and finally to a stop. Ellenberg pulled over as close as she could to the guardrail on the left. The station wagon squeezed in tight and the VW moved over to make room for a fourth car, a new black Jeep Cherokee. The driver of the Cherokee climbed out, hopped around to the back, flipped open the gate. She pulled out a furled banner attached to two sticks.

Ellenberg squeezed out her door and Applegate followed out of his side. A car honked in the distance. The banner was unspooled across the lanes of the interstate, giant bright red letters on a white sheet: *WHO KILLED RAY STERN?*

Applegate looked at the stunning scene behind them, a major US interstate at a complete standstill. Banners were popping up every everywhere, people cheered and chanted.

"Beautiful," said Ellenberg. "What a sight. Let's see how long it takes 'em." She checked her watch.

"Ten minutes, tops," said Applegate. The scene was exactly as he had envisioned it, maybe better.

Two television crews jogged through the traffic and started recording. They had been invited along, let in on the plan. A short, fiftyish reporter named Alex Kirkwood, wearing a tailored suit under his winter parka, came straight for Ellenberg.

"You promise, you deliver," he said.

"I thought you would be interested," she said. "Pretty good visuals."

"We've got a helicopter rented too. There's no way to shoot a sucker like this from the ground. Did you get all three hundred vehicles you wanted?"

"Maybe double that," Ellenberg lied.

"And Dean Applegate to boot. Quite a display here," said the reporter.

The film crew aimed the camera at him and Applegate felt a sudden dry catch in his throat, like he'd swallowed chalk.

"I understand this was your idea," said Kirkwood.

"Nobody seems to care about the death of Ray Stern," said Applegate. His mouth didn't wrap around the words the way it should. "We can't let society forget the price he paid."

A helicopter screamed above them heading east. A cameraman leaned out of the open side door, his feet braced on the skids.

"Who the fuck is in charge of this goddamn mess?"

The booming voice broke through the din as the helicopter droned. The cameraman kept rolling as Ellenberg turned to look at the man who had spoken. He wore a dirty white T-shirt and grease-stained jeans. Long dark hair flowed from underneath a yellow baseball cap. The youthful elements masked a man in his mid-forties.

"You can't fucking stop in the middle of the goddamn interstate!" he yelled. He came storming at Ellenberg, his face red. "I'm half an hour late as it fucking is! I've got zero time for political bullshit. Is this your stupid idea of a joke?"

"We won't be here all day," said Applegate.

"I don't have time for anything, never mind all day."

"You must have cared about something in your life, believed something needed changing," said Ellenberg. Her tone was cool, nonthreatening.

"Like the fucking Vietnam War."

"Exactly. Did you go, or did you protest?"

"Fuck. Both. Went first. Came back and joined the other army that marched on DC."

He was inches away from Ellenberg, glaring down at her calm, centered expression.

"You helped save thousands of human lives by protesting. By voicing your opinion, standing up for it. It's on your record. And you deserve credit. We've got an issue with the police up here in Glenwood Springs and an issue with hunters and hunting. Somebody shot and killed—"

"Yeah, yeah, I remember hearing about that." His tone had eased.

"We are trying to exert a little pressure on the local government here so somebody will decide to deal with whoever killed Ray Stern."

"Okay, okay. Christ," said the driver. "Ten minutes?"

"Max," said Ellenberg. "Unless the cops are slower than we expect."

The man departed, resigned to the situation. One news crew followed him, asking his name and badgering him for more of his story.

Ellenberg smiled.

"This is our day," she said, "I can feel it."

Good, thought Applegate—as long as that includes both of us.

\*\*\*\*

Trudy showed her driver's license to a man who controlled a buzzered door that led out to the tarmac. Allison told the security man that her own name was Mrs. Ferguson and she was thinking of buying an airplane. The man said he wasn't aware that George Grumley had put the plane on the market, but told them that if they needed any technical questions answered he would be glad to come out and poke around with them, though he said you couldn't really judge a plane until you took it up for a test flight.

The concrete apron was a cold sink. They walked past a dozen planes tied to their moorings. The wind picked up. Loose tethers snapped in the breeze.

"Now pretend you're doing lots of talking, the good sales pitch routine, in case old Mr. Anal Airport Security Man happens to be watching," said Allison. She was starting to get a feeling that this bout of sabotage would feel pretty good.

Allison dug into her coat for the all-purpose Leatherman and folded out the needle-nose pliers. Trudy opened the doors on both sides of the plane and Allison reached around underneath the dash. She pulled down a few wires, unsure of what was what, but remembering an old trick—do not snip a wire in half, but rather cut away a whole long section to make patching more difficult. She cut off a foot-long section of blue wire and a couple of yellows, lifted up the side flaps of the cowling and did the same to a bundle of wires that went around the distributor. She also lopped off a couple of sections of vacuum tubing.

"Nice plane you've got here, Ms. Grumley," said Allison, "but its value seems to be dropping as we speak."

Tethered down, of course, the airplane was harmless, but Allison felt a woozy wave of queasiness from sitting inside the metal machine with wings. They were now sitting in the cockpit, side by side.

"This should hold him up a bit," said Trudy. She was hiding a smile. "How much messing around should we do?"

"You're the one in the pilot's seat," said Allison. "Say when."

"When," said Trudy.

"While we're here . . ." said Allison.

"What?"

"I want to take a peek and see if there's anything of interest."

The rear of the Mooney was seatless and spotless, an open area with two storage bins.

"What's to find?" said Trudy.

"Worth a look," said Allison. On her hands and knees, she lifted up one of the lids on the bin and found a flashlight, rope, mess kit, dried food, a gallon of water, a gallon of fuel mix, a box of shot-gun shells and a funny-looking insulated orange hat with ear flaps.

"Hardly George's style," said Trudy, trying it on.

"Hardly been used," said Allison.

Trudy opened the other bin. "Nothing," she reported, "unless you count an empty cardboard box."

"We could use it to carry our parts," said Allison, referring to the pile of wires and tubes by the front seats.

Trudy lifted the box out.

"Slater?"

"Huh?"

"Isn't that your boyfriend's name?"

"What are you talking about?"

Trudy held up the box so Allison could see the label. It had a bright red business logo on the return address and in smaller black ink the typed name: D. Slater.

Allison blinked.

"Mercy," she whispered incredulously. "Plain old fucking mercy."

****

Police cars with blue lights flashing cruised toward them, driving eastbound in the empty westbound lanes.

Applegate counted eight, a variety of paint jobs—city, county and state. It was as if they had been waiting to make their move. Cop cars pulled up nose to nose with the blockade, lights flashing.

"Don't worry, we've got lawyers standing by," said Ellenberg. "How many can they arrest?"

Dozens of people had worked their way to the front of the line and joined hands, chanting: "Who killed Ray Stern? Who killed Ray Stern? Cops don't care, does anyone care? Who killed Ray Stern?"

The state patrol deferred to the local cops, who were cuffing the protesters holding the largest banner.

"So they arrest 'em, but how are they going to move all the cars?" said Applegate.

"I doubt if they've thought it through," said Ellenberg.

The news crews were right on top of the scene, filming it all.

Sheriff Jerry Sandstrom emerged from the pack of cop cars and walked slowly up as if everything was going according to plan. He hooked his thumbs in his belt buckle, waited through a few more cycles of chanting. He held his hands up like a politician encouraging quiet from an adoring throng.

The protesters raised their voices. The chant went to full shout. Ellenberg was right with it, her voice shrill and piercing. She stepped forward, turned around to her troops and encouraged the voices to crank it up. The din reached a new depth and finally she waved her hands overhead and the chorus broke down to weak fragments and finally stopped.

"Any car without a driver will be impounded," Sandstrom announced. "We have tow trucks standing by." A few more police cars zipped up the highway. "Return to your cars now. Your point has been made."

Nobody moved. A few sat down on the pavement, linked elbows. Ellenberg sat down, crossed her legs.

Applegate didn't feel like sitting. The scene went slightly hazy, unfocused. Sandstrom looked calm, unconcerned.

"We have an announcement on this very matter," said Sandstrom.

Kirkwood snapped his fingers and his cameraman, who had been taking close-ups of protesters on the highway, spun around. Sandstrom apparently knew to wait for the cue.

Applegate had the urge to slip away, start running.

"We have a suspect," said Sandstrom.

A gasp went up. Somebody whistled. Another started clapping.

"It has taken lots of hard work by the staff, but we have a suspect," said Sandstrom.

"How about an arrest?" The voice was shrill, female.

"Yeah, an arrest." This voice was half growl and male.

"We can make that happen," said Sandstrom, but only loud enough for those in the front row to hear.

Sandstrom stepped out from the phalanx of uniforms.

Applegate's legs said *spring*. His heart and mind said the same but he stood there. Climb over the guardrail and dive into the river? His legs flinched to go. Ellenberg stood up.

Sandstrom took three steps to Applegate. They were nose to nose.

"Dean Applegate," said Sandstrom.

Ellenberg stepped closer, looped an arm around Applegate's elbow.

"You are under arrest—"

Cameras were in his face.

"Dean," said Ellenberg, "what is going on?"

"—on suspicion . . . of first degree murder in the death of—"

"Dean?"

"—Ray Stern."

Sandstrom spun him around and clamped a pair of handcuffs on his wrists.

Applegate manufactured a serene look of confidence and leaned down to whisper in Ellenberg's ear. "Don't worry. It's a mix-up."

"What?" said Ellenberg. "What do you mean?"

"It was Fishy's rifle that killed Ray Stern."

"Who?" said Ellenberg. "What?"

****

A whirling series of dire possibilities spun through Allison's head. She imagined Slater doing business with the man who had chased her down, killed Bear and tried to kill her. The same man who probably had something to do with the death of Mr. Deer Suit and Rocky.

She piled up clothing as she fought the tears. She opened the closets and dug under the bed, winging things into a laundry basket as she went, wanting every scrap of her belongings out of Slater's trailer. And her life.

She found a beer, took four long pulls. She started combing through the rest of the place. Pictures, letters, phone numbers—anything might help. She wanted to find the obvious thing she had missed, evidence that had been right under her nose all along.

Allison had swung by 101 East Creek, the address on the label. It was at the edge of a relatively empty street. 101 sat off by itself, a few city blocks from any trailers, tucked down in a stand of old-forest aspens. There were no trailers, just one prefab concrete building thirty yards square with a light green exterior, no signs or windows. Just "101" in cheap stick-on lettering on the door and a large plastic storage bin propped out front. There were three boxes inside the bin, labeled and ready to go: two for Hong Kong, one for Taipei. Waiting for UPS.

The building stayed with her as she went to Slater's trailer and dug around: a stack of letters in a straw box; bills; gas station credit cards; phone, electric, Visa statements; a few scraps of paper with names and numbers. Nothing sinister. In the bedroom, she dug through the built-in dresser, four drawers in a stack. All clothes and no surprises. She had met lots of hunters in the camps and out on the trail. His type was rare. Too soft, right? Too with-it, right? Too complex. No. She had mistaken terse for complex. Boy Scout? Right.

She ripped through a closet, thinking back to whether she'd

been manipulated and remembering times he'd talked about his philosophy. She'd been duped. She started to cry, frustrated by her failure to have seen the real David Slater.

In the kitchen, checking the cupboards for the hell of it, she fought the compulsion to bolt. Trudy had said she would follow in an hour, after swinging by to check on the cats. But how long would she really be? What if she had a seizure? What if George found her?

Allison found a round paper tag the size of a quarter dangling on a nail on the inside of a cupboard. "101" was written in pencil, and a key was attached.

Allison was back inside her car without remembering how she got there. Her world was doing that flippity-flop thing again, and she thought she tasted saltwater. She took a quick breath and tried to bring things back into focus.

David Slater. A screwed-up ranger. She had heard stories about antler dust, rumors that you could move the stuff if you wanted, rumors that you could pad your income. But nobody really knew how or where. It was one of those whispers in the wind, nothing she had ever tried to pin down. Jesus, the money. Where were the profits stashed? Why the cheap trailer housing?

The key fit into the lock. The room was dark. Her fingers groped for the light switch along the cool concrete wall.

The interior was like somebody's messy basement, except for the scale of the operation. The work area was confined to a corner of the interior. Tall steel shelving defined the space on one side. Stacks of empty boxes, not much bigger than those needed to mail wristwatches, were stacked on the shelves. She found spools of twine and other threads, straight needles and round ones, and a series of knives and heavy-duty scissors. She squatted down in the middle of the room and picked up a clump of brown hair. Straight hair, tipped white. Deer fur.

In the middle of the workspace stood a piece of industrial machinery with a motor at the bottom of a huge steel bowl, like a bread mixer. Through a fist-sized hole at the bottom of the bowl, two gears with sharp teeth were hooked to the motor. Below the bowl, a collection bin. Light tan dust coated both the bowl and the bin. In the other corner there was a shelf full of plastic vials, nothing special. Also empty. There was a giant plastic bag full of Styrofoam peanuts, strung upside down from the ceiling. A flexible tube at the bottom of the bag worked as a dispenser. She kept getting whiffs of her high school biology class: formaldehyde. She realized Slater saw more profits in the pieces than in the whole. Her head buzzed with fury. Equipment went toppling and flying. Her vision blurred with tears and anger.

✱✱✱✱

"You found a rifle and it isn't mine," Applegate said.

"We've also got Mr. Marcovicci willing to testify that he sold it to you three years ago during one of your annual trips up here. Where were you on the day Ray Stern died?"

Sandstrom had his foot hitched up on a chair. Another cop stood by the door.

"Off on a hike," said Applegate.

"Oh right," said Sandstrom. "All the other boys are cooling their heels in the tent and you decide to go out and take a stroll. We're supposed to buy that one, special discount for stupidity? You didn't take a rifle along just in case? What if your luck changed while you were out there and you saw this good-looking animal and you didn't have your rifle? What then? You'd feel kind of silly, wouldn't you?"

They had been at it for over an hour, in an empty office near the building where the parking-lot protest had been held. A plain metal table separated him from Sandstrom, who was working up a good rage. The trip in the police car to this place had been a blur. He couldn't wipe Ellenberg's puzzled look from his mind.

The rifle was supposed to have been in the barn. Now the police had it? Or said they did. He wanted to look relaxed, but couldn't begin to find that gear.

"I took a hike," said Applegate. It sounded good, but he didn't hear the level of confident assertion he wanted.

"We got everybody else accounted for at the time Ray Stern was killed, about noon. He was shot before it started snowing. And the route he took, it must've taken three or four hours for him to get from his tent to there. It ain't like auto mechanics, figuring this stuff out. So we got everybody else accounted for, every other person in Ripplecreek, except you. And you're out for a stroll."

"Except Grumley."

Sandstrom stopped, straightened up, hitched up his belt, walked around in a small circle and leaned back against the wall.

"And how exactly do you know *this*?" he said.

"He left that morning too."

"And didn't come back?"

"Nope."

"At all?"

"No—"

"But you're off on a hike smelling the pine cones."

"I ran into him."

"Where?"

"On the main trail."

"What time?"

"It was snowing pretty good by then, two or three maybe."

"And where was he going?"

"I don't know."

"Or coming from?"

"Farther up on top, I suppose."

"And what difference does any of this make?" said Sandstrom.

"He seemed agitated," said Applegate. "Very."

"Okay," said Sandstrom. "We'll talk to the world-class hunter and see what he knows."

"No, really."

"Look," said Sandstrom. He opened the door, disappeared for a count of no more than five, stepped back into the room and swung the butt end of the rifle around so it was an inch from Applegate's face.

"We got Marcovicci's testimony," said Sandstrom. "He sold it to you." Sandstrom glowered. He stared and waited. Applegate said nothing while his mind raced away, looking for a way out.

"All the guys in the tent remembered," said Sandstrom. "George Grumley uses a different caliber rifle, a .270. The caliber on this Sako matches exactly the caliber of the bullet we pulled from Ray Stern's body. The bullet was resting against his spine. It plugged. It matches. You gave us this yarn about walking with your rifle back up the hill and tossing it off an unknown cliff. Pure bullshit."

Sandstrom tossed the rifle down on the table. The noisy clatter made Applegate jump.

"Fucking wasted our time," said Sandstrom. "Your whole charade. Joining the animal rights bozos because you had a change of *heart*? How about the guilt factor bursting your head?"

From deep inside him, the stored-up fear was unshackled. It floated up from a dark interior holding tank, an underwater cave where the air bubbles had fought for years for a path to the surface. He couldn't prolong the inevitable any longer.

He had done what Ray Stern had fully intended him to do.

It wasn't cold-blooded murder. More like entrapment or assisted suicide. He knew that.

But now, the embarrassment.

"Okay," said Applegate.  He started to blubber. "Can we make a deal?"

\*\*\*\*

No question that Allison had taken the Sako from the rifle rack. Grumley couldn't figure out why her nose had to be shoved so far into it. Was it a thrill? He couldn't imagine that she would return to her A-frame any time soon. The Sako was already in the hands of the cops.

Time to go. All-the-way go. He should have put the screws to Allison when he had a chance. And Applegate. And Popeye. Like he did with Alvin.

His own house was too depressing, with Trudy's cats in charge. The chorus of meows was nonstop. He couldn't believe he had bothered to check to see if they had enough food. It pissed him off to see that their bowls were topped off. By whom? When?

He needed the fucking banks and his lawyers to get the properties sold, to liquidate. The thought of all the fucking paperwork was a headache, the government making it so complicated, sticking their mitts fucking everywhere. Grumley picked up the phone and dialed his lawyer. He waited through two whole songs and part of a third. How could his own bootlicking lawyer put him on hold?

"George?"

Finally.

"I don't pay you for the privilege of listening to elevator music on the fucking telephone."

Bennie Murdock was small-time, barely legal and on a tidy retainer to advise him on the side about shady transactions.

"Sorry," said Murdock. "Practically everybody down here's been watching the activity up in the canyon. Complete cluster fuck. News footage going viral." Murdock's office was above a restaurant near downtown. "Looked like something out of the goddamn movies. Don't see that too much."

"What's that?"

"They busted this guy out in the middle of the highway, this big traffic jam, I guess it was some sort of animal rights protest. The cops busted one of 'em and carted his butt away."

Applegate. Gone. And he'd be singing soon.

"It's time," said Grumley. He'd have to swing by the barn and grab his favorite rifles.

"Time for what?"

"Bennie—"

"Oh man, punch-out time?"

"Gotta go." There was an old Winchester that had been very reliable.

"All the account numbers the same? Nothing's changed?"

"Yes."

"Prices?"

"I could get more for the store, of course, if it was on the open market. But a deal's a deal."

"I'd give it 120 days for the money to show up in the accounts, once all the deeds get recorded. And then there's the closing dates, all that stuff."

"And you can sell the house, too," said Grumley.

"Your wife going with?" said Murdock, no different than if he was planning a vacation at the beach.

"She's got her own plans," said Grumley. "Besides, to you it doesn't matter where I'm going, right? I could be right here watching you the whole time, a member of the ethics panel of the Colorado Bar Association, here to make sure you ain't fucking your clients."

Grumley heard a snort-like laugh, a cautious one.

"And how will I know I've got the right buyer?" said Murdock.

"Because he'll walk in one day soon, probably within a week. His checkbook will be wide open and he'll know the exact price. He'll be the only one. I guarantee it."

"Well, safe travels."

He slammed down the phone, dialed another number and told whoever answered, as calmly as he could, to get David Slater.

"Can I help you?" answered Slater.

"Hey little buddy, you fuck."

"Always nice to hear your voice, Grumley. Did you hear that your good friend, the animal rights prince, got picked up?"

"Yeah, yeah, what's he saying?"

"I'd have to be a cop to know the answer to that one."

"Thought you had access."

"Only when I need it."

"The kid's clueless."

"What did you have against Rocky Carnivitas?" said Slater.

"He was going to blow my fucking head off. Thought he was standing up for Trudy, for Chrissakes, and he wanted a piece of the action for his troubles. Totally self-defense."

"I'm sure the world's a better place."

"Where's my wife?" said Grumley.

"Wouldn't have a clue," said Slater. "So you're out of here?"

"See Bennie Murdock in about a week. Money goes into the right accounts, it's all yours."

Slater would be king, thought Grumley. He would inherit all the custom hunts, all the hot shots, all the antler traffic. He would control the market.

"Is Sandstrom cool?" said Grumley.

"I should think so," said Slater. "He's got his plum. The media boys have the picture of the sheriff collaring his man."

Grumley thought about mentioning how pissed off he was at

Slater's little buddy, Allison Coil. But let him find out on his own that she was piecing things together. By then, he'd be trading in his plane for scrap in Spokane, Alaska-bound.

Grumley wildly packed clothes in a big laundry bag and dug out a small stash of twenties from a cigar box. He'd been building up a supply for years. The last time he checked it was fifteen thousand dollars, enough to keep him liquid for a few months, pay for plane fuel and cover whatever else would come up. He climbed into his truck and sped first to the barn and next to the airport. Only a matter of minutes now, he told himself, and he would be soaring above this mess.

He bolted through the doors to the tarmac, hustled out, but could see from a distance that the cowling was up and wide open to the sky.

"Fuck!" he yelled.

Back to the terminal. The asshole, that meek little airport man, stood by the door quaking.

"Your best mechanic. Now."

"It's his day off."

"Now," said Grumley.

"He doesn't live too far—"

"And I'm leaving a pile of stuff here. I want it loaded when he's done. I'll call in a couple hours when it's finished."

"Couple?"

"Yeah, two. Couple. One, two. Who fucked with my plane?"

"Nobody. Your wife came by, wanted to show it to this other woman. I didn't know you had it for sale."

"How long ago was this?"

"A few hours ago."

"I'll be back in two hours," said Grumley. "An extra hundred for you if it's working by then. Whatever it takes. Fix it. Good as fucking new, okay?"

Back in his pickup he concentrated on the loose ends, imagining Applegate talking and wondering if anybody would make anything of it. And who was there to hear it?

At some point, Applegate would think clearly enough to hire a decent lawyer and offer a trade of information. Even Applegate would have to take that bait, tell 'em how his old pal George helped eat the dead guy's lunch and took the Sako off his hands.

His truck skidded and bounced as he flew. He would leave it all behind, that was for sure. At a gas station Grumley slammed the truck to a stop near a phone booth. He put two quarters in and dialed.

"Slater, please."

"Just left. Can I take a message?"

He crunched the phone back in the cradle, dug for more quarters, dialed Slater's number, listened to it ring and the voice mail beep.

He spoke: "My wife's going back in the bottle. I think I know how to find her. She's not going to like the fit. You might want to take care of that little Coil chick. Okay?"

The second he hung up he realized he should never have left such a stupid message anywhere. He kicked the truck door with his boot, good enough to make a dent and rattle his ankle. It would cost him an hour to and from Slater's place to fix the mistake.

\*\*\*\*

The radio switched from Dwight Yoakam to national network news. Top of the hour. Trudy tweaked the dial to improve the reception as she maneuvered through the canyon.

Bombing in Tel Aviv, floods in Virginia, the president worried about unemployment numbers. The announcer said there was an arrest, an update on the case of that "odd, somewhat bizarre, so-called creative suicide by the animal rights activist last month near Glenwood Springs, Colorado."

Trudy reached for the volume.

". . . Police here in Glenwood Springs are now questioning thirty-eight-year-old Dean Applegate, arrested during a massive protest on the interstate inside Glenwood Canyon. The one-time hunter turned activist was leading the demonstration for FATE when he was arrested. Police have not yet indicated if he is coop-erating. Other activists said they were sure it was an unfortunate mix-up, but FATE leader Dawn Ellenberg, who has not usually been difficult to find, was not available for comment tonight in Glenwood Springs."

Allison's rifle, no doubt, thought Trudy. It paid off. She wondered if the pieces would come around and grab up George in Applegate's mess and Stern's death. If they could find George. The key now was to hook back up with Allison; it was unsafe to hang around the house alone.

The first stop was Wal-Mart. Trudy had checked George's handgun, which was curiously empty.

"I need ammunition for this," said Trudy. She looked around, not wanting anyone other than the salesman back in sporting goods to see. She lifted the pistol from her pocket a bit so the kid could get a look at it.

"Ma'am, really, it's not a good idea to be walking around with a concealed—"

"Tell me what I need, please." She smiled as calmly as she could manage.

"In Colorado it's not legal to—"

"Help me, please," said Trudy.

The kid eyed the gun. "44 mag. Jesus. I could get in trouble; just remember I never saw that."

Back in the 4Runner she loaded the gun below the dashboard,

keeping an eye on shoppers coming and going. She felt as if she had swallowed a large stone that was growing in her stomach. Oddly, even as her hands shook, her head felt clear and serene. Things were coming to a head.

****

On top of the television there was an envelope, ragged at the seam and open. Allison picked it up, still searching for what she had missed, determined to uncover any scrap in the trailer. Jitters chewed at her insides. She read the return address. She had to read it twice before it sank in.

Pete Weaver. The Weaver Ranch. 40 Ripplecreek.

"*Mr. Slater.*"

Her eyes flicked down to Pete's signature. She recognized the distinctive cursive from her paychecks.

"This letter is to confirm acceptance of your offer."

Her eyes absorbed the date. The letter was a month old.

"*. . . I know it's been six months since we broke off talks. If you are still interested . . .*"

Her brain would not let her digest every word.

"*. . . purchasing my property. I'm ready . . . The last price you offered is acceptable . . .*"

Her eyes leapt to the only figure on the page.

"*. . . $1.5 million . . .*"

There was discussion of earnest money, ten percent. How to deliver it and when. And if not delivered in two weeks, "*I'll put the property on the open market . . . Let me know . . . Sincerely . . .*"

Weaver was selling the largest property in the valley to a man with an antler dust factory. Allison thought of Weaver's prime property and the fact that permits for guides were not held by individuals; they were sold with property as part of the package.

That was the way it worked. Weaver would have no idea about Slater's real business, would he?

She dialed Weaver's number while she stared at the blinking light of the old-fashioned answering machine, one of those separate boxes that attached to the line and recorded messages on a tiny cassette. A light blinked. It was a light that had not been there earlier when she'd headed down to the factory. She stood in the kitchen getting a whiff of something moldy from the sink, steadying herself for an answer she couldn't stand to hear, searching for the words to ask the question.

Three blinks of the red light for each ring in her ear. Another ring.

*Blink . . . blink . . . blink.*

No answer.

Hang up.

*Blink.*

She pressed play.

"My wife's going back in the bottle."

The unmistakable voice.

"I think I know how to find her. She's not going to like the fit . . ."

She shuddered at the venom in the words.

"You might want to take care of that Coil chick. Okay?"

The door opened behind her and she spun around.

"David! I was just . . ."

"You were just . . .?"

It was Grumley, dripping ugly.

"Find anything?" He looked at the pile of stuff on the bedroom floor.

"Why are you here?" she said.

"What did you see on the mountain?"

"I saw you. Dragging Rocky."

"Rocky was a loser and an asshole."

"You killed Bear."

"Just another animal."

"So it's any animal any old day? You and Slater both?"

"So what?"

"All the land and all the animals are there for you and you alone?"

"No. For whoever gets 'em first. Winter gets 'em. A wolf gets 'em. Or I do."

"I think you got more problems than me seeing you dragging Rocky. There's Applegate. Between the two of us . . ."

"The fuck I care."

He stepped toward her. She backed up to the bedroom, thinking weapon or windows. Those options were so weak they were practically nonexistent.

# 16

Stopped at a traffic light, snug up behind a big RV, Trudy studied the stickers on the bumper in front of her. *My Family Dug The Grand Canyon. You'll Feel Peachy in Georgia.* And others: *Carmel, Seattle, Juneau, Parris Island.* The RV's plates were from Arkansas.

She couldn't imagine a life on the road yet, a home on the highway. Too much dread blurred that vision.

The lane of cars next to her started to move, but the large land yacht didn't budge. Now its flashers came on. Trudy slapped the wheel with her palm and checked the rearview mirror as the line behind her began to peel off from the rear and move forward. Eight cars to go.

Trudy felt a cloud pushing its way into her brain, the swirl of excitement loading up. She couldn't tell if this was the brink of a seizure or if she was seeing things more clearly. One blink brought light, the next darkness.

Her breath came in small gulps.

Five cars.

Her mind tried to anticipate what was next, but she worked to stay within the moment. There was a funny taste in her mouth that was either working its way down her throat or working its way up.

Three cars.

She checked the pistol again, resting on the seat underneath a T-shirt.

One car.

Finally she backed up enough to give herself room to maneuver. She came up alongside the RV, ready to gun it, but the light was red again. The elderly driver had the hood up and was poking around the engine. The man's wife caught Trudy's eyes and scowled.

The light cycled around again. Trudy pulled out as quickly as she could manage without causing a stir. The 4Runner whined up, a fine blue mist of exhaust chasing her down the highway.

She turned off toward the Blue Sky Trailer Park. The car shuddered over a cattle guard, hit the dirt road. Her rear window was quickly coated with a swirl of red-rock dust. In the distance she saw the entrance to the trailer park. She tried to picture staying focused, tried to picture staying focused, tried to picture staying focused.

\*\*\*\*

Grumley stepped up and swatted her down, one sweep of his arm knocking her off balance. She grappled for a soft landing on the couch but her head went first and her neck jammed.

The gun was in his right hand by the time she looked up. She grabbed the side of her neck as it pulsed in agony. His fist and gun came through the air and Allison rolled. She tried to jab his leg with hers. She jumped off the couch, staggered to her feet. A lamp on a side table crashed over as she dodged a windmilling arm. Grumley was like a bear standing one-legged on a rock in the river swatting at a bee. Allison dove at him, hitting his shoulder. He went down, his head slamming a shelf with an ugly thud.

The pistol went off. Allison's ears rang and it suddenly she was underwater, slow motion and flipperless, unable to find a center of gravity.

She checked herself for bullet holes. None. No blood.

Grumley got up on his knees. Allison turned for the door. He grabbed her legs. She kicked backwards, felt her boot land a satisfying blow to his face.

"Fucker!" Grumley growled.

Allison raced for the door, bounded through.

And encountered a beautiful sight.

\*\*\*\*

Trudy startled as the door burst open, but held her ground. Allison ran behind her.

George was right behind, staggering.

He stopped.

"What the f—"

She raised the gun so the muzzle was square with his nose.

"Trudy," he said with disdain. "You've been sticking your nose where it doesn't belong."

He was shifting now, moving away, daring her to shoot.

"Shit, Trudy, whatchya' doing?"

"The obvious."

"Nobody saw nothing," he spewed.

A tear shuddered up inside her, with anger and images of Rocky.

"For a pittance you could have fixed me up," she said. "A little scrap. And you'd be on your way outta here. Gone. Do you believe that? Do you know that?"

"Always knew it was an option. And Rocky pressed the point, although he wanted a huge chunk of cash for his troubles to keep quiet about something or other."

"So you saw—"

"Never said I saw anybody anywhere."

"A pittance, George."

"Shit," said Grumley. "You have it easy. What are you gonna do?" He turned and headed to his truck. "Nothing is what you're gonna do."

Aiming was easy.

So was pulling the trigger.

She watched him reel and flop down to the dirt. She kept the gun on him as he crumpled and yelled in agony.

"Don't worry," she said, "it's only an ankle."

She stepped over to her husband, who was scraping his way along the dirt. He winced in pain, his face a wicked snarl. He dug into the ground with his hands and good leg. He crawled toward the truck, attempted to stand and collapsed. Blood oozed from his ankle.

"A scrap," shouted Trudy

"Shit. My leg."

"A scrap," said Trudy.

George Grumley spread himself out on the ground, one hand searching for a grip on the tread of the truck tire. His face turned upward, pleading.

Trudy sensed Allison at her side.

Defeat edged across her husband's face. It was a look she'd never seen before.

"You're going where I've been," said Trudy. "Only yours will have real guards and lots of barbed wire."

\*\*\*\*

The neighbors stood around watching, including one grizzled old man in a tight white T-shirt who tried to take charge, fetching bandages for Grumley and telling other neighbors to go down to the entrance and point the way for the cops and the ambulance to make it in as quickly as possible. The man smoked as he worked, keeping others at a distance, barking out orders like he'd seen it all before. The cops had split into two groups: one at 101 East Table, the other with Sandstrom overseeing the search of the trailer.

Allison leaned on Trudy's 4Runner and looked back into the eyes of neighbors who were staring at the scene and wondering what all this could be about.

Trudy was inside her truck, sobbing quietly. Allison went to join her, thinking about Pete Weaver. She had tried his number right after she'd called 911. No answer.

"You heard they arrested Applegate?" said Trudy. "And the reporter said he was cooperating."

"Sandstrom mentioned it," said Allison. "I don't think he's too happy with this happening now, drawing attention from his big bust. You okay?"

"I suppose. How's George?"

"He's hurting. You did what you had to do."

"I could have let the cops chase him, catch him. It felt so easy, shooting him. Too easy."

"George would be long gone if you hadn't shot him. It might have ended up being a bigger mess."

"What about your David?"

"That's next," said Allison. "Finding him."

An hour later, Sandstrom arrived and went over the statements, realizing there would be no way to charge Trudy with anything, realizing that Allison had fought in self-defense and that Grumley would probably face attempted murder.

Slater's boss Bridgers arrived after the ambulance had departed and Sandstrom asked Allison to go over again how she had found out about the secret factory. Nothing about the factory needed explaining. Bridgers had four other rangers in tow and they were quickly on their own radios, calling for an evidence crew. After the tour of the antler dust factory, Bridgers sighed with extreme exasperation.

"Check the Polaroids," said Allison, pointing to the bulletin board. "Couple shots of him grinning with hunters."

The neighbors had all drifted away. The unnecessary cops had gone back to other assignments. The initial furor was dying down.

"This day is like a sack of woe," said Sandstrom. "Trouble follows me wherever I go."

"Been a busy one," said Allison.

They were all huddled around Sandstrom's car, wondering what Sandstrom would do next.

"You gotta find Slater, too," said Trudy.

"Check," said Sandstrom. "We could put out an all points bulletin but Slater's probably listening on his own damn radio, but I don't know how else to alert the others."

Sandstrom barked into his radio. Sandstrom's limits had finally been reached. He was pissed. Sandstrom spoke in code and numbers, but they all got the gist of his message to the others: find and stop David Slater.

"I've got something else to show you," said Allison to Sandstrom.

She led him inside Slater's trailer and pulled Weaver's letter from her pocket.

"I found this sitting on the television," she said. "It was open."

Sandstrom scanned the letter.

"So Slater's profits from his exports were going to buy a base for his empire?" said Sandstrom.

"I've been trying to reach Pete Weaver on the telephone," said Allison. "I'm worried. I'm positive Weaver has no clue what Slater is really doing."

"You'd have an easier time getting a bird to stop flying than you would corrupting Pete Weaver," said Sandstrom. "Everybody knows that."

"Something doesn't feel right," said Allison. "I'm going up there."

"Well," said Sandstrom, "I think we're done here anyway. Hard to believe this day has one more surprise, but right about now I wouldn't bet more than a nickel on that."

Allison took a minute to tell Trudy they were going to check on something back up in the valley and that she'd catch up with her soon. Trudy said she'd head back home and they hugged. Trudy started to cry. She patted her heart as if she might be able to find the handle to the faucet, to turn off the tears. But it wasn't anywhere to be found. In fact, it had the opposite effect. And Allison gave her another hug.

"I'm not sure I did the right thing," sobbed Trudy.

"When it comes time to hurt somebody, I don't think most good people know," said Allison.

Allison climbed into Sandstrom's police car, slowly letting go of Trudy's hand, knowing there was at least one person she could trust.

✳✳✳✳

Sandstrom drove within the speed limits. Allison wanted him to dig in his spurs and give it a kick. They had turned off the interstate and were heading up toward Ripplecreek.

"I say you go up to Lizard's Tongue next spring and dig around after the snow's melted," she said. "Look where Rocky landed. Near where that elk was, you'll find the shells from the bullets that killed Rocky. They'll be Grumley's."

"We got Applegate," said Sandstrom. "One step at a time."

Allison had tried her how-Grumley-and-Applegate-might-have-hooked-up theory on Sandstrom. He mulled it over like a professor digesting a crazy theory from a challenging student.

"He's a steady fountain of interesting information," said Sandstrom. "Just like that, information just flowing out of him. But I'm having trouble figuring out David Slater."

"We can form a club," said Allison. "I'll be president."

"Ranger wages aren't much, but forest rangers are usually straight arrows who love the outdoors. You're more likely to encounter a corrupt cop in the city."

"You've never been tempted?" said Allison.

"Sweetie, the world is full of people who try to influence you. Some days you feel like nailing every speeder going a whisker over the limit. The next you couldn't care less if they're turning Main Street into the Indy 500. I can't say I've looked as hard into every questionable allegation as maybe I should have. But you can only do so much. Government in general, it can only do so much. People like Slater, flaunting it, doing their own trip, clearly operating outside the law. That's a different story altogether."

Allison leaned forward and took a deep breath, wishing she could will Sandstrom into picking up the pace, wondering if she was being given a line. Nothing made sense, particularly the greed. She kept seeing Grumley killing Rocky and later running into Applegate, the beginning of the end for Grumley, too many pieces starting to fray.

Sandstrom parked forty yards away from a point where the skirt of porch light flared out from the house.

"It's Slater's pickup," said Allison.

"Forest Service anyway," said Sandstrom. "No jumping to conclusions."

"Shit," said Allison, hopping out.

"Wait," said Sandstrom. He turned to grab his shotgun off the rack.

Allison bounded ahead, then waited while Sandstrom ambled out. It might not be a bad idea to work together. Sandstrom put his hand on the hood of Slater's pickup and nodded his head to say 'yes.' It was still warm.

Sandstrom led the way into the glassed-in porch. Wicker chairs and a wicker couch, large plants, a hammock. The door to the house was ajar. Sandstrom gave it a shoulder and it stopped.

"Christ," he said, giving it a heave so Allison could squeeze under his arm and in.

Pete Weaver was on the floor behind the door. He stared back, but he wasn't seeing anything. His legs climbed the wall, his forehead was gone. His arms went directions they shouldn't.

Allison backpedaled and went faint.

A drawer or door slammed shut and she heard a muffled shout. The cry came from deep within the giant house, maybe upstairs. Dishes and books were piled up on the floor, tossed haphazardly. Stuff was strewn everywhere.

"Weaver's behind the door," said Allison. She was back on the porch, catching her breath. "Dead." Each word was a struggle.

"I'm going in," said Sandstrom, backing up against the door, pushing hard, and squeezing through. Allison followed.

A gentle gurgle came from the kitchen. Sandstrom went first, shotgun at his waist. Allison stayed in the shadow of his frame.

"Something on the stove," said Sandstrom. "Beans."

Sandstrom crossed the kitchen to turn off the gas. "Basic fire prevention there," he whispered. A back door from the kitchen led to a dining room and Sandstrom started that way when Slater stepped out of the shadow holding a rifle by the barrel and the stock already on the move like a baseball bat, catching Sandstrom's head flush and hard with an ugly, wet smack. Sandstrom crumpled in a heap.

"Allison," said Slater. A butcher-block table separated them. He looked relaxed, at ease. "I love these big houses with the back staircases."

Sandstrom lay in a lump. Allison backed away from the table.

Slater plucked the shotgun from Sandstrom's hands and put it up on the counter behind him.

"I had it all arranged for us," he said. "We were going to be set up for life." This was delivered as matter-of-fact. He could have been stating requests for a grocery list.

"We?"

"You and I. The whole valley. We would have run the whole valley."

"What does that mean, run the valley?"

"Make money, enjoy ourselves," said Slater.

"There never were any biologists or researchers."

"Oh, well, probably not," said Slater. "But how do you know? Know for sure? That's government information."

"Do you know who strung me up from that tree?"

"Not me," said Slater. "Not for sure. But you might ask George Grumley. He'd probably have an idea."

There was a taste of seawater in her mouth; was that possible? And a wet sensation from her clothes, but maybe this time she wouldn't be able to swim, keep her head screwed on straight.

"Why?" she asked.

"Why what?"

As if nothing had happened.

"Why all this?"

"Oh, I could tell you a story, little missy, make your hair curl."

"Try me."

Hands behind her, fingers feeling for something useful, anything.

"A story about the government," said Slater.

"Who cuts your paycheck," said Allison.

"Fuckers, that's who," said Slater, still calm. He was spinning a campfire tale, nothing more. "The government. Govern nothing. Swiped my parents' land. Section 9 of the Endangered Species Act of 1973, as amended. But the government wouldn't issue a special rule pursuant to Section 4-d. No 4-d, land gone. 4-d, 4-d, fucking 4-d. Here's your compensation, your land is gone, and they pay a nickel for every dollar it's worth. Timberland. Ten thousand acres of prime timberland, a retirement bank account, ready to sell for harvest. Land that climbed a gorgeous hillside in the western Cascades. Everything mortgaged to the hilt for this tidy little investment. Little, hell. Gone. The owls won. The government won."

"Jesus," said Allison. "Revenge?"

"Revenge, shit," said Slater. "Just playing within the same bendable rules. They rip off my family for their political needs, and that's money. I play with the wilderness, hurt nobody, and that's money. My parents had the bad luck—God rest their weary souls—to buy land in what became an SEA, a Special Emphasis Area. Where the fucking Forest Service had determined that it was necessary and advisable, based on God knows whose advice, to apply broad protection—"

He stopped. He sucked in a sharp breath and let it settle. Allison let her hands drift behind her on the counter, wondering if there might be a knife rack.

"—from incidental take. Incidental take to protect a few spotted owls."

"No different than a little incidental take on the Flat Tops?"

"Where there's plenty of deer and elk and nothing's endangered. Nothing."

"Jesus," said Allison again. "Rocky was 'incidental take'?"

"Ask Grumley about his own damn feelings about Rocky. Not my business. However, based on what I know, I wouldn't say the victim was innocent."

"Just hunt anything anywhere, anytime?"

"You're a stickler like old Mr. Weaver, I suppose."

"Selling antler dust to the Asians?"

"Just another market. And where's the harm?"

Her fingers were coming up empty. She needed a weapon, something. She scooted a couple of inches to the stove, tried to make it look like she was shifting weight.

"It's all come apart. You're done," she said.

"I'm going to find my cash and be gone. You're my last problem."

"Problem?"

"You're certainly not part of the solution, showing up here with this oaf," said Slater.

"You betrayed everything."

"I was waiting until it was all mine."

Feeling the handle of the pot of beans behind her, the question in her mind was whether it had boiled down too much. The mess flew easily. Slater gagged and shouted as the hot beans coated his face. Allison scrambled around the corner of the butcher block and ran for the door, avoiding any glance at Weaver's body. There was no way around it. Weaver's weight had pushed the door shut and his body blocked it. She had struggled to pull it open. His corpse was a perfect doorstop.

Slater was coming after her as she squeezed through.

The ignition in Slater's pickup held no keys. She checked Sandstrom's car. It was keyless too, but a gun, gleaming chrome in a holster, sat on the floor. She grabbed the gun, let the holster drop off.

She ran down the driveway, thinking she might be able to out-hoof Slater to Weaver's barn. Her legs churned, fueled by fear. She gasped for breath but her legs worked as if they didn't really care if they got oxygen or not. The long dirt driveway turned dark, the glow of Weaver's place faded. As she was swallowed up by the night, a rifle shot cracked behind her. She ran harder, waiting for the next bullet to fly. Zig two steps, zag three.

She slowed. A car started up. Allison risked a glance around as headlights flicked on and she was in the crosshairs of the light.

The barn loomed ahead. She tried to outrun the edge of the light, her lungs heaving and burning. The pickup roared, the lights flicking onto high beams and splashing her shadow across the side of the barn. She reached the door, flipped the latch up and stumbled inside.

A light from the inner office cast a faint glow on the far side of the cavern. A horse snorted. She could see the animals in their stalls and wondered if one of them could spirit her away, bareback. She ran across the floor looking for a place to hide and wondering if a stall would do. The horses would give her away. Hayloft? No way out. Tack room? No cover, nothing. She kept moving, searching.

She reached the far door and threw it open, wondering if Slater might assume she had run through the barn if she left it open.

Slater's car skidded to a stop outside, the engine snapped off. He shouted something and she heard her name muffled in the yell.

The barn was open and empty except for the five elk sleeping on the floor in a corner.

Skins—hides spread out in heaps.

She heard the door swing open and she dropped, lying flat on the floor. She rolled over between the fourth and last skins, yanking the clumpy wrinkles of one of them over her body.

The warm, fleshy feel of the hide and the light odor of salt enveloped Allison as she froze, hoping Slater would sprint through the door she had left open, to chase madly after her into the darkness.

"Allison?"

Slater's voice was close, too close. And calm. He wasn't going to be fooled by an open door. She kept a vise-like grip on the gun. She could hear him stepping through the barn and tried to let her weight sink into the straw beneath the skin.

"I know you're in here," he said.

Allison clutched the gun at her knees.

One door opened and slammed shut, perhaps the closet where they hung the rain gear. Next it would be the tack room.

Allison's heart throbbed and she worked to keep its shock waves from rippling through her body.

She heard him rustling around. Two minutes or two seconds, she couldn't be sure. Her mind raced off to a place that was dark blue and peppered with stray, uncontrollable flashes of purple and black. Salt on her tongue. Panic balled up in her throat. Her eyes strained for an opening in the dense skin. She tried not to inhale. She heard the metallic *ching, ching* of knife on sharpener. The sound had to be the Buck knives, stored in slits in a big chunk of wood in the tack room. *Ching.*

But he has a rifle.

What the . . .

"Nice blades."

Her grip on the gun tightened.

"Nice skins, too."

Voice above her.

Something went *whomp* on the ground. Nearby. Very close. Maybe he had dropped to his knees. The sound was to her left. Every muscle in her body wanted to spin away from the noise, to react.

She stayed put.

"Nice skins, all salted out."

She heard the sound of knife cutting through fur and drying elk flesh, a soft but violent sound. He gasped and struggled.

"I smell you. Female mixed with fear," he said. "Very distinct. Well, this one's empty."

Two skins to go. Or three?

"Too bad," he said. "Just too bad. We had it all, Allison."

The next skin was getting carved up. His voice sounded wet and slobbery.

"I had it all figured."

Was he sniffling?

One to go?

She heard him stand up, or thought she did. She listened to the terrible silence for a long second and heard him drop to the elk skin next to her, plunging the knife, jabbing and ripping and flailing the skin and grunting as he worked to slice it.

She aimed in her mind first. She stuck her head out and poked the gun upwards from beneath the skin. Slater stared at the spot that rose toward him like a leather volcano. His mouth opened and he started to raise the knife. And started to say something.

Allison fired.

Slater staggered back, his body slammed into the wall. He sagged to the floor.

Allison slumped, shuddering.

She crawled away and stood up, didn't look back. This time, for once, she realized she wasn't wondering whether all the pieces should be put back together.

# 17

It was high noon, and the streak of warmish air teased them with spring, still months away. Allison wanted something to melt, something around her to change dramatically, but that would be many moons away.

Trudy sat bundled up next to her on Allison's front porch. They sipped giant cups of strong black coffee. An old quilt was wrapped around their legs. Allison tipped her head back against the wall to soak up the low-slanting sun, which added an ounce of warmth to the midday breeze.

The authorities had all come running when Allison called in breathlessly for help from Weaver's house. Sandstrom was making his way to his feet, groggy and plenty pissed. He needed attention from an EMT, a few bandages. The interviews had lasted all evening, well into the night.

When they were finally done, Allison had shared her bed with Trudy, who had come up the valley after hearing the commotion on the news. Trudy slept, at least for awhile. Allison hadn't managed sleep. She was unable to shake the idea she'd taken a life, no matter the situation.

Now, the coffee helped. Allison knew she needed rest, but that would come eventually. An occasional police car cruised up and down the road. They counted four news trucks, too.

"How are you doing?" said Allison.

"Okay," said Trudy. "Better. You?"

"Weird. Sad," said Allison. "Mostly sad. Very, very sad. Pete Weaver deserved so much better. And it's so hard to understand why I never saw what Slater was up to."

"Don't beat yourself up," said Trudy. "You've got competition when it comes to being a bad judge of character."

"I should have stopped to put a few things together, really taken a hard look," said Allison.

"You did good," said Trudy. "You were right all along. Don't forget that."

"If you insist," said Allison.

"You took off his mask," said Trudy. "Their whole scheme is done."

"Until someone else decides to find a way around the law," said Allison. "Quite the racket they set up."

Trudy shook her head. "Terrible," she said.

Some day down the road, Allison knew deep remorse would surface, most likely when she least expected it and when it was most inconvenient. For now, there were too many *what ifs* to run down and digest in order to nail the appropriate emotion. Feeling good about being right was in the mix, too, and that didn't suck.

"Now it's time for me to get back," said Trudy.

"Back home?"

"Back to my animals."

"A good idea," said Allison. "I'll take you. Can I help?"

"Sure," said Trudy. "I also want to make a few calls down to Denver, see about an appointment to get this brain fixed."

Allison smiled, offered Trudy a hug. "Seems like a reasonable idea to me," she said.

\*\*\*\*

In the late spring, when the snows up high had given up their grip on the warming earth, Allison rode up to Black Squirrel Pass. She came up the long way around. She stopped her horse, McCartney, about where she figured she had been when she saw Grumley dragging Rocky's limp body across the rocks.

Allison matched her memory with her current field of view, now on the cusp of green. The air was clear. She imagined Rocky and Grumley tangling on the trail, the shot being fired. Heard it in her head, the dull echo.

She walked McCartney down and around, a faint wisp of apple or pear and muddy earth in the air.

Everything was wrapped up. Grumley's federal trial for illegal exports was a few months off. But nobody argued the resolution of that case, especially with the murder charge tacked on. Bobby Alvin's body had been found. Applegate had been dealt with a few minor charges and faced a suspended two-year sentence while he was out on probation. He was fined twenty thousand dollars. Grumley's ranch was sold.

Trudy had made it for two whole months without a seizure. Before the sale of her house, Trudy's kitchen had become a frequent tea stop for Allison, who was starting to get to know the cats by name. Plants, too, by type. She'd never met anybody who defined the phrase "new lease on life" as much as Trudy did. In fact, Allison had taken her on a cool, late-spring camping trip on horseback. They wound up around a campfire in a high clearing and shared stories late into the night. Trudy confessed it was her first night out in the open since high school.

Allison stood on Lizard's Tongue and gazed out over the valley. She wound her way down to the picked-over elk carcass, now a mess of bones. The bulletless elk surely indicated where they had tangled, where Grumley had confronted Rocky.

She stood away from the heart of the bunker, wondering how many paces Grumley might have taken before aiming his rifle at Rocky. She strolled around, her eyes casually glancing down here and there, thinking it would be a small miracle if she spotted anything, but it was possible. The bullet shells that held Rocky's fate were right here, in this spot. Grumley had probably tied Rocky up and dragged him to get him off the main trail.

Allison studied the grass around her boots and pushed aside the leaves on a small bunch of alumroot where she couldn't see the ground. It was possible the earth had swallowed them up. Or a chipmunk had decided to take them back to its den and placed them on a chipmunk mantle, over a chipmunk fireplace. Souvenirs from the big bad world above.

She found nothing, of course nothing. And what difference did it make? Just another piece of the world she couldn't pick up and put back together.

Allison backed up a few paces, stood square. She sighted her rifle down over the elk carcass, saw Rocky there, pleading for mercy. She checked Black Squirrel Pass and imagined herself coming over the ridge. She looked at McCartney looking back at her and made sure there was nothing in her line of fire.

She fired three rounds and on the last two looked for the shells ejecting and twirling. Both arced up, bounced off a rock and hopped down and away.

She followed them, studied them, a few feet apart from each other. The third was there, too. The three shells formed a gold-tipped triangle on a scrap of barren earth. She crouched and picked up each one and let her eyes go soft-focus, searching for anything else man-made in her field of view.

There. Worn down by winter. Not so bright. A much larger shell, pointing downhill. The shell with Rocky's name on it. She held it up to the sky between index finger and thumb and wondered about the sound it had generated. Rocky had heard it . . . or maybe not. And George.

And her. She heard it. And what if she hadn't?

Then what? Maybe somebody would have found Rocky's shot-up body in the spring and maybe all the same questions would have been asked, maybe all the same answers would have been found. On the other hand, maybe Grumley would have returned and found time to dig an even deeper, more permanent grave. Maybe Rocky would have disappeared forever.

What if she had left it alone? What about Weaver, Alvin? What about Bear? Did her questions lead to their . . . ?

She couldn't answer that question. She wouldn't answer that question. How far back in the phrase "chain reaction" did one have to travel to find the source? The airplane crash had led to years of legal hassles and assigned blame. An arbitrary dollar amount was set to balance the big scales in the sky, to make her whole. Nearly half of the nine hundred thousand dollars was now committed as a hefty down payment on Weaver's ranch. Justice, in theory, was done.

Really? Was it?

Had she sought more, she realized now, studying the beat-up shell from the bullet, she might actually think the government was the enemy or, at least, a fearful master. She made a silent promise. The money would be used for a perfectly good government cause. The money would underwrite her time on the Flat Tops. She would be an unofficial sentry, an extra pair of ears and eyes. The money would be invested, essentially, in protecting a government asset. It was money well spent. Even if nobody ever knew her role, it would be her way of justifying the fact that she'd cashed the check.

She put the bullet in her pocket as a reminder and headed off. She would find a place for it on her own little mantle.

\*\*\*\*

# Acknowledgements

Thanks to all my friends in writing and fiction: Mark Graham, Gary Reilly, Mike Keefe, Phil Reed, Ted Conover, Laura Snapp, Mike Booth, Bill Briggs, Ralph Beall, Mark Eddy, Diane Carman, Irv Moskowitz, Allyn Harvey, John Hickenlooper, Helen Thorpe, Mark and Wendy Klemick, Steve Metzger, Gregg Mundt, Ann LaBotz, Bruce Caughey, Dixie Good, Phil Good, Marilyn Saltzman, Ted and Susan Pinkowitz, Dan Slattery and Parry Burnap. Thanks also to Nick Zelinger for inspired imagery for the cover and to Melanie Mulhall and Betsy Zelinger for their tenacious, thoughtful editing. Many thanks also to Catherine Lutz for a solid read-through and spiffy improvements for this paperback edition.

CPSIA information can be obtained at www.ICGtesting.com
Printed in the USA
BVOW08s1624071015

421433BV00004B/44/P